After reading *The Anniversary Waltz*, the scenes and characters continue to linger in my memory, even though I opened the pages some four weeks ago. First-time author Darrel Nelson has captured the universal traits of great literature. Throughout the read I felt what it is like to be really loved and all the emotions love brings with it. I could not put the book down; each page held the mysteries of love and life. If you like Nicholas Sparks's novels, *The Notebook* comes to mind, you will love what Mr. Nelson has written.

—Sharon Gibb Murdoch
Cofounder of Heritage Makers

Every girl wants a knight in shining armor. That is what First Lieutenant Adam Carlson became for Elizabeth Baxter. Author Darrel Nelson masterfully transports the reader back to the days following World War II when the soldiers lucky enough to survive returned home to put the war behind them yet apply the lessons they had learned toward building a future full of happiness. *The Anniversary Waltz* is a heartwarming story that will bring tears to your eyes and a smile to your face as Mr. Nelson writes a story filled with laughter and love, tragedy and tears. You will be sad to have this reading experience end.

—M. J. Evans
Author of *Behind the Mist*,
Book One of The Mist Trilogy

The Anniversary Waltz is a thoroughly enchanting story, full of a wide range of emotions. The characters leaped from the pages straight into my heart.

—Lena Nelson Dooley
Author of *Mary's Blessing*, *Maggie's Journey*,
and the Will Rogers Medallion Award winner
Love Fin.

D1508801

The ANNIVERSARY WALTZ

A novel

DARREL
NELSON

ReALMs

MOST CHARISMA HOUSE BOOK GROUP products are available at special quantity discounts for bulk purchase for sales promotions, premiums, fund-raising, and educational needs. For details, write Charisma House Book Group, 600 Rinehart Road, Lake Mary, Florida 32746, or telephone (407) 333-0600.

THE ANNIVERSARY WALTZ by Darrel Nelson
Published by Realms
Charisma Media/Charisma House Book Group
600 Rinehart Road
Lake Mary, Florida 32746
www.charismahouse.com

Cover design by Nathan Morgan
Design Director: Bill Johnson

Visit the author's website at www.darrelnelson.com.

Library of Congress Cataloging-in-Publication Data:
Nelson, Darrel, 1950-
The anniversary waltz / Darrel Nelson. -- 1st ed.
     p. cm.
ISBN 978-1-61638-715-0 (trade paper) -- ISBN 978-1-61638-865-2 (e-book)
I. Title.
PS3614.E445554A84 2012
813'.6--dc23
                                                    2012001161

12 13 14 15 16 — 9876543
Printed in the United States of America

Prologue

October 2006

WOULD YOU DO me the honor, Miss?"

Adam Carlson stood beside his wife, Elizabeth, who was still seated at the dining room table. He presented her with a single white rose, which he brought out from behind his back. She held the flower close in order to savor its sweet fragrance. Adam extended a wrinkled hand and looked at her expectantly, the question lingering in his smile.

Elizabeth laughed lightly and put the rose on the table beside her plate, pausing to smooth down her white hair and adjust the two-strand pearl necklace around her slender neck. She placed her hand in his, and together they walked slowly into the living room, followed by family members who gathered around the perimeter of the area rug.

The living room was decorated especially for the occasion. A banner that read *HAPPY ANNIVERSARY* stretched above the doorway, and crepe streamers hung from the center of the ceiling, radiating to the corners of the room like the spokes of a wheel. Balloons were taped to the walls in clusters, and below each cluster was a hand-drawn picture that showed two stick figures holding hands, with the words *GREAT-GRANDMA LOVES GREAT-GRANDPA* printed across the bottom in irregular block letters. A brass floor lamp stood in the far corner, casting a warm glow throughout the room. A floral arrangement in a ceramic vase sat on the fireplace mantel, and a small pennant attached to a thin wooden stick protruded from the leaves and bore the message *HAPPY 60TH*, written in glitter paint. An old picture frame holding a photograph of Adam and Elizabeth on their wedding day sat on the coffee table, and an album containing photographs of past anniversaries lay open beside it.

When everyone had assembled in the living room, Adam held Elizabeth in formal waltz position. He cleared his throat and said, "It's only fair to warn you that I have two left feet. I hope I don't step on you with either one of them."

She reached up and gently stroked his cheek with her thin hand. "I'll risk it, sir."

They moved slowly in a small circle in the center of the area rug as he softly hummed "Believe Me, If All Those Endearing Young Charms," a song that had become *their* song years ago. It was a simple waltz to even simpler accompaniment, but tears formed in Elizabeth's eyes. Adam produced a handkerchief from his pocket and gently dabbed her tears.

Several family members brought out handkerchiefs too and wiped their eyes, as they did every year at this moment.

Adam and Elizabeth's youngest great-grandchild, a little girl with a ribbon in her hair and wearing her Sunday dress, glanced up at her mother in concern. "Mommy, is Great-Grandma sad?"

"No, dear," came the subdued reply. "She's happy."

The little girl looked puzzled. "Why is she crying?"

"You'll see."

Turning her attention back to her great-grandparents, the little girl watched them intently.

Adam held Elizabeth close, and their steps became smaller and smaller until their feet stopped moving altogether. They merely swayed back and forth on the spot. Dropping the formal dance position, she rested her head against Adam, and he wrapped his arms around her frail shoulders. Humming in a mere whisper now and pausing more frequently to catch his breath, he held her against him until the song ended. Then he tilted her face up to his, and they exchanged a tender kiss.

The family members applauded, the little girl the most enthusiastically of all.

Several cameras appeared, and Adam and Elizabeth held on to each other so the moment could be captured and added to the photo album.

Conducting his wife over to the couch, Adam helped her get seated. "Thank you for the dance, Elizabeth," he said.

"Thank *you* for the dance, Adam," she replied. "All sixty years."

He sat beside her, and they held hands. The family members gathered around, as they did every year on this occasion, to hear Adam and Elizabeth relate the story of the anniversary waltz.

Chapter 1

July 1946

ADAM CARLSON SHIFTED in his seat on the Greyhound bus and stared wearily out the window. He couldn't remember being this tired, not even during the heaviest part of the fighting in Italy. But he was too excited to close his eyes now. He had finally received his discharge and was almost home. The return voyage across the Atlantic by army transport ship made him seasick, and the four-day journey across the country by train seemed to last forever. But that was all behind him, compartmentalized in his memory along with a thousand other images he would just as soon forget. All that remained was the thirty-mile bus ride north from Great Falls.

Running a hand through his wavy, brown hair, he studied the landscape he hadn't seen in four years—except in his dreams. And he *had* dreamed about his hometown of Reunion, Montana, a great deal, especially while lying under the stars at night and smelling the earthy aroma of freshly dug foxholes. Those were the times he wondered if he would ever see the Great Plains again or feel the wind on his face. He ached to see the Rocky Mountains and gaze at the foothills as they merged with the plains and stretched eastward into infinity. This was the country he loved, the country for which he had fought. Big Sky Country—a corner of heaven.

He noticed a hawk in the distance, riding the invisible current on graceful wings, circling above a stand of cottonwood trees. At that moment, he decided, it had been worth it—all of it.

Even though he had enlisted against his father's wishes.

As the son of Hector Carlson, dry land farmer, Adam hadn't needed to enlist. But he wanted to satisfy his sense of adventure. He wanted to see the world outside the farm's boundaries, to answer the call of plain, old-fashioned patriotism. *Remember Pearl Harbor!* Laborers could be hired to bring in the harvest, he'd told his father, but who was going to go overseas and fight for a cause greater than one family's run of bad luck?

Hector hadn't accepted this reasoning, however. He tried to talk Adam into staying and helping run the farm. When his efforts proved futile, he gave up talking to his son at all. He didn't come to see Adam off, nor did he write once in the four years Adam was away, not even a quick note scribbled at the bottom of the regular letters Adam received from his mother, Maude.

Adam shook the memory away and felt his heart rate quicken as the bus made the last turn leading into Reunion. The anticipation of meeting his parents made him feel strangely nervous. It was dreamlike, as unreal as the world he had just left.

His thoughts went to those who would not be returning. Sixteen of his friends and comrades had fallen in Europe and were now permanent occupants. They would be forever denied the thrill of a homecoming and the anticipation of getting on with their lives. They would never see the mountains again or watch the maturing fields of wheat sway in the wind like a planted ocean. In their memory he closed his eyes, fighting his emotions as the Greyhound turned onto Main Street and headed for the bus stop in front of the Reunion Mercantile.

Several people were waiting on the sidewalk, anxiously craning to see inside the bus. A face appeared in the barbershop window next door to the Mercantile, peering out to study the scene. Two doors down a woman clutching several garments paused before entering Yang's Dry Cleaners and glanced toward the bus stop. In a small rural community like Reunion, where grain prices and the weather were the main topics of conversation, the arrival of the Greyhound attracted attention.

Inside the bus the driver announced, "Reunion. Please remember to take all your personal belongings. I'll set your luggage on the curb." He opened the door, and those who were getting off made their way forward.

Adam remained in his seat, looking out the window. He watched as each person emerged and was immediately engulfed by waiting arms. It was heartwarming to see people embrace, cry, and laugh all at the same time. He wondered if his father would be this demonstrative, but he already knew the answer to that.

The bus driver reappeared in the doorway a few minutes later. "Isn't this your stop, soldier?" He smiled sympathetically. "Sometimes it's as hard coming home as it is leaving, isn't it?"

Adam nodded and eased his six-foot frame out of the seat. He put on his service cap and adjusted his uniform before making his way up the aisle.

"Good luck," the driver said, patting him on the shoulder.

Adam stood in the door of the bus for a moment, watching the happy scene. A woman in a blue cotton dress made her way through the crowd. It took Adam a moment to recognize his mother. She had aged during the past four years and looked so frail that he wondered how she got through the crowd without being snapped like a dry twig.

"Adam…Adam!" she called, her voice filled with so much emotion she could hardly speak. Tears formed in her eyes and ran down her cheeks as Adam quickly descended the bus steps. She took him in her arms and embraced him with surprising strength. "Oh, my son, God has answered my prayers and brought you back to me."

Adam held her for a long time, his eyes closed, his lips quivering. Maude silently wept on his shoulder and rubbed the tears with the back of her thin hand. Finally she held him at arm's length as if unable to believe her eyes. Adam smiled reassuringly and gazed out over the crowd.

"He didn't come," she said, in answer to his unspoken question.

Adam looked into his mother's face. "But at least you came."

She reached up and stroked his cheek, her hand trembling. "Of course I came. Wild horses couldn't—" She changed the topic abruptly, likely realizing it would only serve to emphasize her husband's absence if she didn't. "Where's your luggage?" she asked. "Let's get you home so you can rest. You look exhausted."

So do you, he wanted to say, but he just smiled at her. It was obvious that the intervening years had taken their toll on her too.

Adam led her toward the passengers who were sorting through the luggage, which was now sitting on the curb. He had no difficulty identifying his two suitcases. They bore little resemblance to the ones he'd purchased four years earlier at the Mercantile. They were now held together by rope and packaging tape, and both of them showed evidence of journeys they'd taken aboard buses, trains, ships, army trucks, jeeps, and, on one occasion, an Italian farmer's hay cart.

Maude had no difficulty identifying her son's luggage either. As she reached for one of the suitcases, Adam quickly intercepted her. "I've got them, Mom," he said, picking up the suitcases and adjusting his grip on the sweat-stained leather handles.

"The truck's parked in front of the dry cleaners," Maude said, taking hold of his arm and leading him through the crowd.

Adam nodded to the bus driver, who gave him a thumbs-up gesture, and followed his mother down the sidewalk, answering her questions and asking a few of his own. He realized the words of greeting he practiced on the bus were unnecessary. He hoped it would be the same when he finally met his father. But somehow he doubted it.

As the farm came into view, Adam drew in a deep breath. The surrounding fields of wheat and barley, a vibrant green beneath a robin's egg sky, were a pastoral setting of majesty and peacefulness. But in many ways, returning home was like riding into enemy territory. Several times during the war, he had run into an ambush and barely escaped with his life, using every skill possible to survive. Today he felt like there was no refuge. He could only proceed directly into the line of fire and hope for the best.

His mind raced wildly as the pickup truck rattled through the gate and stopped in front of the house. He reached for the door handle but hesitated, taking everything in one more time in case it suddenly vanished...like a dream upon awakening.

The farmyard had changed. The two-story, clapboard house looked tired and faded, and several shutters hung at odd angles. The veranda tilted slightly to the south, and the railing was missing several spindles. The pump out in the yard had only a stub of a handle, and the clothesline beside it sagged noticeably. The woodshed and the barn were badly weathered, and the poplar tree near the garden now held only remnants of the tree house that he and his father had built years earlier.

Perhaps the farmyard had always looked like this and he hadn't noticed. But a fresh coat of paint would do wonders to hide the wrinkles and blemishes, and he resolved to paint every building before winter. He would shore up the clothesline, repair the front step, fix the shutters, replace the handle on the pump...

A burst of energy surged through him. He would make it up to his father by getting the farm back in shape. It would be like he had never left. He would show his father that he *did* care.

Maude put her hand on his. "Before we go in, there's something I want to say. Despite your father not coming to meet you today, he does love you."

Exhaling slowly, Adam turned toward her. "He has a funny way of showing it."

"He has a hard time expressing his feelings sometimes, that's all."

"He didn't write *once* in four years."

Maude stared out of the truck window, focusing on nothing in particular. She seemed to be searching for the right words. "I can't say I agree with how he's handled things, son. And I'm not trying to make excuses for him. But it's been hard on him too. I just wanted you to know that." She patted Adam's hand. "I just hope the two of you can let bygones be bygones."

Adam leaned over and kissed his mother on the cheek. "You're a good woman, Maude Carlson."

She smiled in appreciation, but her smile faded as the barn

door opened and her husband stepped out into the sunlight. She glanced over at her son, who squared his shoulders and pulled on the door handle.

Adam was struck by how much his father had aged. His hair was much thinner, and his sun-hardened, wrinkled skin was stretched like tanned hide on a pole frame. His complexion resembled buckskin, rough side out, and his leanness added a sharp edge to his features. A permanent scowl creased his forehead, and his mouth sagged at the corners.

Hector remained motionless, as though he was a gargoyle guarding the farmyard. His expression looked equally sullen and fierce, and Adam slowly approached him. Staring down the enemy in the fields and streets of Italy had not been this hard.

Maude hurried toward her husband. "Hec, it's our boy! Adam's home!"

Adam studied his father's face, looking for any sign of welcome...or forgiveness. But Hector's granite-like countenance remained unchanged. Adam stopped several paces away and stood before his father like a disobedient child.

Hector met his son's eyes momentarily, and then his gaze wandered over Adam's uniform. The silence deepened and Adam felt the tension increase.

Maude narrowed her eyes. "Well, Hec, say something."

Hector scratched his stubbled chin and cleared his throat. "They treat you okay?"

What a strange question, Adam thought. Was his father referring to the army or the enemy? In all honesty, neither of them had treated him well. The army had removed four years of his life with the precision of a surgeon's scalpel, and the Germans had been far less subtle than that. They had tried to *kill* him.

Adam felt numb as the memories of the past four years flooded his heart, a trickle at first and then a gush. The experience had been more overwhelming than he ever expected. And with one question his father had reduced it to insignificance.

"You know I don't agree with what you did," Hector said. "But I'm glad you didn't go and get yourself killed."

Adam forced a smiled. "I'm glad I didn't either."

Maude looked anxiously from one to the other. "Hec, this calls for a feast of the fatted calf. Get some beet greens from the garden, and I'll cook a roast with all the trimmings."

Hector remained motionless.

She shooed him away from the barn. "You go on, now." Embracing Adam, she said, "Go have a bath and get some rest, son. I'll call you for dinner. There's so much to talk about."

Adam glanced at the retreating figure of his father and returned to the truck to get his luggage, aware that his mother was reverting to her proven formula for restoring peace on earth, good will toward men: a delicious meal. In the past, good food had settled more arguments in the family than had any line of reasoning, logic, or argument. The way to a man's heart...

CHAPTER 2

S TANDING AT THE steam press in Yang's Dry Cleaners, Elizabeth Baxter paused to wipe the perspiration from her forehead with a handkerchief she kept in the pocket of her uniform. The interior of the shop was a blast furnace, made all the more stifling by the summer weather. On days like this she couldn't wait to get home, fill the bathtub with water as cool as she could stand, and bury herself beneath a soothing layer of bath bubbles. Her hair felt straight and stringy, and a quick glance in the silver plating on the steam press revealed that her makeup needed touching up. By midafternoon, she always felt faded. But a bath would rejuvenate her, and by seven o'clock she'd be ready for Nathan Roberts to drop by, the young man she'd been dating for a year.

She glanced at the clock. Three thirty. Two more hours until closing time. She reached for a pair of wool pants that hung on a nearby rack, determined to keep busy. That always helped the time pass faster.

It wasn't that she disliked working in the dry cleaners. Every job had its pros and cons. The summer heat made the shop unbearable, true. But in the winter, when the temperature plummeted below freezing and stayed there for weeks on end, the interior of the dry cleaners felt as cozy as a warm blanket. Besides, in a small town like Reunion, jobs were hard to come by, and working at the dry cleaners was better than working at the truck stop diner on the highway, where the air was thick with the pungent odors of grease and tobacco smoke, and the waitresses had to put up with the teasing, flirting, and advances of the male patrons.

Elizabeth placed the wool pants on the bottom pad of the steam press and smoothed the wrinkles so they wouldn't get ironed into the material. Reaching up, her hand found the handle, and with a practiced movement, she lowered the top pad. Steam hissed from the edges, and she felt her hair become even straighter. With another practiced movement she raised the lid at just the right moment and adjusted the pants. Once more she lowered the lid, turning momentarily away from the steam. When she was finished pressing the pants, she placed them carefully on a hanger on the rack.

Tucking a strand of hair behind her ear, Elizabeth glanced at her best friend, Julie Landry, who was working on a shirt at the spotting table. Slightly taller than Elizabeth, Julie wore her long brown hair in victory rolls—big, soft curls gathered just above her shoulders. But by this time of the day, the curls were showing the effects of the heat too, and Elizabeth found some consolation in that. *Misery loves company,* she thought.

Reaching for another garment, Elizabeth looked over at Chenglei "Lee" Yang, the diminutive owner of the dry cleaners. He stood at the front counter, sorting though a pile of customer receipts. His black eyes squinted in concentration, and his thin shoulders hunched forward. He was a quiet man who rarely spoke more than two sentences throughout the day. Instead, he hummed tunes from his native China to himself as he worked, seeming to enjoy his own company. Whenever asked a question, he would answer, "Good, good," whether he was commenting on the weather, his health, or his business.

Elizabeth liked working for him. He never looked over her shoulder to check on her, and he wasn't critical of how she did her job. He gave her credit for being responsible and intelligent, and since she'd started working for him two years ago, he had come to rely on her more and more. Her duties had grown to include dealing with repairmen and salesmen, ordering supplies, and keeping the supply shelves stocked, as well as doing her share of the normal workload, which had increased over the past few months. With the war now over, people were indulging in luxuries once more—luxuries such as having their clothes dry-cleaned. Business was booming, and so were Elizabeth's responsibilities.

Three months earlier she'd talked Lee Yang into hiring another employee to help with the growing workload. She'd convinced him it would allow him to do even more business, which would mean he could send for his family sooner. His wife and three children were still living in China, and he hadn't seen them since arriving in Réunion five years ago. He agreed to hire Julie, and, as Elizabeth had predicted, the shop was able to handle more business.

"Good, good," Lee Yang now said to himself as he thumbed through the last of the receipts.

Elizabeth watched him rub his hands together in satisfaction. She wasn't certain how much money he'd been able to save, but he was obviously pleased with how things were going. And based on his thin, bony physique, the arrival of his wife couldn't happen too soon.

The bell above the front door jingled a short time later. An elderly woman marched sprily into the shop and approached the front counter. Elizabeth recognized Eunice Murphy, who at the age of eighty-three still played the organ each week in church. Eunice held a dress over her arm, and her furrowed brow and pursed lips gave her a determined expression. "Mr. Yang," she said, "I've got a bone to pick with you."

Lee Yang raised both eyebrows. "Bone to pick? This is dry cleaners, Mrs. Murphy. Restaurant next door."

She ignored his attempt at humor and wagged a finger at him. "I know where I'm at."

"What seem to be problem?"

A low rattle sounded in the elderly woman's throat. "My dress wasn't dry-cleaned properly."

Elizabeth watched her boss's hackles rise. Although he was a quiet, unassuming man, he was fiercely proud of his work and his reputation.

"How not done properly?" he said. "Is there stain that no come out? Dress shrink?"

She laid the dress on the counter. "See for yourself."

Elizabeth and Julie exchanged glances, and Julie rolled her eyes before turning her attention back to the shirt she was spot cleaning.

Lee Yang examined the dress and shrugged. "I look. See nothing wrong."

"Look closer, Mr. Yang."

Lee Yang narrowed his eyes indignantly. "I tell you—"

"Good afternoon, Mrs. Murphy," Elizabeth said, stepping forward to interrupt the discussion. "Is there a problem with your dress?"

Eunice turned on her. "There certainly is. It still looks thin and worn."

Lee Yang coughed in exasperation, but Elizabeth maintained a neutral expression. She understood how people often thought dry-cleaning restored garments to their original state, magically transforming them to new again. And even though the dry cleaners did minor sewing and repair jobs, nothing could restore threadbare material to its original condition. She had tried to explain this to disgruntled customers in the past, but experience had taught her it was futile.

She held the dress up and admired it. "This is a beautiful dress, Mrs. Murphy."

Eunice hesitated momentarily. "My husband bought it for me for our first wedding anniversary, God rest his soul."

"I remember your husband." Elizabeth lowered her voice reverently. "How long has he been gone now?"

"Ten years this month."

Lee Yang cleared his throat as though preparing to resume the debate, but Elizabeth quickly said, "He had excellent taste."

Eunice's countenance softened. "We hardly had a nickel to our name, but Frank worked overtime for a month to save up enough to buy it."

"And you've had it all these years?"

A faraway look came into the elderly woman's eyes. "I only

wear it each year on our anniversary and on a few other important occasions."

"What a special dress."

"Of course, styles changed over the years, and he bought me other dresses as our financial situation improved. But this one has always remained my favorite."

"When is your anniversary, Mrs. Murphy?"

"A week Friday."

"How perfect. That's when Heritage Days begins. You can wear the dress to the community dance."

"Not in its present condition!"

Elizabeth gently hung the dress on a hanger and placed it on the garment rack. "Leave it with me, Mrs. Murphy, and I'll personally see that it receives the care and attention it deserves."

Eunice scowled in concern, deepening the wrinkles that lined her face. "It won't cost me extra, will it? I already paid you once."

"But—" Lee Yang started to say.

"It won't cost you a penny more," Elizabeth replied, cutting a quick look at her boss.

The elderly woman's gaze went to the dress, then back to Elizabeth. "And it'll be ready in time?"

"In plenty of time. You can pick it up early next week."

The trace of a smile appeared in the corners of Eunice's mouth. "You must think I'm being a fussy old woman."

"Of course I don't," Elizabeth replied, nudging her boss discreetly.

"You customer," Lee Yang replied flatly. "We take care of you."

"It's just that the dress is very dear to me," Eunice said. "Did I mention that my husband bought it for me for our first wedding anniversary?"

From her place at the spotting table, Julie stifled a giggle.

"That's so sweet," Elizabeth said, walking the elderly woman to the door and holding it open for her. "Your dress will be fine, Mrs. Murphy. Early next week, remember."

When Elizabeth came back to the front counter, Julie said, "And just how do you intend to restore that old dress?"

"I don't."

"Then what you going to do?" Lee Yang asked.

"Keep her focused on the *memory* of the dress."

Julie laughed lightly. "The dress may be worn and faded, but her memory of it is as bright as ever, right?"

"And a little sincere flattery can go a long way."

Lee Yang shook his head. "I hope you know what you doing. Mrs. Murphy one tough lady."

"Don't worry," Elizabeth said reassuringly. "Everything will be good, good."

He still looked doubtful as he turned and walked away, muttering to himself in Mandarin.

At closing time the bell announced the arrival of another customer. Elizabeth was standing just inside the boiler room, doing a quick inventory of the cleaning supplies. She sighed inwardly when she heard the bell. There was always someone who waited until the last possible second to drop off dry cleaning.

She started when she heard a familiar voice say, "Hello, Chop Suey. How's business?"

"Good, good, Mr. Roberts," Lee Yang replied. "I keep up on bank payment."

"I know you do. You're one of our best clients."

Elizabeth fussed momentarily with her hair and ran a hand down the front of her uniform. Stepping in from the boiler room, she smiled at Nathan Roberts, her steady. He was the loan officer at the bank, and he held in the palm of his hand the fate of many local businesses and farms. He wore a white dress shirt with silver cuff links, a broad necktie that was held by a tie clip, suit pants, and polished black leather shoes. His hair was neatly groomed, parted on the side in a perfect line, and he held a double-breasted pin-striped suit over his arm. Obviously working in his office with its window-mounted air-conditioning unit had its advantages. He appeared fresh and well groomed, even at the end of the long workday. But that was Nathan, always immaculate.

"There she is," Nathan said, winking at Elizabeth.

"Hey, I didn't think I'd be seeing you till tonight."

"I was tied up at the bank all day and couldn't get here sooner. I want this suit dry-cleaned for the Heritage Days opening ceremony next week."

Julie joined them. "And here I thought you wanted it dry-cleaned for my birthday party on the eighteenth. You two are coming, aren't you?"

"Wouldn't miss it," Elizabeth replied.

"I'll wear the suit just for you, Julie," Nathan said. "If I can get it dry-cleaned in time." He turned toward Lee Yang. "That shouldn't be a problem, should it, Chop Suey?"

"No problem for you, Mr. Roberts," Lee Yang answered.

Elizabeth stepped around the counter and picked up the suit, nudging him with her elbow. Dropping her voice to a whisper, she said, "I wish you wouldn't call him that. His name is Lee Yang."

Nathan waved a hand dismissively. "He doesn't mind," he said, calling over Elizabeth's shoulder. "It's our little joke. Right, Chop Suey?"

"Little joke," Lee Yang replied. "Mr. Roberts very funny man."

"See?" Nathan replied, beaming at Elizabeth.

"I sweep floor," Lee Yang said, reaching for the broom. "Julie, put sign in window."

"Gladly," Julie said, wiping her glistening cheeks with the back of her hand.

Laying the suit on the counter, Elizabeth said, "I still think it's rude. I shouldn't be so accommodating to you. It's closing time, you know."

Nathan straightened himself up to his full height. "You'd say no to me?"

She folded her arms and gazed at him narrowly. "Sure."

"I hold the mortgage here, in case you've forgotten."

"How can I? You remind me all the time."

Looking pleased with himself, Nathan put a finger under Elizabeth's chin and lifted her face toward his. "So are you going to accommodate me or not?"

"I'm still thinking," she said, returning to the other side of the counter.

Nathan leaned an elbow on the counter. "I'll make it worth your while."

"What, drop the interest rate so we can get a raise?" Julie said as she put the *Closed* sign in the window and locked the front door.

"Even better," he said.

Elizabeth looked at him in pretended distrust. "What do you have in mind?"

"How about a movie tonight and an ice cream soda afterward?"

"You're letting him buy you off that cheap?" Julie said, pulling down the window shades.

"And then we can plan a shopping trip into Great Falls on the weekend," Nathan added.

Elizabeth tore off a claim stub and handed it to him. "I think we can accommodate you after all, Mr. Roberts. I'll be ready at seven o'clock."

CHAPTER 3

LTHOUGH HIS MOTHER encouraged him to go up to his bedroom and lie down, Adam was too restless to relax. He made his way outside and strolled around the farmyard, reminiscing. Memories washed over him, triggered by everything he saw. The farmhouse, the woodshed, the corrals, the remnants of the tree house, the pump, the garden—each was a single drop that grew into a torrent of memories that threatened to overwhelm him. A casual glance in any direction rekindled scenes from different stages of his life: he and his cousin Ty sneaking cigarettes and smoking the whole pack in the barn, then getting sick afterward and lying in the hayloft in misery; building the tree house with his father and later taking refuge there—which included pulling up the rope ladder—whenever his father threatened to march him out to the woodshed for a spanking; fetching water from the pump in all kinds of weather and hauling bucket after bucket into the house for Saturday night baths in order to get ready for church; weeding the garden by the hour and complaining by the minute...

Adam rubbed his eyes wearily and leaned against the top rail of the corral.

Arriving in Reunion and greeting his mother had been exhilarating. However, driving out to the farm and having to stand before his father had been emotionally draining. The unresponsive welcome he'd received from his father weighed heavily on him, although in all honesty he hadn't expected open arms and a gush of apologies. But looking into his father's eyes and seeing the condemnation and sense of betrayal there—the same as four years earlier—was worse than Adam had expected, and it deflated the joy of his homecoming.

Noting the changes that time had wrought—the aged appearance of his parents, the weathered condition of the buildings and corrals—further drained him and brought a sense of loss. He might be able to fix up the farm and restore some of its former glory, but there were certain things he would never be able to undo. They were lost to time and change, beyond restoration.

A whinny caught his attention, and a white stallion and a smaller bay plodded around the corner of the barn. "Snowflake! Babe!" he called, clicking his tongue to call them over. "I thought you guys might be out in the pasture."

As Adam extended a hand, the white stallion snorted and backed away. "Easy, Snowflake," he said. "It's me." He climbed between the rails and slowly approached the stallion, holding out his hand and speaking softly. "Looks like you haven't been ridden in a while. Has my dad been neglecting you guys? Well, I'm back, and things are going to change."

He gently patted Snowflake on the neck. A shiver ran through the stallion, but the horse stood its ground. "That's better," Adam said. "Now you remember me, don't you?" He ran his fingers through the mane, frowning as he noticed the collection of snarls and burrs. "You need a good grooming." He glanced over at the bay. "You too, Babe. You both look like a couple of wild horses. Well, I'll fix that soon enough."

At that moment he saw his father round the corner of the barn and go inside. Hoping to take another stab at reconciliation, Adam walked over to the weathered structure and peeked through the window. He noticed his father holding a pitchfork and cleaning one of the stalls. "Hey, Dad, it looks like you're hard at it," Adam said, leaning on the windowsill.

Hector continued working without looking at his son.

"Got another pitchfork?" Adam asked after a moment's silence.

"Nope."

"Let me take over. I can clean this stall and the other one before supper."

"Did the other one yesterday."

"Okay, let me finish this one for you."

Hector still refused to look at his son. "I can manage." He cleared his throat and muttered, "Been doing it for four years."

Adam opened his mouth to reply but then reconsidered. What had he expected? That his father would suddenly break down and apologize? He knew Hector Carlson better than that. Adam looked at his father a moment longer, but Hector remained lost in his own thoughts and continued working as though no one else was there. "I'll go see if Mom needs any help," Adam said. "I'll call you when supper's ready."

He crossed the yard and entered the house, grateful that the interior of the farmhouse still offered hospitality and familiarity. He was also grateful it didn't show the same effects of time as the exterior did. The patterned wallpaper, the faded curtains, the antique furniture, and the squeaky hardwood floor were largely as he remembered them. The kitchen still had the same arrangement—the coal stove along the far wall and the wooden kitchen table on the opposite wall. The living room furniture was also the same, including the couch that sagged noticeably in the middle and sat across from the stone fireplace.

Maude stood at the kitchen sink, peeling potatoes.

"Anything I can do?" he asked, coming up behind her and peering over her shoulder.

"I saw you talking to your father," she said, glancing out of the window above the sink.

"*Trying* to talk to him."

"He'll come around, son. I'm sure of it. Things just have to run their course." She reached for another potato. "I know it's hard on you, but try to be patient with him."

Adam leaned against the kitchen counter. "I'm trying."

"I know you are, son. Now why don't you go upstairs and get some rest?"

Running a hand wearily through his hair, he said, "I tried, but I can't seem to lie still."

"Old habits die hard, don't they? I'm sure there were days,

probably weeks, you didn't dare relax. Well, permission granted to go upstairs, lie down, and do nothing, soldier."

Adam stood at attention and saluted smartly. "Sir, yes, sir."

Maude wiped her hands on her apron and embraced her son. "It's going to take awhile to adjust back to civilian life. You'll have to retrain yourself."

Giving her a quick kiss on the cheek, Adam went to his bedroom. When he'd earlier carried his suitcase upstairs to unpack, he'd noticed that his bedroom was just as he'd left it four years earlier. The photographs of his school days and community activities still hung on the wall, and his high school yearbook still sat on the small stand along the far wall. The Tarzan books he'd collected over the years sat on the bookshelf near his dresser, and one look inside the top dresser drawer told him that his baseball card collection was still intact. A pair of work boots sat beside the bed in the exact position he'd left them when he'd stepped out of them and changed into his army uniform. In one of her many letters to him, his mother had explained how it had been three weeks before she could bring herself to move the boots. Four years later she'd replaced them in the same position. It was a gesture that touched him more than if she'd hung a banner of welcome between the front gateposts.

He bent down and picked up the boots. Tears that he'd been holding back for days, weeks, and years began to form. They collected in the corner of his eyes and trickled down his cheeks as he thought about everything that had transpired since he'd last stepped out of the boots. He tried vainly to hold his emotions in check, but finally he gave in to them. Burying his face in his pillow, he sobbed until he fell into a dreamless sleep of total exhaustion.

It had been four *long* years since Adam had tasted his mother's cooking. As he savored each bite of roast beef, mashed potatoes and gravy, beet greens from the garden, and homemade bread, he realized his memory had not done it justice.

Many nights he'd lain awake, reliving the memories of his life before the war. They had become jumbled in the chaos, and one of his favorite pastimes had been to try and put them back together. And his starting point was often the memory of his mother's cooking.

"So, Dad," Adam said, reaching for a second helping of potatoes, "I notice the buildings could be spruced up. Now that I'm back, I thought I'd paint them." He looked over at his mother who, in turn, looked at her husband.

Hector concentrated on his vegetables. "Paint costs money—money we don't have."

"I've got some money coming, and I qualify for military benefits. I can even get a special veteran's loan from the bank, if need be."

Exhaling in disgust, Hector said, "Loans hit you with interest, and that ends up costing more money."

Maude laid a hand on her husband's arm. "It would improve the value of the farm, Hec."

"I was in middle school when we last painted the barn," Adam said.

"And putting a little money back into the farm will make a difference in the long run," Maude added.

"It's like closing the barn door after the horse gets out," Hector muttered.

Adam looked genuinely puzzled. "I don't understand."

Hector glanced at Maude, who shook her head discreetly, and focused his attention back on his plate.

"I think it would be a blessing to get this old place looking good again," Maude said.

"And it's not like I'm completely out of practice," Adam said. "I helped a farmer in northern Italy paint his barn during a break in the action."

The instant he said it, Adam realized his mistake.

Hector's fork stopped midway to his mouth. "You helped a farmer paint his barn?"

Adam shifted uncomfortably. "We had a layover for a few days

25

in the Po Valley, and I helped a farmer who had been kind to us. He'd given us a ride in his cart and—"

"You couldn't stay and help me, but you could help some guy that you didn't even know, in some far-off country?"

"Dad, it wasn't like that."

The food fell from Hector's fork. "What *was* it like?"

"I didn't leave here to go work somewhere else. It was just a one-time thing. I had a few days, and he needed help."

"And I didn't?" Hector grunted, spearing the food that had fallen from his fork.

Adam cleared his throat. "I know you think I betrayed you...that everything you've done around here alone proves what an ungrateful son you have."

Hector pounded the table with his fist, causing the fresh milk in the glasses to ripple. "I won't have you talking to me in that tone. You're not so big that I can't take you out to the woodshed."

Instinctively Adam felt something tighten within at the mention of the woodshed. His father was not an abusive man, but he firmly believed in the adage: *Spare the rod and spoil the child.* On occasion he'd firmly demonstrated that belief by marching Adam out to the woodshed, where he kept a leather strap he used to make sure Adam didn't turn out spoiled.

But for all his sternness, Hector did possess a sense of humor...of sorts. It lay buried somewhere deep below the wind-chiseled wrinkles and farm-hardened calluses. Adam decided there might be a chance to diffuse the tension by appealing to it now. "If you try to take me to the woodshed," he said, "I'll climb up into my old tree house and you won't be able to catch me."

There was a silent pause and Maude studied her husband, attempting to decipher his mood.

Hector glanced around the table, and the smallest trace of a smile flickered in the corners of his mouth. "You think I couldn't climb up there...what's left of it?"

Adam arched an eyebrow. "Nope." He felt on more familiar ground now, bantering with his father as he edged away from disaster. That was one defense tactic he'd learned in his youth, to sidetrack his father and get his mind on other things. It hadn't always worked, but it had meant fewer trips to the woodshed.

Maude picked up on her son's cue. "Remember the time you told Adam to weed the vegetable patch and he went fishing instead? My, you were upset. When he got home, you went to march him out to the woodshed, but he climbed up into his tree house and wouldn't come down."

Adam slapped his knee. "I remember that. We used to have milk cows, and you'd hurt your foot because one of the cows— what was her name, the one who got tangled in the barbed wire fence?"

"Three Teats."

"That's right. Ol' Three Teats had stepped on your foot the day before and you could hardly walk, let alone climb up into the tree house."

Hector grunted. "You stayed up there until you were sure and certain I'd cooled down."

"I was there until dark."

Maude sighed. "I might as well make a confession now that it's all water under the bridge. After you went to do chores, Hec, I snuck supper out to Adam. He had a pail tied to a rope that he let down, and I put his meal in there. I couldn't bear the thought of him going hungry."

"And I'll tell you a little secret, Mom. I ate *two* suppers that night."

"Two suppers? But I only brought—" She broke off and looked at her husband. "Well, Hector Carlson, if that doesn't beat all."

Hector suddenly got busy with his fork again. "It was just a few weeds in the garden. Nothing to starve a boy over."

Adam smiled at the memory, although at the time it had been *much* more than just a few weeds in the garden. Normally it would have meant a trip to the woodshed. But somewhere during the evening, Hector had mellowed enough to sneak his son supper. His anger had gradually disappeared, but it had taken him the rest of the afternoon and early evening to get to that point. How long would it take this time over something far more significant than weeds in the garden?

Adam received a clue moments later when Hector spoke again, almost to himself, drawing his fork through his food. "It wasn't anything to get all hot and bothered about. Not like—" He stopped mid-sentence and left the thought dangling.

Adam knew what his father was going to say, though. *Not like deserting the farm and me.*

Hector's face grew grim, and the mood turned heavy again.

Adam felt his heart sink. All roads up memory lane seemed to lead to the same intersection: the corner of Resentful Feelings and Unhealed Wounds.

CHAPTER 4

THE FOLLOWING FRIDAY Elizabeth emerged from Yang's Dry Cleaners holding a freshly pressed double-breasted suit by the hanger. She glanced at her reflection in the shop window and paused to fix her hair. When she finished primping, she drew in a deep breath. Mingled fragrances of summer hung deliciously in the air, and she felt excited to be out of the shop. Even though it was only noon, she was finished with work for the day. The dry cleaners was closed in the afternoon for Heritage Days, but the Mercantile and other stores remained open. The sidewalks had been swept, the litter picked up, and the storefront windows washed in anticipation of the community celebrations.

Heritage Days occurred annually on the second weekend in July to commemorate Reunion's birthday. The community had been founded in 1892, one year after the Great Northern railroad opened up northern Montana to settlement. Ranchers and homesteaders began to arrive, thrilled at the prospect of staking a claim in one of the last open grassland areas in the country. An uneasy truce developed between the two groups, which allowed Reunion to grow and flourish. Reunion—so named when two business acquaintances from back east met to establish a town—went from virgin prairie to a full-fledged community within a short time. And by the turn of the century, the population had increased to 1,300 residents. Oil was discovered in northern Montana in 1921, bringing more people into the area, and Reunion practically doubled in size over the next decade. Businesses continued to spring up, rivaling those already established in the larger center of Great Falls, thirty miles to the south.

Even the war had helped the population increase. An air force base was constructed outside of Great Falls, which housed and trained bomber crews of the Second Air Force. The influx of construction workers, training personnel, and civilians spilled over into Reunion, which increased in population to 3,500 residents.

And now that the war was over, the residents—minus the sixteen young men killed in the war—were celebrating a new era of peace, the end of rationing, and a return to normalcy.

This year an opening ceremony was being held at the town office to commemorate the end of the war. The stores were running specials both days, which included sidewalk sales. A carnival had also been arranged at the fairgrounds, consisting of rides, game booths, novelty races, a horseshoe competition, and a quilting bazaar. A community dance was scheduled for Friday night—tonight—and fireworks were planned for Saturday evening to cap off the celebrations.

The mood of the entire community bordered on giddy, particularly with the young women, who were excited about the increasing number of available young men. The dance was the perfect occasion for the young women to model their newest dresses.

Elizabeth had bought a dress especially for this evening, and she was anxious to see Nathan's reaction. Her almond-shaped green eyes, auburn hair, and high cheekbones had captured his attention a year ago. She was certain her new dress would help maintain it.

She let her gaze wander past the town office to the dance pavilion next door. With its covered roof and framed walls, the pavilion had windows that could be opened for ventilation in the summer and closed so the interior could be warmed by a gas heater in the winter. Situated near the center of town, the pavilion had hosted many community dances over the years. She knew that members of the Heritage Days committee were already there, setting up the refreshment tables, hanging crepe streamers, and adding other decorative touches. A tingle of excitement ran through her as she thought of the pavilion coming to life tonight with the sounds of Kenny Jones and His Moonlight Orchestra.

Elizabeth continued toward the town office, where her uncle

was hard at work on his speech for the opening ceremony, scheduled for two o'clock on the front lawn. She noted with satisfaction that preparations were almost complete. A portable stage and a lectern had already been set up, with a row of chairs across the front for honored guests and local dignitaries. And members of the high school band were assembling a small bandstand nearby.

She hurried up the front steps and entered the foyer. Proceeding down a short hallway, she knocked on the door that read WIL JACKSON, MAYOR.

"Come in," came the reply.

Elizabeth opened the door and stepped inside.

Wil Jackson was pacing back and forth in front of his desk, toying with his moustache while studying a piece of paper. His tie was loosened around his fleshy neck and his collar was open. Perspiration glistened on his forehead, emphasizing a receding hairline, and an ample stomach protruded over his belt.

"Here's your suit, Uncle Wil. I thought I'd save you a trip and drop it by on my way home."

"Thanks, Elizabeth. I'd almost forgotten about it. I've been so busy trying to get my speech finished. Listen to what I've written so far and tell me what you think."

He held the paper in front of him as though standing at a podium and cleared his throat. He read the first three paragraphs, pausing briefly to gauge his niece's reaction before continuing. "We're anxious for the return of Reunion's men of the armed forces. We're—"

"Don't forget the *women*, as well," Elizabeth said, interrupting him.

Wil busied himself with his pencil for a moment and looked up. "You don't think I'm being too wordy, do you?"

"The speech is very good—" She arched an eyebrow. "—now."

He set the paper and pencil aside and wiped his forehead with a large handkerchief. "There are going to be a lot of people in town today. I want my speech to be perfect."

"It will be. Especially if you pay tribute to those who made the supreme sacrifice."

"We're going to have two minutes of silence to honor them. Nathan, representing the Chamber of Commerce, will lay a wreath in memory of the fallen."

"It sounds like everything is under control."

Wil glanced down at his notes. "Almost. I just have to finish my speech."

"And I've got to go get ready myself. See you at the opening ceremony."

Wil sat down and began writing briskly, waving without looking up.

Elizabeth burst through the front door and hurried down the hallway toward her bedroom, where her new dress was already laid out on the bed.

"Elizabeth, is that you?" came a voice from the adjoining bedroom. "Will you step in here for a minute, dear?"

Appearing in the doorway, Elizabeth said, "Are you about ready, Aunt Lenora?"

Lenora was sitting in front of her vanity mirror, scowling in frustration. "It's my hair, Elizabeth. I can't seem to do a thing with it in this heat. I don't want to show up looking like something the cat drug in."

Although anxious to get ready herself, Elizabeth knew there'd be no peace until she helped her aunt. She reached for a comb and began styling her aunt's hair, working quickly and efficiently.

Lenora folded her fleshy arms across her full-figured bosom and stared straight ahead. A scowl accentuated the wrinkles on her forehead. "Your uncle was up half the night working on last-minute details for Heritage Days."

"It's a big event this year."

"But he kept me awake on top of it. I just know I have bags the size of steamer trunks under my eyes."

"You look fine, Aunt Lenora." Elizabeth paused to examine her aunt's hair from several angles. "It's funny why Uncle Wil ran for mayor when he's so busy with his firm."

"Some members of the Chamber of Commerce talked him into it because he's a certified public accountant. They said the town needed someone to get the books back in order. And Wil has done that—I'll give credit where credit's due."

Elizabeth resumed working on her aunt's hair. "The town is in good hands."

Lenora held up her hands, studying her neatly manicured nails. "Yes, it is, isn't it?"

They both laughed, and the mood lightened.

Lenora watched her niece in the mirror for a moment before speaking. "You know, Elizabeth, there's only so much two people can talk about before they start repeating themselves."

"I think we're doing fine, Aunt Lenora."

"I meant your uncle and me. Because we didn't have any children of our own, it was just the two of us at first, talking about the same old things. But when my sister died and you came to live with us, things changed. You brought something into our lives that was missing."

"Variety?"

"That's a good way to describe it."

"Like the time I turned beautician and gave the neighbor's cat a haircut?"

Lenora laughed softly under her breath. "Land sakes, Eunice Murphy was upset. She didn't talk to us until that old tabby's hair grew back. It was the quietest the neighborhood had been in ten years."

"Or when Julie and I snuck your car and went for a midnight joy ride?"

"Oh, my goodness. I'd forgotten about that. You girls were only twelve or thirteen at the time. You ended up crashing into a fire hydrant and denting the front bumper. That cost your uncle two hundred dollars, if memory serves me correctly."

"And four weeks of my life. I was grounded for a month, remember?"

Pursing her lips at the memory, Lenora sighed. "But despite everything, Elizabeth, you have turned out all right. You're a sensible girl, and your uncle and I are grateful that you're dating a sensible young man. Nathan has a good career and is a prominent citizen in the community. And he attends church with us."

Elizabeth understood how her aunt felt about church attendance. Lenora maintained that you could lie about your age, cheat on your diet, and steal from your savings account. But to not attend church on Sunday was unacceptable.

"Nathan is an excellent prospect," Lenora added.

Pausing over her aunt, the comb poised in midair, Elizabeth said, "I know, I know. You tell me all the time what a lucky young woman I am to have him for my steady."

"He could have his pick of any girl in town. But he picked you!"

"And I should be grateful, I realize. But it's just that he's so—"

"What...? Handsome? Wealthy?"

"Possessive."

Twisting around in her chair, Lenora said, "Of course he's possessive. He doesn't want to lose you, that's all. And you surely don't want to lose him!" She sighed and settled back in her chair. "It does my heart good to know you'll be well provided for. With Nathan, you'll want for absolutely nothing."

Working in silence, Elizabeth considered her aunt's words. Wanting for absolutely nothing sounded appealing. But was a home filled with more possessions than she knew what to do with the basis for a good marriage? Did the scale that measured financial prosperity also measure happiness?

She put the finishing touches on her aunt's hair and left the room, the questions resonating in her mind. She didn't know the answers, at least not yet. And perhaps that was why she was holding back, reluctant to make a commitment. Wanting for nothing seemed like an enviable situation. But was it...enough?

CHAPTER 5

ADAM SET THE hammer down and stretched his cramped fingers. The corral fence was almost finished. There was just the top rail to secure and the sagging gate to repair. Despite the leather gloves, the palms of his hands felt sore and chafed. He had been fighting the blisters for days. Farm-hardened calluses took time to reacquire.

Still, he was grateful that his father had agreed to let him put some money into fixing up the farm. A coat of paint and some urgent repairs were a start. And hopefully his father would welcome the improvements and agree to let Adam do even more. You couldn't twist Hector Carlson's arm, Adam realized. But if you applied leverage gently and subtly enough, you could sometimes get it to bend. Especially if you convinced him that the idea was his in the first place. The art of gentle persuasion—a technique Adam had attempted to master long ago.

Maude arrived carrying an egg basket and a container of water. "I'm just on my way to the chicken coop to gather a few eggs for lunch. Thought you could use a drink."

Adam gratefully accepted the container and drained the contents in one long swallow. The sun had been relentless all morning, and he hadn't yet readjusted to the dry Montana climate. Perspiration beaded on his forehead, and he wiped it with the back of his glove. "Thanks. Just what I needed."

Maude looked at him in concern. "What you need is some rest. Sleep in for a change. Quit before sunset. Take Snowflake or Babe for a long ride. Go fishing down at the river. You've been working like a house-a-fire since you got home."

Adam smiled guiltily. What his mother said was true. He'd begun working on the farm the day after his arrival home, one week ago, rising each morning before the sound of the rooster and working each night long after the setting of the sun. It had become a cycle of work and more work, with little variation. Conversation at breakfast had been brief because he would hardly sit still long enough to eat. And conversation at the evening meal had been limited because he was simply too tired. He had repaired, patched, and replaced, pausing only to attend church services with his mother on the Sabbath.

He knew his mother was elated to have him accompany her to church again. He'd quit attending in his youth, choosing to stay at home, like his father, and use the time to do things other than sit on hard pews and listen to Pastor Wight's lengthy sermons. Maude had continued to attend, however, but hadn't nagged him or his father about neglecting their spiritual duties. And that was something Adam admired and appreciated about her.

Following church services—in which Adam had discovered that the pews weren't as hard nor Pastor Wight's sermon as lengthy as he remembered—he'd changed his clothes and got back to work. But for all his efforts, he still felt unsatisfied. The more he did, the more it seemed there was to be done. The front steps were badly weathered and in need of repair. The coal shed was dilapidated and looked like it might fall over in the next stiff breeze. The pump was rusty and required attention…the garden needed weeding…the chicken coop needed new shingles. On and on it went.

He went to bed each night with sore and aching muscles, but he knew it was his own doing. During basic training, a seventeen-week experience that had almost killed him, a drill sergeant had been in his face, yelling directives and making the group run five extra miles because someone hadn't assembled a rifle correctly. They had been forced to climb ropes, scale walls, scamper under coils of barbed wire, endure hours of bayonet practice, shoot at targets until their shoulders throbbed, and march endlessly in formation with full packs on their backs. But now Adam was being harder on himself than the drill sergeant had been. And yet, as he looked at what he'd accomplished on the farm, he realized he was merely scratching the surface.

As if reading his thoughts, Maude laid a hand on his arm. "Things take time, son. Rome wasn't built in a day."

Adam nodded in resignation.

"Lunch will be ready in twenty minutes," she added. "Then we need to get ready. The opening ceremony of Heritage Days begins at two o'clock, and I've invited Sid and Alice and their family to go with us."

"They're back from the cattle auction in Billings?"

"Yes, Alice called last night to say they just got home."

"It'll be good to see them again. Is Ty coming, too?"

"Of course! He was so upset that he couldn't be at the bus stop to greet you. He's coming ahead in his own car so he can drive you around and spend some time with you."

Adam tossed his work gloves aside. "Then I guess I'd better go in and get ready. The fence will have to wait."

He was anxious to see Ty again. But he was nervous too and couldn't help wondering if they'd be as close. So much had changed during the time they'd been apart, and perhaps their relationship had been altered forever as a consequence of the war. But as he thought about the experiences they'd shared over the years, he instinctively felt that the bond between them was timeless.

Hurrying into the house to shower and get dressed, he chuckled in anticipation of meeting his cousin and best friend. In the past, being with Tyrone Hansen had always been an adventure. And there was no reason to expect otherwise today.

The sound of a vehicle pulling up in the yard, gravel skidding and a horn blaring, caused Maude to jump. Hector looked up from the kitchen table as Adam half rose from his chair, staring at the door expectantly.

Moments later there was a loud knock, and the front door flew open. A stocky young man with short, sandy hair, a tanned complexion, and brown eyes appeared in the doorway. Adam grinned at the sight of his cousin, who lived with his parents, Sid and

Alice, on their family ranch five miles north of Reunion. Maude and Alice were sisters, and they had given birth to their sons only two weeks apart. Ty and Adam had been practically raised as twin brothers.

Ty bellowed a greeting, causing Hector to flinch. "Adam, you old son of a gun! Welcome home." He wrapped his arms around Adam and gave him a giant bear hug. "If you aren't a sight for sore eyes."

Maude slapped Ty playfully on the arm. "My goodness, Tyrone. We didn't get Adam back in one piece just to have you break him in two."

Ty let go of Adam and reached for her. "Come here, Auntie. I've got a hug for you too." He picked her up but held her as he would a glass ornament. She protested, but only in fun. When he set her down, he nodded at Hector. "Uncle."

Hector nodded in return and almost smiled.

"Are your parents far behind, Tyrone?" Maude asked, glancing out the kitchen window.

"They'll be along in a few minutes," he replied. Turning back to Adam, he looked his cousin over from head to toe. "Man, it's good to see you again. You haven't changed a bit."

Adam embraced Ty again and then held him at arm's length. "Neither have you."

Without warning, Ty spun Adam around and put him in a headlock. The two wrestled for a minute, testing each other's strength, while Maude looked on in concern.

Suddenly releasing his grip, Ty paused and sniffed the air. "It sure smells good in here. Is that roast beef sandwiches, with scrambled eggs on the side?"

Maude crossed to the cupboard and got a plate. "Care to join us?"

Ty pulled up a chair without hesitation. "Maybe just a bite. Could you pass the sandwiches, Uncle?"

The others watched as Ty tore into the meal. The food disappeared with astonishing speed. Maude offered him seconds, which he readily accepted.

Hector pulled a face. "Doesn't your mother feed you?"

Ty chuckled. "I'm still a growing boy."

"Yeah, sideways," Adam said, ducking a retaliatory swipe.

Finally pushing himself away from the table, Ty groaned contentedly. "Thanks, Auntie. That's the first meal I've eaten since the last one."

Maude laughed. "You're such a kidder, Tyrone Hansen."

"But I'm not kidding when I say it was delicious." He winked at Hector. "You're one lucky man, Uncle."

Hector grunted in reply.

Ty patted his stomach. "I'm so full, I don't know if I'll be able to dance."

Adam glanced at him quizzically. "You're going to dance for us?"

"Very funny. There's a dance tonight at the pavilion."

"The annual Heritage Days community dance," Adam said, almost to himself. "I'd forgotten."

"You've been away," Maude said matter-of-factly.

Hector studied the scrambled eggs on his plate. "Well, I'm not going to any dance."

"Don't be a stick in the mud, Uncle," Ty commented.

"Besides, it's celebration time, dear," Maude added. "And we have so much to be grateful for." She took Adam's hand and squeezed it.

Hector slid his chair away from the table. "What about the chores? All the celebrating in the world won't help get them done."

"We'll finish up when we get back," Adam said. "There are *three* pairs of hands now."

Ty winked at his cousin. "Well, maybe two and a half."

Adam ignored the remark. "How about it, Dad?"

"You can all go if you want. I'm staying right—"

He was interrupted by the arrival of another vehicle. This was followed by the sound of rapid knocking on the door, and three children—a boy and two girls—burst into the kitchen. Adam looked at them in disbelief. "Are these who I think they are?" he said, glancing at Ty.

"The tornado trio in person," Ty replied. "Tim, Judy, and Rachel."

"They've grown so much."

A tall, lanky man and a slightly overweight woman appeared in the doorway. Adam broke out in a wide grin when he saw his uncle Sid and aunt Alice.

"Where is he?" Alice called out, scanning the interior of the kitchen. Her eyes fell on Adam, and she rushed forward, arms extended. She clutched him tearfully, locking him in an embrace that rivaled Ty's fierce bear hug. "Welcome home! Welcome home!"

Sid rushed forward, his large shoes clapping on the hardwood floor. He pounded Adam on the back repeatedly. "Good to see you again," he said in a loud voice that echoed off the kitchen walls. "Welcome home, soldier." He motioned toward the three younger children. "Come on, you guys. Give him a hug!"

Tim, Judy, and Rachel joined their parents, milling around and getting in their fair share of the celebratory hugs and back-slaps. They mauled Adam mercilessly and finally released him, only to grab him moments later and start all over again.

Adam finally managed to extricate himself and hurried over to his mother, who stepped forward to form a line of defense. The bus driver's words—*Sometimes it's as hard coming home as it is leaving, isn't it?*—had just acquired new meaning. Adam's back stung and his ribs ached. Fortunately, there were no other relatives living in Montana, so he wouldn't have to endure another overzealous reception.

"It's so good to see you home, safe and sound," Alice said, her voice quivering. "We haven't drawn an easy breath the whole time."

Me, neither, Adam thought.

"Did you shoot anybody?" Tim asked, his youthful curiosity overriding tact and propriety.

Sid cuffed the boy lightly on the back of the head. "Now, what kind of a question is that?" he said, looking at Adam, the same question lingering in his eyes.

"We were just finishing up lunch," Maude said to her sister. "Can I offer you anything?"

"No, thanks," Alice replied, determined to hug Adam once more. "We ate just before we came."

"Besides, there's no time now," said Ty, suppressing a guilty grin. "We need to get going. The opening ceremony starts soon."

"You coming, Hec?" Sid bellowed, noticing that his brother-in-law didn't make a move to get up from the table.

Hec shook his head. "Too much to do around here."

"And it'll still be here waiting for you when you get back," Sid laughed.

Alice nudged her husband. "Leave him be, Sid." She knew her sister's husband well enough to realize that cajoling him into coming would just make everyone miserable.

"I'll stay and help Dad with the chores," Adam said.

"I won't hear of it," Maude said firmly. "If your father doesn't want to come, that's his decision. But the rest of us are going. I'll ride with Sid and Alice. They can bring me back before the dance so I can help your father with evening chores. You and Tyrone go on ahead." Adam tried to protest, but Maude patted him affectionately on the arm. "And wear your uniform, son."

Adam glanced at his father, who was sitting sullenly at the table, and then turned toward Ty. "Guess I'm going with you. Come on, we can spruce up in my room."

"Hey, I'm already as spruced as a goose," Ty replied. "Just hurry."

Adam followed his mother up the stairs, reappearing a short time later dressed in his uniform. He tugged at his jacket and put on his service cap, pausing for his aunt Alice's appraisal.

"Well, look at you," Alice gushed, about to start another round of celebratory hugs. "You look so handsome in your uniform."

"So handsome," Ty mimicked.

Adam eyed his cousin narrowly. "You ready?"

"I was born ready," Ty replied, causing Sid to roar at his son's joke.

As Adam and Ty headed toward the door, Alice watched them go. "Just look at the two of them together again," she said, a catch in her voice. "Just like old times."

"That's what's so worrisome. Right, Hec?" Sid said, sitting down at the kitchen table with his brother-in-law.

"The two of them on the loose," Hec muttered, shaking his head.

Ty paused in the doorway. "Hey, Uncle. No loud partying and carrying on while we're gone."

Hector actually smiled. "You can count on it." His eyes met Adam's, and the smile faded.

Noticing his cousin's hesitation, Ty yanked him out the door and into the front yard. Motioning dramatically, he pointed to a red '34 Oldsmobile with faded chrome trim that sat in the driveway. "Your chariot awaits," he said.

Adam whistled under his breath. "This old jalopy still runs?"

"Like a top, but it cost an arm and a leg to have the transmission overhauled last month."

"An arm and leg, huh? You're going to have a hard time at the dance tonight, aren't you?"

Ty reached for his car door. "Very good, soldier. Keep it up. The ladies love a man with a sense of humor."

Adam climbed in the passenger's side, hoping they also loved a man with two left feet.

Chapter 6

MAYOR WIL JACKSON stood behind the portable lectern that had been set up on the front steps of the town office. Fleshy jowls practically hid the knot of his necktie as he perused his notes, making sure the pages were in order. When he was satisfied, he glanced at his wife, Lenora, who sat in the front row with a group of other fashionably dressed women. When she gave him the signal with her eyes that it was time to begin, he tugged on the lapels of his double-breasted suit and leaned into the microphone. "Ladies and gentlemen, it is my pleasure to—"

The public address system began squealing. Nathan Roberts, who was standing nearest the unit, leaped to the controls. He adjusted knobs and turned dials and motioned for Wil to try again.

"Ladies and gentlemen, it is my pleasure to welcome you to Heritage Days," Wil said, eyeing the microphone as though daring it to act up again. "It's all the more special this year because the war is finally over."

An enthusiastic round of applause followed. Wil paused and gave a thumbs-up to Nathan, who beamed in self-satisfaction and picked up the commemorative wreath he'd been holding for the ceremony.

From his place in the crowd, Adam recognized Nathan. They had gone through school together. "What's Nathan up to these days?" he whispered, nudging Ty.

"He's your best friend or your worst nightmare." When Adam looked at him curiously, Ty added, "He works at the bank. Loans."

Adam nodded in response. "Nathan was always good with figures."

"Especially one *figure*, in particular," Ty added, outlining the shape of an hourglass with his hands.

Adam noticed the young woman with her back to him, standing beside Nathan, and he nodded in comprehension.

Wil's voice boomed through the square just then, drowning out further conversation. "With the date that will live in infamy," he said, referring to Japan's surprise attack on Pearl Harbor, "the United States was brought into the war that cost more money, claimed more lives, and affected more people than any other war in history."

A subdued murmur went through the crowd.

"Who, within the sound of my voice, can claim they haven't been touched by the war in some way?" Wil continued. "We have all made sacrifices. Some have paid the ultimate sacrifice. I'm thinking today of Winston Brown, who was lost in the Northern Atlantic, victim to a German torpedo. I'm thinking of Carter Brimley, who was shot down over France; David Ranger, who fell in North Africa; and Sam Tunney, who was reported missing in action during the invasion of Iwo Jima." He named Reunion's other twelve young men who had died in the war. "They believed in the cause of freedom and gave their lives defending it. We will never forget them, and we honor them this day."

An atmosphere of reverence settled over the town square. Here and there handkerchiefs appeared as women dabbed their eyes, and men stared solemnly at the ground.

"They fought in the belief that military aggression and political oppression could be overcome. In the words of President Roosevelt: 'No matter how long it may take...the American people, in their righteous might, will win through to absolute victory.' And victory has come, ladies and gentlemen. We have seen the defeat of the German forces in Europe and the ultimate triumph in the South Pacific over Japan."

The applause that followed built into a wave of rejoicing and celebration. Women began embracing one another, and several men pounded each other on the back. Some of the children took advantage of the break in the formalities and scurried among the adults, laughing and chasing one another in a game of impromptu tag.

Adam felt an arm wrap itself around him, and he looked down into the face of his mother. She had somehow found him in the crowd, and her eyes glistened as she embraced him. She didn't need to vocalize her gratitude that Adam wasn't one of the sixteen who would not be returning home.

Wil appeared pleased with the enthusiastic reaction to his speech and looked at Lenora, who nodded at him in approval. He waited for order to be restored and said, "This truly is a day of celebration, isn't it? And it will be all the better when the last of Reunion's men and women of the armed forces return home."

Without warning, Ty pounded Adam on the shoulder and called out, "Here's a returned soldier right now!"

All eyes turned to Adam, who shifted uncomfortably.

"Adam Carlson got home just last week," Ty added.

"Adam Carlson!" Wil said. "Come up here, soldier."

Adam cut a glance of disapproval at Ty.

"Go ahead, dear," Maude said encouragingly.

Adam squared his shoulders and reluctantly made his way onto the podium to loud applause. Wil grabbed him by the hand and pumped vigorously. "Welcome home. We're mighty proud of you. We're mighty proud of *all* of Reunion's men and women in the services."

Adam made a move to return to his place in the crowd, but Wil maintained his grip. "Stay up here and represent them, son." He nodded to the high school band, seated in the temporary bandstand nearby. Upon cue from the director, they began playing "Happy Days Are Here Again."

During the song Adam shifted uncomfortably, feeling conspicuous. He saw tears in the eyes of several people in the crowd, and he realized that for their sakes he needed to overlook his own feelings of discomfort.

When the song ended, Wil returned to his notes.

As Adam listened to the speech, he let his gaze wander out over the crowd. He noticed Nathan had moved closer to the center of the podium, and he nodded to him. Nathan nodded back, his arm around the young woman beside him. Adam had a better look at her now and observed she had long auburn hair, which framed her high cheekbones and accentuated her green eyes. She wore red lipstick and had on a light yellow dress. Adam finally recognized her as Elizabeth Baxter, the adopted daughter of Wil and Lenora Jackson. She had been only a gangly teenager when he left, and now...she wasn't.

His eyes continued to scan the crowd, and he smiled in response as old classmates waved to him. They now had spouses and little children of their own, and Adam could only wonder at the changes time had wrought.

He came back to the moment when Wil coughed into the microphone and referred once more to Reunion's sixteen sons who had been killed in the war. The mood became silent and solemn. Adam fought his emotions as Nathan, on behalf of the Chamber of Commerce, laid a wreath at the base of the portable stage in their memory. Heads bowed as Wil led everyone in two minutes of silence.

Following this, a young man from the band stepped forward and played *Taps* on the bugle. He was flat on a few notes and didn't sustain others long enough, but it didn't matter. It was one local son honoring sixteen other local sons, and it was a worthy tribute.

Wil stepped back to the microphone. "This concludes our ceremony. Everyone's invited to the fairgrounds to check out the activities. And don't forget to come to the pavilion tonight, at eight, where we can dance to the sounds of Kenny Jones and His Moonlight Orchestra."

Applause echoed through the square.

"And remember to stop by the stores today and tomorrow and check out all the specials," Wil said in conclusion. "Enjoy Heritage Days, folks."

Smiling faces greeted Adam wherever he went, and hands continually reached out to slap him on the back and welcome him home. He had to stop frequently to answer questions and listen to comments about how good it was to see him again.

As he and Ty reached the fairgrounds, a voice called out, "Adam. Adam Carlson."

It was Nathan, standing at a booth that said *Shooting Gallery* in flaming red letters. Elizabeth stood beside him.

Adam extended his hand. "Long time, no see, Nathan."

Nathan shook his hand. "Nice to be back, I bet."

"Sure is," Adam said, glancing at Elizabeth.

Nathan gestured toward her. "You remember Elizabeth Baxter, the mayor's niece."

"Of course," Adam said, holding out his hand. "Our families attend the same church."

"That's right," Elizabeth said, putting her hand in his briefly. "You and Ty and Nathan were several classes ahead of me in school. But you didn't pay attention to us little kids then."

I am now, Adam thought, surprised how warm her touch felt. A brief pause followed before he realized he was still holding her hand and staring into her eyes. He released his grip and dropped his hand to his side.

Nathan motioned toward the booth. "Remember going gopher hunting when we were boys? You couldn't hit the broad side of a barn. Learn anything overseas?"

Adam shrugged. "A little."

Pulling a handful of money from his pocket, Nathan selected two nickels and dropped them on the counter. "How about a friendly competition...for old-time's sake?" Picking up one of the pellet rifles, he handed it to Adam. "It's not your regular army issue, but let's see what you can do, anyway. Ten shots each, the winner gets a prize."

"What's the prize?" Ty asked.

Nathan glanced at Elizabeth from the corner of his eye. "How about a kiss from Miss Elizabeth Baxter?"

"Nathan!" Elizabeth protested.

Ty gave a catcall under his breath. "You must feel very confident, Nathan."

Nathan put an arm around Elizabeth and looked down into her face. "Can I have the kiss now, Elizabeth, or wait until after I've shown Adam a thing or two?"

Elizabeth turned her face away and glanced at Adam. Something in her expression told him that she wouldn't mind if Nathan was shown a thing or two either.

Adam motioned to Nathan. "After you," he said, as a group of people crowded around to watch.

Nathan removed his jacket and handed it to Elizabeth. Loosening his necktie, he placed the rifle stock against his cheek and sighted down the barrel. He drew in a deep breath and pulled the trigger, narrowly missing the first target. He adjusted the sights and hit the second target dead center. The crowd responded and more people gathered, attracted by the contest.

He hit the third target and received congratulatory slaps on the back.

Adam glanced over at Elizabeth. Their eyes met briefly again before she turned to watch Nathan line up his next shot.

Nathan hit four more targets in slow succession, each one accompanied by increasingly loud cheers. On the eighth shot, however, he nicked the target but it didn't go down. "It's rigged," he said, scowling.

The man running the booth spoke up indignantly. "It is not!" He walked over and tapped the target, which immediately dropped.

The crowd began buzzing: "It's a miss, it's a miss."

In frustration Nathan fired his next shot too quickly and missed the target. Hissing through clenched teeth, he drew in a deep breath and squeezed off his final shot, hitting the target squarely. He pumped his fist amid the cheering and winked at Elizabeth, wetting his lips.

"Seven out of ten," Ty noted. "Not bad." He turned to Adam. "You've got your work cut out for you."

As the man in the booth reset the targets, Nathan readjusted his necktie and gestured toward Adam. "No pressure, my friend," he said, grinning.

Adam took the rifle and balanced it in his hand. It was nothing more than a toy, really, and he wondered how accurate the sights were. Choosing not to use them, he nestled the stock against his cheek, fixed both eyes squarely ahead, let out his breath, and gently squeezed the trigger.

Ten shots sounded in quick succession. Before anyone could react, it was over. Adam put the rifle down on the counter and stepped back.

There was a momentary silence, and then the man at the booth let out a whoop. "He got 'em all! By golly, he got 'em all!"

Nathan lurched forward to check for himself. All ten targets *were* down. He turned and stared hard at Adam, unable to find his voice.

Ty patted Nathan on the back and shook his head in mock sympathy. "Ten beats seven, I'm afraid. Looks like he *did* learn something overseas, all right."

"I just got lucky," Adam said.

Ty nudged Nathan in the ribs. "What was the prize again?"

Nathan responded by grabbing his jacket from Elizabeth and putting it back on.

Adam tipped his hat to Elizabeth. "Don't worry about it, Miss. All in good fun. I won't hold you to it."

Without warning, Elizabeth stepped forward and kissed him on the lips. Adam was too surprised to react. But Nathan jumped as though a wasp had just stung him, and Ty whistled a loud catcall.

When the kiss ended, Elizabeth backed away and placed a hand to her throat, as though surprised by her own impulsiveness.

She drew in a deep breath and let it out slowly. Her green eyes narrowed, and she flashed Nathan an inscrutable look.

Nathan took her by the arm and spun on his heels, pulling her behind him. She glanced over her shoulder at Adam before disappearing into the crowd.

Ty placed a hand on Adam's shoulder. "You may have surprised Nathan with your sharp shooting, but I'd say Elizabeth Baxter got the drop on you."

A low murmur rumbled in Adam's throat.

"You learned how to handle a rifle in basic training," Ty added, "but obviously there are some basics you *haven't* learned."

Glancing at his cousin, Adam said, "And you're going to teach them to me?"

Ty flexed his fingers until his knuckles cracked. "Watch and learn, soldier boy."

CHAPTER 7

A BREEZE SIFTED THROUGH the open windows and stirred the streamers that hung from the ceiling as Adam followed Ty into the pavilion later that evening. Paper lanterns added an intimate glow to the room, where Kenny Jones and His Moonlight Orchestra were in full swing. The music rose and fell like swallows chasing each other. A table with a large punch bowl and glasses stood along one side, and a dessert table filled with cookies and bars sat next to it. Small groups of people were gathered around the tables, visiting and laughing.

Several young women stood nearby in a tight-knit circle. They kept looking toward the young men who lined the far wall, waiting for one of them to make the first move. But the young men remained in place, as though their job was to keep the wall from falling over.

Ty recognized one of the young women and nudged Adam. "That's Julie Landry, the tall brunette in the middle. I took her out on a date a while back. She was a lot of laughs." He smoothed down his hair. "I'm going to ask her to dance."

"You don't let the grass grow, do you?"

"Let me show you how easy it is. I'll introduce you to one of them."

Adam restrained him. "I'd like a drink of punch first," he said, wishing his mother had come to the dance so he could start out with a less intimidating partner.

"Coward," Ty laughed, walking toward the young women.

Adam headed for the punch bowl and poured himself a glass. Several people greeted him warmly and asked the usual questions. He answered each one, all the while glancing at Ty, who was now talking to the brunette.

Moments later he saw Ty lead her onto the dance floor and swing her gently into the air. When her feet touched down, Ty gave a dramatic gesture and glanced over. Adam waved in feigned appreciation and refocused on his conversation.

His gaze wandered to some people who were standing in a group. He noticed Nathan and Elizabeth among them. Nathan was talking to several men and gesturing with his hands as though making a significant point. Elizabeth was talking animatedly to a young woman, and Adam noticed the way she wrinkled her nose when she laughed.

He put a hand to his lips as the memory of the kiss returned. It was seared in his brain as though it had been applied with a branding iron. He could still feel the softness of her lips and smell the fragrance of her perfume.

A moment later their eyes met, and she walked over to him, an air of apology gathering around her. "About what happened at the shooting gallery today," she said. "I hope I didn't embarrass you. I was just trying to teach Nathan a lesson. He made me feel as though I was a prize at a carnival booth, like a stuffed toy or something."

"Believe me, you're no stuffed toy at a carnival booth," Adam replied.

She waved a hand dramatically in front of her face. "You're going to make me blush."

Adam smiled at her antics and motioned toward the punch bowl. "Can I get you a drink?" he asked, filling a glass and carefully handing it to her.

"Thank you," she said, taking a sip and leaving a trace of red lipstick on the rim. "By the way, that was pretty good shooting at the arcade this afternoon."

"Like I said, I just got lucky."

"I doubt that."

Adam filled a glass for himself and drank in silence for a moment.

Elizabeth studied him. "You certainly surprised Nathan."

Toying with his glass, Adam chuckled. When Elizabeth looked at him questioningly, he said, "Nathan and I go back a long ways."

As if aware he was being talked about, Nathan appeared beside them. "Here you are," he said, taking Elizabeth by the hand and glancing only perfunctorily at Adam. "Let's dance."

She quickly handed her glass to Adam, good-bye written in her expression, and followed Nathan onto the dance floor.

Adam watched them sift into the crowd and begin to jive in rhythm to the music. Not knowing what to do with the half-filled glass, he drained the contents in one swallow, aware that her lips had been pressed to the glass moments earlier.

A break occurred in the dance a short time later, and Ty escorted Julie over to him. "Hey, wallflower boy," Ty said. "Ready to dance yet?" He turned to Julie conspiratorially. "Julie Landry, may I introduce General Adam Carlson, recently returned from overseas."

She rolled her eyes at Ty and held out her hand to Adam. "Nice to meet you, *General*."

Adam extended his hand, which she grasped with a firmness that surprised him. Her smile revealed perfect teeth, and her hair hung softly around her shoulders. She was attractive...but she wasn't Elizabeth. "First Lieutenant, actually," Adam said, scowling good-naturedly at his cousin.

Ty tapped him on the shoulder. "Would you do her the honor of the next dance?"

Adam smiled stiffly. "Sure."

Julie pulled him onto the dance floor. The orchestra began a jive number, and Adam moved awkwardly to the music, trying to avoid stepping on her feet or tripping over his own.

Laughing good-naturedly, Julie took his hand and guided him along. She twirled as if he was leading and added several more moves. He began to feel more comfortable and managed to avoid maiming her or making a fool of himself.

He bumped into someone and turned to apologize. It was Nathan, who twirled Elizabeth and continued dancing without acknowledging him. Suddenly, Nathan was all around him— circling, gyrating, doing fancy footwork, swinging his arms, and spinning Elizabeth vigorously. He was a whirling dervish of flashing feet and pumping arms.

Adam did his best to not get drawn into an unofficial dance contest. He may have beaten Nathan in the shooting competition, but he was obviously no match for him on the dance floor. As soon as the song ended, he escorted Julie back over to Ty. "Thanks for the dance, Julie," he said. "Hope I didn't step on you. I felt like a bull in a china shop."

"You did swell," Julie replied.

"Now ask someone else," Ty said. "The night is still young."

Adam faked a nod as Ty and Julie returned to the dance floor. He watched them until his attention was diverted as Nathan and Elizabeth crossed his line of vision. He saw Nathan twirl Elizabeth, causing her dress to levitate to her knees, revealing a pair of shapely legs in nylon stockings. Nathan obviously noticed them too, because he twirled her repeatedly and fixed his gaze beneath the rising hem of her dress.

At the end of the song Kenny Jones, the orchestra leader, approached the microphone. "For our next number," he said, his voice echoing through the pavilion, "we're going to liven things up a bit. When you hear this sound"—the trombone player gave a sustained sliding note that dipped and returned to the original pitch—"you have to switch partners. Okay, everyone, onto the dance floor. Let's get ready to jive and make this place come alive."

Adam stepped back to the refreshment table, prepared to sit out the dance. But Ty and Julie emerged from the crowd with a young woman in tow. "Adam, this is my friend Susan Godfrey," Julie said. "She needs a partner for this next dance."

Stepping forward and extending his hand, Adam replied, "I'm not much of a dancer, but I'd be happy to be your partner."

"Thank you," Susan said. She was short and slightly overweight, and wore a pair of black cat-eye glasses, which were now attentively focused on Adam's uniform.

Adam led her onto the floor and took up a dance position. Kenny Jones raised his baton, and the orchestra kicked into high gear. The rhythm pulsed through the pavilion as the bass drum pounded out an infectious beat.

The dance floor was crowded, and it was impossible not to bump into one another. Adam kept his movements small, almost dancing on one spot. Ty, on the other hand, was all over the place, matched only by Nathan, who seemed determined to be in several different places at once.

At length, the trombone player blasted out a long, sliding note. There was a flurry of activity, to the accompaniment of boisterous laughter, as everyone frantically exchanged partners. Ty grabbed Susan and handed Julie off to Adam.

Adam noticed that Nathan kept Elizabeth for his partner. When a large man, with an even larger woman, tried to barge in between them and force a trade, Nathan pulled Elizabeth to another section of the dance floor. The music resumed, and the couple was forced to find different partners.

A short time later, the trombone player gave the signal to switch again and another mad scramble ensued. Adam felt a tug on his sleeve and peered down into the face of Eunice Murphy, who was wearing an old-fashioned, faded dress. She looped her arm through his and smiled up at him. Adam thought she appeared to be too frail to be out on the dance floor at all. But she surprised him by gripping his arm firmly and whispering, "Try to keep up, sonny."

Adam patted her hand. "Hello, Mrs. Murphy."

"Do I know you?" she asked.

"I'm Adam Carlson. My mother and I used to deliver milk to you when we had dairy cows."

"I don't need milk today," she said.

Adam was about to explain they didn't operate the dairy business any longer but the music started back up. As the dance resumed, he quickly discovered that Eunice Murphy's injunction to try and keep up had not been spoken idly. He was unable to match her step for step, and she more than proved she belonged on the dance floor. He felt cloddish in comparison and was grateful when the trombone finally sounded once more. He shook his head in wonder as she spryly latched onto another young man and issued the same injunction.

His aunt Alice appeared by his side and grabbed hold of him—he was an easy target in his uniform and service cap. "Would you do me the honor, soldier?" she asked.

"Of course," he replied as the dancing continued. "Where's Uncle Sid?"

"He and Judy and Rachel are taking your mom home. Tim was anxious to come to the dance so I could teach him how to fox trot."

"He's sure growing up."

"And doesn't he think so. He's out on the dance floor right now."

When the trombone sounded once more, Adam discovered he was standing beside Nathan and Elizabeth. He gestured to Nathan to trade partners, but Nathan shook his head.

"Aren't you supposed to have a different partner each time?" Adam said good-naturedly above the cacophony of laughter and music.

"Who's keeping track?" Nathan answered, pulling Elizabeth into the thick of the crowd.

His aunt Alice had disappeared in the chaos, so Adam was forced to look for a new partner. He noticed a young girl milling around in the crowd and held out his hand to her. She willingly accepted the invitation.

On the next signal from the trombone player, Mayor Wil Jackson and his wife, Lenora, approached Nathan and Elizabeth. Nathan graciously gave Elizabeth to her uncle and bowed to Lenora, extending his hand to her. Lenora, wearing a two-strand pearl necklace and a new dress that suited her full figure, smiled and tilted her head in acceptance, taking his hand and sashaying into dance position.

As the dance got underway again, Adam eased his way toward Elizabeth and her uncle. He wanted to be ready to make his move when the trombone sounded again. His time with her at the punchbowl had been all too brief.

When the trombone signal came, everyone scattered to find a new partner. Adam quickly made his way toward Elizabeth. From the corner of his eye, he saw Nathan heading in the same direction. He quickened his pace, careful not to knock anyone over in his headlong rush to reach her first.

The two men reached Elizabeth at the same moment. As Nathan attempted to budge in front of him, he tripped over Adam's foot and pitched forward, striking his head on the edge of the dessert table. The music continued, the dancers blissfully unaware of the incident, as Elizabeth leaned over Nathan in alarm and touched his forehead.

He grimaced and brushed her hand away. "Don't!" he said. "It hurts."

Adam helped Nathan to his feet. "You okay?"

Nathan shook his head in an effort to get his eyes to focus. "You didn't have to tackle me."

"I didn't tackle you. You tripped over my foot."

Nathan grunted under his breath and tried to take a step, but he wobbled and almost fell. Adam and Elizabeth both reached out to steady him.

"Let's get you outside for some air," Adam said.

Nathan pulled his arm free from Adam's grip. "I'll be all right, no thanks to you. Just leave me—" His knees buckled and Adam grabbed hold of his arm again. Nathan pulled his arm free once more, but he remained unsteady, leaning heavily on Elizabeth.

"Actually, we'd better get you home," Adam said. "I'll get Ty and we'll drive—"

"Nathan has his car here," Elizabeth said.

"Okay, I'll drive. Let's get him out to the car."

"I can drive myself," Nathan said, attempting to walk on his own.

"Not tonight you can't," Elizabeth said.

Nathan started to protest but suddenly grabbed his head. "I feel dizzy."

Together, Adam and Elizabeth walked him toward the front entrance, negotiating their way through the energetic crowd.

"Which is his car?" Adam asked, once they were outside.

"The blue one," Elizabeth answered, pointing to the four-door Chevrolet sedan with whitewall tires and shiny chrome hubcaps.

She hurried ahead to open the rear door. Adam paused to get a better grip, finally tossing Nathan over his shoulder and carrying him bodily the rest of the way.

"Is he going to be all right?" Elizabeth asked.

With a final exertion, Adam flopped Nathan onto the backseat. "I've seen men hit on the head by a lot worse things than a dessert table," he replied.

Elizabeth climbed in beside Nathan and leaned his head on her shoulder.

Adam hurried around to the driver's side. "Where are the keys?" he asked, running a hand under the front seat.

"Jacket pocket," Nathan mumbled. "I don't remember which one."

Elizabeth searched his pockets and handed the car keys forward, touching Adam's hand as he reached for them.

"Where to, Miss?" Adam said, putting on the airs of a chauffeur. He looked at her in the rearview mirror and smiled, noticing how her auburn hair framed and accentuated her eyes.

"Head north down Main Street and take the second right turn."

Adam started the car and backed away from the curb. As he drove down Main Street, he glanced in the rearview mirror again. The pavilion had receded in the distance, and all he could see now was Elizabeth, gently stroking Nathan's hair as she cradled his head on her shoulder.

Adam focused his gaze back on the road, struck by the thought that Nathan Roberts, despite the dizziness and the purplish goose egg above his right eye, was one lucky man.

Elizabeth stepped out through the screen door and joined Adam, who was standing on the front porch, leaning on the railing.

"How is he?" Adam asked, turning to face her.

"He has a headache, so I gave him some aspirin and put a cold compress on his forehead. He's resting comfortably now."

"I'm sure he'll be okay. The Nathan I remember had a thick skull."

Elizabeth looked at him questioningly.

"One day when we were kids, a few of us decided to play Tarzan," Adam explained. "My cousin Ty challenged Nathan and me to a race to the top of one of the old poplar trees in the park. We were about halfway up when the branch Nathan was standing on broke. He fell and lay there moaning and crying, but eventually he got to his feet and climbed right back up into the tree."

"That's Nathan," Elizabeth said. "And he's still climbing."

Now it was Adam's turn to look at her questioningly.

"He works at the bank, but his goal is to eventually own it," she explained. "Actually, he wants to own several of them."

"Knowing Nathan, he'll probably do it, too."

She murmured and stood beside Adam at the railing. Together they stared at the evening scene, momentarily lost in their own thoughts. The night was cloudless and the stars glinted overhead, giving the sky the appearance of a studded velvet curtain.

"When I was overseas in Italy," Adam said at length, "I used to look at the North Star at night. It was a constant point in all that was going on around me. And no matter how much the landscape changed, no matter where I found myself, I could always get my bearings by looking up."

Elizabeth folded her hands and stared at him.

"It was comforting to know that it was the same point of light I had looked at many times as a boy," he continued. "It was a reminder of home, of better times." He paused for a moment. "I used to dream about being back and gazing at the North Star—" He turned and looked into her eyes. "—and now, here I am."

She reached over and squeezed his arm, allowing her hand to linger. "Welcome home," she said, smiling appreciatively. "Uncle

Wil spoke for all of us today at the opening ceremony. We're grateful—I'm grateful—for what you did."

"And I'm grateful for what you at home did too. Letters from my mom, along with other news from home, reminded me that we were all in this together."

"The newspapers reported the *facts* about the war. But I'm sure only those who were in it can really know what it was like."

"But that's behind us now. Tonight there are only the community celebrations to think about. Would you like to go back to the dance?"

"I'd better stay with Nathan, in case he has a concussion."

Adam looked at her in concern. "I don't think it's a good idea for you to walk home alone afterward."

Arching an eyebrow, Elizabeth looked at him and said, "This is Reunion, not the big city."

Just then, Nathan called out, "Elizabeth!"

"I'd better check on him," she said.

"And I'd better get back to the dance," Adam replied. "Ty's my ride home."

She stared up into his face. "Thanks for helping Nathan."

"It was the least I could do."

As he stepped off the porch, she called after him, "Think it's safe for *you* to walk back alone?"

He turned and grinned at her. "This *is* Reunion, right?"

They looked at each other for a moment.

"Elizabeth!" Nathan called again, his voice urgent and demanding.

"Thanks again," she said, disappearing inside.

Adam made his way down the sidewalk. The leaves chattered in the trees along the boulevard, harmonizing with the mourning doves calling to one another from the dark recesses of the branches. But he didn't notice. His mind was on the events of the day, and he was hardly aware of traversing the five blocks to the pavilion.

Nathan lay on the living room couch, his head resting on a cushion. Elizabeth sat beside him, holding his hand. "Feeling any better?" she asked.

He rolled his eyes toward her. "You didn't have to do it, you know."

"Do what?"

"Kiss him today at the shooting gallery."

She released his hand. "Hey, you're the one who made the deal."

He dropped his gaze and looked miserable.

She leaned down and stroked his cheek. "Look, just don't treat me like I'm a prize in a contest. I hope I'm more to you than that."

"Of course you are, Elizabeth. Come here."

He gently pulled her down until their lips met. But he quickly turned away and put a hand to his forehead. "It feels like someone's beating the inside of my skull with a hammer."

Elizabeth lifted the cloth from his forehead. "I'll run this under the water again."

Nathan settled back on the cushion and closed his eyes.

Standing at the kitchen sink, Elizabeth held the cloth under the cold water. Then she turned off the tap and leaned against the sink, watching the water drain. Her thoughts went to the events of the day. She had so looked forward to Heritage Days—to wearing her new dress, attending the carnival, and going to the dance. Especially the dance. But things hadn't turned out as she had envisioned. Nathan had pulled her away from the carnival after the incident at the shooting gallery, and the dance had ended prematurely when he got injured. Still, it had been an eventful day, one she wouldn't soon forget.

Wringing out the cloth, she made her way back into the living room.

CHAPTER 8

A DAM PAUSED IN repairing a hole in the wire mesh around the chicken coop and wiped the perspiration from his face. It had been five days since the dance, and he had allowed the events of that evening to occupy his thoughts a great deal as he worked. It had been easy to talk to Elizabeth on Nathan's front porch, and the way she had teased him about *his* personal safety in walking back to the pavilion alone still made him smile.

He had gone to church with his mother on Sunday and had seen Elizabeth there, sitting with Nathan and her aunt and uncle. During the service he had found his attention shifting to her, and as a result he had missed portions of Pastor Wight's sermon. And once when he glanced at her, he found that she was looking directly at him.

On Tuesday, when he had gone into town with his father to get some farm supplies, he'd noticed her step into Yang's Dry Cleaners, to pick up some dry cleaning, he assumed. He could only see her from the back, but there was no mistaking the color of her auburn hair and the shape of her figure. He was tempted to walk into the shop and feign surprise at meeting her, but he couldn't think of a valid excuse to enter the establishment, considering he didn't have an item of clothing to drop off or to pick up. So he had helped his father load the supplies and had climbed into the truck, all the while scanning Main Street for another glimpse of her. She hadn't reappeared, however, and he was disappointed as he and his father drove back to the farm.

Now, setting his tools aside, he reached for the glass of lemonade and plate of cookies that sat on a sawhorse in the shade. His mother had brought the refreshments to him a short time earlier. He drank the lemonade and consumed three cookies.

It felt good to have his mother fuss over him again—something he had missed in Italy. On more than one occasion he'd seen seasoned soldiers lying wounded and dying in the foxholes, calling out for their mothers.

He thought back to the day he'd come upon a German soldier who had gotten separated from his unit. The soldier was no more than a youth, and Adam had easily disarmed him. The young man fell to the ground and cried, *"Mutter! Mutter!"* As Adam was about to take him prisoner, a stray bullet hit the German in the head, scattering his brains on the ground. Adam ducked for cover, and as he lay there, he imagined a woman in a distant village in Germany opening a letter that reported her son's death.

Adam turned toward the farmhouse. While overseas he'd often dreamed of walking through the front door and greeting his mother. Or sitting at the kitchen table and enjoying the aroma of bread baking in the oven or stew simmering on the stove. Now he no longer had to be content with just dreaming about it.

He grabbed another cookie and on a whim headed for the house, not because he needed a break...but because he could. His ability to do something this casual had been restored— something forever denied the young German soldier.

Maude was standing at the kitchen counter kneading dough and listening to Doris Day singing "Sentimental Journey" on the radio. Adam noticed a dab of flour on his mother's cheek and wiped it off with the dish towel.

She frowned in concern when she noticed his glistening forehead and the sweat stains on his shirt. "You're working too hard, son."

"Now that's the pot calling the kettle black," Adam said.

Maude laughed lightly and returned to her work. "It seems so familiar to have you working here again."

Adam sat down at the table. "It's like I was never away."

"Your father commented on it too."

Adam perked up. "He never said anything to me about it."

"He's a man of few words. You know that as well as anyone. He doesn't pay compliments very often."

Grunting under his breath, Adam leaned back in his chair. "There's so much more I want to do around here. A fresh coat of paint would do wonders to the place. The chicken coop needs new shingles, and the old woodshed should be torn down before it falls down. We can salvage the wood to build a storage shed. But every time I bring up the subject, Dad gets testy."

Maude looked up at Adam sharply. "He hasn't said anything in particular, has he?"

"What do you mean?"

"Nothing," she said dismissively. Continuing to knead the dough, she added, "I just want you to know that we *both* appreciate the work you're doing, son. You're an answer to prayer."

Adam leaned forward in his chair and propped his elbows on the table. "When I was a kid, work seemed like slavery. But it's funny what four years away can do to a guy. It feels good to be fixing up the place."

"And it's looking better already. A fresh coat of paint will spruce it up even more. That can't help but increase the value of the farm."

"It'll be like turning the clock back ten years for the farm."

Maude gave a half-smile—to Adam there was an expression in her face that he couldn't interpret—and reached for the bag of flour. "Oh, dear," she said. "I was going to make some more bread, but there isn't enough flour."

"I'll get a new bag from the pantry."

"We're out. This is the last one."

Adam pushed away from the table. "I can run into town and get some flour, if you like. I need to go to the Mercantile for some paint anyway. Anything else you want me to pick up?"

Maude thought for a moment, rubbing her cheek with her hand and putting a streak of flour back where it had been. "Get a bag of salt. And also some kerosene."

Adam raised both eyebrows. "New recipe?"

Maude laughed. "No, silly. The lamp in the chicken coop needs refilling."

"So flour, salt, and kerosene. Anything else?"

"We should have your uniform dry-cleaned."

Wrinkling his brow, Adam said, "Isn't it just going into the closet, with mothballs?"

"You'll still be wearing it to formal events and veterans' ceremonies," she said, rummaging through her purse and handing him some money.

"Keep it, Mom. I'll take care of things."

She looked at him for a moment. "I want you to know, son, that your father and I appreciate the money you sent us each month. Although I admit that neither one of us could bring ourselves to spend it at first, knowing the price you were paying for it. But I convinced him it would dishonor you if we didn't. And heaven knows we needed it."

"So he agreed to use it?"

Maude nodded. "Your father's a complicated man, Adam. A lot of it is his own making, I admit. But in his own way, I know he's proud of you too."

She replaced the money in her purse, turning her back so Adam couldn't see her face.

He came up behind her and laid a hand on her shoulder. "He and I'll work things out, Mom. We'll be fine."

She patted his hand without turning around.

He went upstairs and changed into a clean pair of jeans and a short-sleeved cotton shirt. When he reappeared, he had his uniform draped over his arm. "Today will be the first time I've driven into town on my own since I got back," he said, reaching for the keys that hung on a nail by the door.

"You just be careful, dear."

"I know. The old truck isn't much, but it's all we've got, right?"

"No. *You're* all we've got."

The bell above the door of Yang's Dry Cleaners jingled as Adam entered.

Julie stood with her back to the front counter, hanging up a freshly dry-cleaned dress. "Be right with you," she called, taking a moment to adjust it. "Now, what can I—" She stopped abruptly when she saw Adam. "Well, hello. Haven't seen you since the dance."

Adam returned her greeting. "I didn't know you worked here," he added.

"I've been here for three months now." She glanced toward the garment racks. "But there's someone else who's worked here a lot longer than me."

Adam looked at her questioningly. Julie motioned him to wait and stepped behind the garment racks, reappearing moments later with Elizabeth.

"You work here too?" Adam said, grinning when he saw Elizabeth. Now he understood why he'd seen her enter the dry cleaners the other day.

"She's the supervisor," Julie said.

Lee Yang came in from the back room in time to hear Julie's comment. "But I boss," he said, pointing a thumb at his chest. "Welcome home, soldier. I see you at opening ceremony the other day."

"It's good to be home," Adam replied.

"Any dry cleaning you have today. Free."

"That's nice of you," Adam said. "Thanks."

"You go overseas, fight, help everybody. You deserve it." He glanced at the uniform draped over Adam's arm. "Elizabeth see to you."

The work routine quickly returned to the dry cleaners. Julie went over to the steam press, and Lee Yang went to the spotting table to refill a container of cleaning fluid.

Adam laid his uniform on the counter and looked at Elizabeth. "So you're the supervisor here?"

She lowered her voice secretively. "Until I can decide on a permanent career."

Adam scanned the interior of the shop, noticing steam billow from the steam press, where Julie was working on a dress. "I can't imagine why you'd want to leave here," he said, wiping his forehead.

"It's not that bad, really. Although it *is* hard to keep the curls in your hair."

He glanced up. "Your hair looks fine to me."

She tucked a strand of hair behind her ear and smiled at the compliment.

After a moment's hesitation, Adam cleared his throat. "So how's Nathan doing?"

"Good. After you left, he finally settled down." She held up a hand as Adam opened his mouth to reply. "And, yes, I made it home safely."

Adam hid a grin. "That was my next question."

Elizabeth motioned toward the uniform. "Do you want it deep cleaned or spot cleaned?"

"Better give it the works."

While he waited for her to write his name on the claim stub, he noticed a poster taped to the front window. "I see there's a community hayride tonight. I hadn't heard about it."

"Posters are up all over town."

When Elizabeth handed the stub to him, he asked, "Are you and Nathan going?"

"Nathan has to meet with a client in Great Falls, so he can't make it." She turned toward Julie and spoke in a loud voice, so her friend would hear her over the sound of the equipment. "But Julie is trying to talk me into going on the hayride with her."

"It'll be fun," Julie said, lifting the top pad of the steam press and removing the dress. "And you're just going to sit around the house otherwise."

"Why don't you go, Elizabeth?" Adam asked.

Julie stepped away from the steam press. "Because Nathan doesn't like her to go places without him."

Over at the spotting table, Lee Yang shook his head and muttered something to himself.

"I can make my own decisions, thank you," Elizabeth said, directing a scowl at Julie, who retreated back to the steam press and continued working on the dress.

Adam eyed Elizabeth curiously, considering Julie's comment. Elizabeth hung the uniform on a nearby rack and came back to the counter. "How about you? Are you going?"

"I don't think so. There's so much work to do on the farm."

"You know what they say: *'All work and no play...'*"

Adam chuckled. "Have you been talking to my mother?"

"Well, the other night you sounded like my uncle, so it's only fair."

"Touché," Adam replied.

"Your mother's right, though. The break would do you good."

Adam gestured toward her. "Look who's talking."

An expression of sudden determination crossed Elizabeth's face. "All right, I'll tell you what. I'll go if you go."

"What time does the hayride start?"

"Seven o'clock. At the community center parking lot."

"I can finish things up by then. All right, it's a date."

She put her hands on her hips in mock disapproval. "If you're asking me on a date, it's only fair to warn you that I'm already going steady with Nathan."

Adam looked at her narrowly. "You're a tease, you know that?"

"Really?" she replied, keeping a straight face.

He backed toward the door, fighting with the doorknob. "See you there at seven," he said.

Outside, he pocketed the claim stub and paused to consider the situation. By inviting one another, he and Elizabeth were committing to meet at the hayride tonight. What exactly were they thinking would happen? The question narrowed itself to a single point in his mind. What was *he* thinking...or hoping? Uncertain of the answer, he climbed into the pickup truck and started the engine.

As he headed down Main Street, he reminded himself that it was just a hayride. He'd been on one many times before. The participants would travel around town or out into the country on a hayrack, laughing and socializing as they went. Nothing more. Still, he was in unfamiliar waters this time, and the thought of showing up alone made him feel uneasy. His mind churned as he considered the situation. He needed backup. He decided to call and ask Ty to accompany him. His cousin was fun and would keep things lively. Safety in numbers.

Adam was almost to the farm when he realized he'd forgotten the grocery items and the paint.

CHAPTER 9

THE COMMUNITY CENTER parking lot was already crowded when Adam and Ty arrived. People milled around, talking and laughing in anticipation of the hayride. A flat rack, hooked up behind a '38 Dodge pickup truck, sat in the center of the parking lot. A mound of loose straw was in the middle of the rack, and bales had been placed around the edges. Elizabeth and Julie sat on some bales near Susan and a few other young women, who were talking and gesturing to one another.

Ty nudged Adam and pointed at the girls, giving a devilish grin as he hopped on the wagon. He picked up an armful of loose straw and crept toward the unsuspecting duo. Moments later Elizabeth and Julie disappeared in a shower of straw. Julie screamed and made a grab for Ty, who deftly moved out of the way. She chased him around the pile in the center, giggling as she stated what she'd do to him when she caught him.

Adam came around to the back of the hayrack and looked up at Elizabeth, who was still shaking straw out of her hair. "This seat taken?"

Elizabeth smiled and patted the bale. "It is now."

He hopped onto the rack effortlessly and sat beside her. "Glad to see you made it."

As she was about to respond, a pile of straw descended on them.

"Let's get him!" Adam called, helping Elizabeth to her feet. "You help too, Susan. You're on our side." The three of them picked up an armful and threw it at Ty.

"Hey!" the driver called, sticking his head out of the truck window. "Let's keep *some* on the rack. Places, everyone. We're moving out."

There was a scramble to get seated. Adam slid closer to Elizabeth to make room for Susan. As he brushed some straw from Elizabeth's shoulder, Ty and Julie crowded onto the next bale.

71

Glancing in the rearview mirror, the driver popped the clutch and the truck lurched forward. Everyone yelled and grabbed onto the nearest person. Elizabeth and Susan clung to Adam, and he allowed himself to enjoy the sensation of their arms clamped around his.

"Who's driving?" Adam called to Ty.

"Alf Whitehead," Ty answered. "And he's never sober at this time of night."

"In that case, hang on for dear life," Julie said, looping her arm through Ty's as the hayrack swung into the street.

"I am," Elizabeth said, tightening her grip on Adam.

"Everyone okay?" Alf called, looking back and coming dangerously close to hitting a parked car.

As the hayrack swerved toward the center of the road, Elizabeth fell against Adam. They clung to each other and laughed like they were on an amusement park ride. The doubts he'd had earlier about what to expect when he and Elizabeth met at the hayride began to disappear. He found himself relaxing with her.

Until Ty set his sights on them again.

Adam had just turned to say something to Elizabeth when he found himself buried beneath a pile of straw once more. He fought his way out of it in time to see Ty reaching for another armful.

"Hey, truce," Adam called.

"And spoil all the fun?" Ty said, scooping up more straw. "Come on, Julie. Straw fight!"

"I thought we were on the same side," Elizabeth said, appealing to her friend.

Julie glanced at Ty. "If you can't beat 'em, join 'em."

At that moment, Alf slowed at an intersection for an oncoming car, skidding to a stop in the loose gravel and sending up a cloud of dust.

Realizing that Ty and Julie weren't going to relent, Adam leaped off the hayrack and held out his arms to Elizabeth. "Jump!" he called.

Through the swirling dust Elizabeth glanced from Ty and Julie, with their arms loaded, to Adam, who was beckoning to her.

Giving a cry of uncertainty, she leaped off the rack as the straw descended on the spot she had just occupied. Adam caught her and steadied her in the uncertain footing on the gravel road.

He turned in time to see the truck lurch forward, sending Ty and Julie tumbling into the straw.

Adam grinned as Ty scrambled to his feet and shouted, "You haven't seen the last of us!"

"We have for now," Elizabeth shouted back.

Adam held her against him and waved goodbye to Ty, laughing as the hayrack receded in the distance, finally disappearing altogether.

Strolling along the tree-lined boulevard, Adam and Elizabeth laughed at their escape. The sun slanted westward toward the Rocky Mountains, lengthening the shadows. A breeze sifted through the treetops and brought relief from the stifling heat that wrapped northern Montana as snuggly as a woolen blanket. A flock of geese honked in answering calls as they flew overhead, and a gray cat padded its way down the sidewalk before disappearing through a gap in the hedge that fronted one of the yards.

"Shall I walk you home?" Adam asked.

Elizabeth shook her head. "Let's walk for a while. The evening is so pleasant. Unless you want to get rid of me."

"No, of course not," he replied quickly. "But it's going to be dark in a while, and a young woman shouldn't be alone when—"

"I'm not alone. I'm with you."

Adam smiled in chagrin. "I'm sounding like your father, aren't I?"

She touched his arm. "You don't feel like a ghost."

"I'm sorry. I wasn't thinking. How old were you when you lost your parents? I remember it was a terrible tragedy."

"I was three when they were involved in a car accident. Dad was killed instantly; Mom died two days later in the hospital."

Subdued by the information, Adam simply said, "I'm sorry."

"Aunt Lenora and Uncle Wil took me in and raised me. They're the only parents I've ever really known."

"I notice that you call them *Aunt* and *Uncle*."

"Aunt Lenora insisted on it from the beginning. She wanted to make sure I kept my heritage, I guess. They never legally adopted me, so I've always gone by Baxter instead of Jackson."

"Why didn't they have any children of their own?"

Elizabeth laughed lightly. "Raising me discouraged them from wanting any more children, I'm afraid."

"You couldn't have been that bad."

"I'm not sure Uncle Wil and Aunt Lenora would agree with you." When Adam looked at her doubtfully, she added, "You want an example? Julie and I once snuck Uncle Wil's car when we were thirteen and went for a joyride. We did all right until I got the brake and the gas pedal mixed up. We ended up driving over the curb and crashing into a fire hydrant. You should have seen the water!"

"I did something worse. I once drove the tractor into the side of the cowshed and punched a hole in the wall. It frightened one cow so badly that it ran into the barbed-wire fence. After that, the cow was known as Three Teats."

Elizabeth laughed and said, "I was grounded for one month."

"Instead of being grounded from driving the tractor, my dad made me drive it out to the fields and plow them all by myself. I went from morning until evening for a solid week."

"You didn't have any brothers who could help out?"

"No. Like you, I'm an only child."

"So you discouraged your parents from wanting any more children too?"

Adam made a face. "Actually, yes. When my mom was expecting me, she told my dad that she would wait until the coldest night of the year to go into labor. She was good to her word. Her labor pains began in the middle of a January blizzard. Dad had to hitch the horse up to the sleigh and drive three miles into town for the doctor. On the way back, the storm was so blinding that my dad dropped the reins and gave the horse its head, fearing they would be found frozen to death the following morning in the middle of a pasture. But the horse led him and the doctor safely to the farm. The labor was longer and more difficult than the journey to get the doctor, however, and my mom and I almost didn't make it. It was an experience my father vowed never to repeat. And he kept his word. So, yes, I guess you could say I discouraged my parents from having any more children."

They continued to share stories back and forth, laughing at some incidents and growing serious at others, all of which unfolded like chapters in twin autobiographies. Adam found himself opening up to her like a vault door, expressing things he had never shared with anyone else. He was amazed at how easily she unlocked the combination to his innermost thoughts and feelings. Perhaps it was their common background. Although separated in age by four years, they had attended the same church and the same schools, and they could laugh about the same townspeople. Being with Elizabeth felt like coming home.

The sun dipped below the jagged horizon, backlighting the Rocky Mountains and tinting the sky with shades of crimson. The moon came out, and Adam paused to look at it as it hung in the sky like a silver dollar. He had often watched it in Italy and longed for the time when a casual glance upward didn't have to be followed by a quick peek over his shoulder to make up for the momentary distraction. Tonight was such a time.

"It's beautiful, isn't it?" Elizabeth said, pausing beside him.

He glanced at her from the corner of his eye. "Yes, it is," he replied, wanting to add more than he dared say. *She* was beautiful, too, but for now the compliment would have to remain buried in his simple response.

Elizabeth drew in a deep breath and let it out slowly. "It's so peaceful tonight. You probably didn't have much of a chance to enjoy evenings in Italy, did you?"

"Not much."

"I can't imagine how hard it must have been for you. For all of you," Elizabeth said, as they resumed walking. "Why did you enlist, if you don't mind my asking?"

Adam considered the question before replying. "I joined the army the day I turned nineteen to escape farm life and the drudgery, I guess. Part of the reason was to get some new clothing, including leather boots. The Depression hit my family hard, and we had nothing except the food we produced ourselves. I decided that by enlisting and having half of my monthly pay sent home, it would go a long way in helping out, since it would mean one less mouth to feed. But I wasn't able to make my father understand. He felt betrayed, claiming that I was deserting him when I was needed most. And he emphasized that opinion by not coming to see me off or writing to me even once."

Elizabeth looked at him sympathetically. "I'm sure he loves you in his own way. He just doesn't know how to express it."

Adam smiled wryly, remembering their earlier conversation at the dry cleaners. "You *have* been talking to my mother."

Laughing and nudging him with her elbow, Elizabeth said, "You'll never know." She turned serious and added, "But if that's what she said to you, I'm sure she's right. Mothers can be pretty perceptive, you know."

Adam plucked a blade of grass that was growing in a clump along the sidewalk and stuck the stem in his mouth. "I know for a fact that my mother is. She's always been able to look right into my soul."

Nudging him again, Elizabeth said, "See? So listen to what she's telling you about your dad."

"I'm trying, believe me. But it takes more than that. Words are just...words."

"But they're a start. Things take time."

Adam spat out the grass stem. "If you say 'Rome wasn't built in a day,' I'll know you're conspiring with my mother."

Elizabeth's eyes twinkled in the moonlight. "All right, I won't." Then in a whisper she added, "But it wasn't."

They walked aimlessly, continuing to talk. At length they turned down Main Street and approached the dance pavilion. Motioning toward the vacant structure, Adam said, "As I recall, the last time we were here, I tried to dance with you."

"We didn't get the chance, did we?"

He tried the door and found it unlocked. "Would you do me the honor, Miss?"

She gave a curtsy and accompanied him inside. The interior was lit with a silver sheen from the moonlight that streamed through the open windows, and the air felt cool and refreshing. Together they walked to the center of the dance floor.

Taking up a formal dance position, he hesitated. "It's only fair to warn you, though, that I have two left feet."

"I'll risk it, sir."

He took the first step, trying to recapture the mood and the music of Kenny Jones and His Moonlight Orchestra. Hesitant at first, and encouraged by her when he *did* step on her foot, he danced with increasing confidence, and soon they were moving as one.

He picked up the tempo. The waltz became a jive, and he twirled her around. Then to make her laugh, he pirouetted under her arm.

"You're improving, Mr. Astair."

"Thank you, Miss Rogers."

Deciding to risk a bolder move, he attempted a more dramatic twirl. As she spun under his arm, they bumped into one another and Elizabeth lost her balance. He grabbed her before she could fall, and she locked her arms around his neck. For an instant they resembled a sculpture of a woman reclining in her partner's out-stretched arms.

"Are you all right?" he asked, helping her back up.

"Clumsy me," she laughed.

"No, I've got two left feet, remember?"

She smiled. "You just need more practice."

"I wasn't invited to too many dances in Italy, that's true."

Her smiled faded. "How did you endure it? The war, I mean. The newsreels always showed so much suffering and damage. How did you witness all that and not get...depressed?"

"Who says I didn't get depressed?"

Elizabeth looked at him apologetically. "I'm sorry. I shouldn't have said anything. It's just that you're so positive and strong."

He squeezed her hand. "It's because I'm here with you," he replied gently, brushing a strand of hair from her cheek.

She dropped her gaze suddenly and stepped away from him. "Maybe we'd better get back. The others will be looking for us." She headed for the door.

Adam followed, and they walked in silence for a moment. As they crossed the intersection, he said, "Hope I didn't spoil the hayride for you. I thought flight was better than fight, considering the situation."

"It's all right. I enjoyed the evening."

"So did I."

"I liked our talk. And what I said earlier about your father? I really hope you can work things out."

Adam fell silent as he considered her words. She made it seem believable...possible. Just like his mother did, and he trusted his mother more than anyone else on earth. Elizabeth had now joined that circle of trust, and he regretted the evening was coming to an end.

The community center was dark when they arrived. The parking lot was vacant, and even the straw that had fallen from the hayrack during the straw fight had been cleaned up. There was no evidence that the hayride had ever occurred.

"We were gone longer than I thought," Elizabeth said, looking around in surprise.

"I'll walk you home," Adam said.

A red '34 Oldsmobile came roaring down the street and pulled into the parking lot. Ty unrolled the window and stuck out his head. "Where have you two been? We've been driving around looking for you."

"We went for a walk," Adam answered.

Julie leaned across Ty and said, "Elizabeth, Nathan was here."

"He's back from Great Falls already?" Elizabeth said, genuinely shocked.

"His client forgot about the appointment, so Nathan turned around and drove straight back to your place. When your aunt said you went to the hayride, he tracked us down. He got here just as we were returning from the hayride."

"And no Elizabeth," Ty said, wagging a finger.

"What did you tell him?"

"That you ditched the hayride with Adam," Julie replied. "Well, what were we supposed to say? He caught us by surprise. You said he wasn't coming."

Elizabeth hurried toward the car. "I'd better call him."

Adam held the door open and climbed in the backseat beside her. She slid across to the far side and said little as they left the community center. He glanced at her several times, but she didn't make eye contact. Something had changed between them, and he understood what it was. She was going steady with Nathan. What business did he—Adam—have spending time with her? If it was the other way around and he was going steady with her, what would he expect from Nathan? Hard questions—ones he didn't have answers for.

When they arrived at her place, Elizabeth got out before Adam could get the door for her and quickly headed up the front walk.

Adam watched her go and sat back in his seat. "It was just an innocent stroll," he said, almost to himself.

"You know what they say?" Ty said. "Innocence is in the eye of the beholder."

"That's *beauty*," Julie said.

Ty glanced in the rearview mirror at Adam. "I like my version better."

Adam met his cousin's eyes briefly before looking away.

As Elizabeth passed her aunt's open bedroom door, Lenora said, "Nathan came by. Twice, actually."

Elizabeth stopped abruptly. "Twice?"

"He dropped in the first time to surprise you, but you weren't home. I told him you went to the hayride with Julie. He left to find you but apparently wasn't able to because he came back to see if you had arrived yet. When you still weren't here, he went home."

"What did he say?"

"That he'd see you tomorrow."

"I'd better call him."

"Frankly, he sounded tired. I think he was going home to bed."

Elizabeth's mind began racing as she attempted to draft the explanation she was going to give Nathan. Julie's comment earlier today that Nathan didn't like Elizabeth to do things without him was no idle observation. And as Elizabeth had already explained to her aunt, Nathan was possessive. But so far she had been able to keep a balance between her needs and his demands. Still, she didn't want to hurt him.

As Elizabeth turned to leave, Lenora said, "I know it's late, dear, but let me ask your opinion. I can't decide which necklace goes best with this dress I'm wearing to my social club tomorrow evening."

Elizabeth sighed inwardly, thinking how insignificant her aunt's quandary was in comparison to her own. Still, looking at the necklaces would provide a distraction from her present dilemma.

As she studied the assortment of silver and gold chains and the strings of pearls, she remembered the times she'd secretly looked through them as a young girl, playing dress-up and wearing as many of them as she could fit around her neck. If her aunt only knew the abuse her necklaces had taken over the years! Elizabeth reached for the two-strand pearl necklace, the one that always seemed to glow with an inner light. "This one will be perfect," she said at length.

Lenora eyed it affectionately. "That's my favorite. It belonged to my mother and to her mother before that. And one day it will belong to you."

Elizabeth looked at her aunt in surprise. "Thank you, Aunt Lenora." She held the necklace up to her. "I'll always treasure it."

"I know you will. You have ever since you were a little girl."

"Why, whatever do you mean?" Elizabeth replied, doing her best Scarlett O'Hara impersonation.

"My necklaces were often in a different arrangement than I had left them. Especially this one."

Elizabeth grimaced guiltily. "And here I thought I was being so clever."

Lenora placed the necklace around her niece's neck and looked at her in the mirror. "You'll look beautiful wearing it on your wedding day."

"My wedding day?"

"Yes, when you get married, I'm giving it to you as a wedding gift." She held up a finger to interrupt Elizabeth. "Not that I want you to rush things, mind you. But sometimes a person can take things too slow, as well."

Choosing to ignore the implications of that comment, Elizabeth removed the necklace and handed it to her aunt. "I'm going to go to bed now, Aunt Lenora. It's late, and I've got to go to work in the morning."

"Good night, dear. Sweet dreams."

Elizabeth left the room without replying.

After dropping Julie off, Ty drove Adam out to the farm. He pulled into the yard and killed the headlights.

"Adam, I went along with you on the hayride tonight to help you get a social life. But remember that I told you there were some basics you hadn't learned yet? Well, one of them is to know who's on the market and who's not."

"So you're a Realtor now?"

Ty put on an air of mock sophistication. "When it comes to the ladies, think of me as the voice of experience."

Adam rolled his eyes. "I know you mean well, Ty, but I don't need the lecture."

"I think you do. We're not little kids anymore. Back then you could take Nathan's aggie in marbles or he could take your Babe Ruth baseball card and get away with it. But things have changed now. When it comes to matters of the heart, it's a different ball game."

"As in three strikes, I'm out?"

"As in ball four...walk. And keep walking."

"Speaking of which, I'm going to walk into the house now."

Ty cuffed him on the shoulder. "You know I'm only trying to help. And just to show you that I have your best interest at heart, I'm going to take you to Julie's birthday party tomorrow night."

"I'll pass, thanks."

Ty winked at him. "Several *available* young women will be in attendance."

"I've got too much to do around here."

"I'll pick you up at eight."

Adam looked at his cousin intently. "You're not going to take no for an answer, are you?"

"Eight sharp."

Pursing his lips, Adam got out of the car and climbed the front steps. Several treads creaked in protest.

Ty spun the tires and pulled away, honking the horn eight times.

Adam waved in acknowledgment and bent down to examine the bottom treads. They needed immediate attention. Like everything else. His to-do list was growing longer, not shorter. There weren't enough hours in the day to accomplish everything.

He glanced at the receding car in time to see the taillights disappear over the crest in the road. In less than twenty-four hours the same car would reappear, coming for him. He decided to get up earlier than usual and start work. Because like it or not, he was going to a birthday party tomorrow evening.

CHAPTER 10

THE FOLLOWING MORNING dawned dull and gray. Thick clouds hung in the air, promising rain, and a cool wind descended from the mountains to the west. A fresh scent rode the current, arriving as a harbinger of the moisture that would surely follow, and the tall mixed grass surrounding the farm stirred in anticipation.

Hector stepped onto the front porch, doing up the straps on his bib overalls. He studied the sky for a moment, then let his gaze wander to Adam, who was hunched over the bottom step, pounding a shim under one corner to level it. "You're hard at it," Hector said.

"Morning, Dad," Adam replied, setting the hammer aside and standing on the bottom step to test it. "That's better. The corner had settled. I was afraid you or Mom might slide off when it gets icy."

"We're not that old and decrepit, thank you."

"I just meant—"

Hector held up a hand. "It'll be nice to have the step fixed up."

Adam smiled and said, "Would you stand on the other end of this board for a minute? I need to cut it to replace the bottom tread."

Hector scratched his stubble chin and stepped onto the end of the board. Adam marked his line and reached for the saw, cutting vigorously into the wood. Sawdust swirled up in the morning air, followed by the sweet aroma of spruce. The stub end dropped to the ground as Adam made the last pass with the saw and Hector stepped off the board. Rubbing the hair-like splinters that stuck out from the cut end, Adam laid the board in place and tried to position it to match the other treads.

Hector looked at the board critically. "Too short."

Adam stared in disbelief. "But I measured it."

"Measure twice, cut once."

Adam reached for a new board and attached his tape measure to the far end. He made a mark with a pencil and reached for the saw again. Making a starting groove, he cut determinedly into the wood.

Hector stopped him as Adam finished the cut and got ready to nail the board in place. "You've got the cut end out. You don't want the jagged edge to be seen. Here, let me do it."

"No, I got it, Dad. You go ahead with the chores. I'll finish up here."

Hector shrugged and started for the barn.

Adam watched him go and shook his head grimly. The day was not getting off to a good start, and it looked like it was only going to get worse as the clouds darkened and raindrops began to land in the yard.

His mind reverted to the events of the hayride and his evening stroll with Elizabeth, and how they had ended up at the pavilion. It had been a special time for him—the culmination of four years of longing for just such a carefree evening. It had been so easy to talk to her, and he had hated to see the evening end. Especially the way it did. He could still see Elizabeth sitting in the backseat on the way home, pressed against the far door. He had felt so distanced from her.

Like he did from his father.

He reached for the hammer and pounded a nail in place, hitting it repeatedly, long after it had buried itself in the wood.

Elizabeth peered out the window of Yang's Dry Cleaners, watching the rain dance on the sidewalk. She'd arrived before Lee Yang and Julie to open the shop, just ahead of the downpour, and was grateful to be indoors. There was a coziness she always experienced during a summer rainstorm, a certain nostalgia that filled her with memories of childhood when she would press her nose against her bedroom windowpane and listen to the sounds of the rain.

Her thoughts turned to the hayride and the walk she had taken with Adam. She had enjoyed the stroll and their dance in the vacant pavilion. But a sense of guilt washed over her as she thought of Nathan unexpectedly returning from Great Falls, only to discover that she and Adam had gone AWOL. What message did that convey to the man she had gone steady with for a year?

She crossed to the front door and flung it open, allowing the cool morning air to wash over her. Looking at herself in the window, she noticed the stress lines in her countenance. Obviously guilt was an accessory she did not wear particularly well.

She hadn't had a chance to explain things to Nathan yet. He needed to know that she and Adam had bolted from the hayride in fun and that their stroll was an innocent walk, nothing more. It was like the kiss at the shooting gallery—a physical exchange between two people without any strings attached. And the dance was simply closure to a request she'd been unable to grant Adam on the night of the community dance. The situation was simple enough, and yet she knew Nathan would not see it that way.

A hiss from the steam press called her back inside. The pipes were now singing as steam coursed through them, and the shop began to heat up. The familiar odor of cleaning solutions filled the air.

She walked to the clothes press and tested it to see if the steam was ready. Taking a coat from the check-in rack, she placed it on the bottom-ironing surface, careful to keep the fur collar out of the way so the steam wouldn't turn it brittle. She reached up and grabbed the handle, lowering the top pad. Steam hissed out from under the edges. Then she raised the top pad at just the right moment and adjusted the coat. The press was working well; the shop was ready to do business.

Deciding to finish the coat before Lee Yang and Julie arrived, she turned it over and spread it out on the bottom pad. While she worked, she ran the events of last night through her mind again.

In this moment of inattention she brushed against one of the steam pipes. Gasping in pain, she clutched her bare arm, angry with herself. She had gone weeks without burning herself, and she felt quite proud of her track record. Now she would have a painful welt as a reminder not to let her mind wander when working around the equipment.

She hurried over to the sink and ran cold water over the burn, grateful that no one had witnessed her carelessness. Grimacing in exasperation, she gently dried her arm with a towel. The shop hadn't even opened yet, and already it was shaping up to be a long day.

The telephone rang moments later, and she answered it on the second ring. "Yang's Dry Cleaners," she said with practiced cheerfulness.

"Hello, Elizabeth."

"Nathan." She took a deep breath to calm herself. "I'm sorry about last night. Julie said you came to the hayride looking for me."

"I had to deliver some forms to a rancher near Great Falls, but he must have forgotten about our appointment. No one was home. I drove all the way there, only to turn around and drive back. I thought I'd surprise you and show up for the refreshments after the hayride."

And I wasn't there. Elizabeth cleared her throat. "I was going to call you and explain what happened at the hayride."

"Listen, I've got a client arriving in just a few minutes and I need to get some paperwork ready. Can we talk later? Let's go out for dinner. I'll pick you up at your place at six. Got to run."

The line went dead, and Elizabeth hung up the phone, a little annoyed at his demands and expectations. Didn't he realize that left her only half an hour to get ready, and it was Julie's birthday party tonight too? Plus she knew he would quiz her on the details of the hayride. She sighed and glanced at the clock, almost dreading the arrival of six o'clock.

By the time Lee Yang and Julie arrived, the throbbing in her arm had stopped. Elizabeth approached Julie and greeted her cheerfully. "Everything ready for the party tonight?"

"What party?" Lee Yang asked.

"Her birthday party," Elizabeth said.

Lee Yang looked surprised. "It's your birthday? Good, good. Work hard, I let you go early today."

"Without docking my pay?" Julie asked.

"I didn't say that," Lee Yang replied. He chuckled to himself and went into the boiler room. The boiler had been acting up lately, and he went to monitor the reading on the pressure gauge.

When they were alone, Julie asked, "Have you spoken to Nathan yet?"

"Yes, he called me a few minutes ago."

"What did he have to say about the hayride? Was he upset?" Then she paused in contemplation and answered her own question. "He was upset."

Elizabeth picked up a garment and pretended to examine it. "He didn't say anything about it...yet. But he wants to take me out to dinner tonight." When Julie opened her mouth to object, Elizabeth added, "But don't worry. We'll hurry. I wouldn't skip my best friend's birthday party."

"Good. Because you don't want to miss the games." Julie emphasized the word *games* and winked at Elizabeth playfully.

Elizabeth understood her meaning. There were certain games they'd played at parties since they were teenagers. Ones they had perfected over the years.

But as excited as she was about the party, a nagging feeling settled over Elizabeth and tempered her anticipation. What was she going to say to Nathan? How was she going to raise the topic of the hayride and sound convincing and sincere? And what about her dance with Adam in the empty pavilion? Should she even mention that?

Her mind flooded with more questions, and she glanced up at the clock. Her long day had just gotten longer.

By the time Maude called him for lunch, Adam had the front step finished and the porch railing repaired. Hector was already in the bathroom, washing up. Adam joined him and scrubbed thoroughly, careful not to leave dirt streaks on the towel.

Although they stood side by side, Hector didn't acknowledge his son or make pretense at conversation. Not even a comment on the rain. The two men silently sat down at the table to the aroma of homemade vegetable soup and fresh-baked bread.

Maude went to the icebox and returned with a bottle of soda pop, pouring it into two glasses.

"Orange Crush," Adam said.

"For the working men," Maude replied.

"What about for the working *lady*?"

Maude shook her head. "I'd prefer a cup of tea."

Adam raised the glass to his lips, remembering the drink of punch he'd taken from Elizabeth's glass at the dance. He took a sip and set the glass back down. "When I was in Italy, I got this craving for soda pop," he said. "I hadn't had any in a long time. Anyway, my unit came across an abandoned country store, and we found a case of Orange Crush in the storeroom. I couldn't believe it. It was like an angel of mercy had delivered it to us. The soda pop was warm, but it still tasted like Orange Crush. We drank the whole case."

"You must have enjoyed that," Maude said.

Adam laughed under his breath. "Actually, the incident cured my craving for Orange Crush. I got sick on all that warm soda, and now I can only handle it in small amounts. Like this."

Maude listened to him, fascination written over her face. Adam had not spoken much about the war since his return, nor had she pressured him for details, for which he was thankful. He would open up when he was ready. A flower needed to blossom in its own time.

Adam looked over at his father, noticing how preoccupied he seemed with his meal. So far Hector hadn't said much. His silence hung over the table like a storm cloud.

Maude glanced at Hector. "The front step and the railing look good, don't they, Hec?" she said, attempting to draw him into the conversation.

Hector muttered something indecipherable.

"I'd like to tear down the old woodshed and build a storage shed after I finish the painting," Adam said. "What do you think, Dad? And I noticed the root cellar needs some attention before winter. Give me a few months, and I'll have the place looking like new."

Hector's expression darkened, and he set his fork down in a determined manner. "Maude, we can't do this any longer."

"Yes, we can," she replied. "And we will."

Adam looked at his parents, puzzled.

"He needs to know," Hector muttered.

"Needs to know what?" Adam asked.

Maude laid a hand on her husband's arm. "Let it alone. Now you listen to what I'm saying."

"Let what alone?" Adam asked.

Hector pushed away from the table and got to his feet. "I'm going out to the barn," he grumbled, heading for the door.

Adam watched his father exit, then turned back to his mother. "What did Dad mean by 'He needs to know'? Needs to know what?"

Maude began to clear the table. "It's just something between your father and me, son."

Helping clear the table, Adam said, "When I was little, you and Dad used to talk in code to keep things from me. Things like Grandpa Carlson's health and how it was failing, or what we were going to do because it hadn't rained for months and the crops were burning up. Things you didn't want me to worry about." He paused and looked at his mother evenly. "Is there something I should be worried about?"

Maude huddled over the sink and got busy washing the breakfast dishes. "No, everything's fine," she said.

But the stiffness in her shoulders told him she was not telling the truth. When she didn't turn, he shrugged. No sense pressing her. She would talk in her own time too.

CHAPTER 11

NATHAN, PUNCTUAL AS ever, picked Elizabeth up at six sharp. He wore a pin-striped suit, silver cuff links, and a colorful tie. His hair was neatly combed, and his shoes were polished, although they were freckled with beads of moisture from the incessant rain.

She huddled under his large umbrella as he walked her out to the waiting Chevrolet. Climbing in, she brushed a few droplets off her dress as Nathan ran around to the driver's side, shook out the umbrella, and placed it on the backseat. She glanced over at him, unable to read his mood. Or his intentions.

Nathan pulled away from the curb. But instead of driving to the restaurant downtown, as Elizabeth had anticipated, he headed for Great Falls, ignoring her protest that they needed to be back in time for Julie's birthday party. He seemed preoccupied and only made small talk on the way. Elizabeth made several attempts to talk about the hayride, but Nathan changed the subject each time. Finally she settled back in her seat and decided to do it Nathan's way. A short time later she blinked in surprise when they pulled up in front of the nicest restaurant in the city.

Under the protection of the umbrella, he escorted her inside. "I have a table reserved for us," he said, leading her toward a table that had an elegant place setting for two.

Holding her chair while she got seated, Nathan sat across from her and placed his hands on the edge of the table, interlocking his fingers.

The waiter arrived with two menus and went through a short spiel about the evening's specials, offering his recommendations. Nathan ordered sirloin steaks for himself and Elizabeth, and in moments the waiter reappeared with their salads.

"Bon appétit," Nathan said, reaching for his salad fork.

Elizabeth picked through her salad, glancing frequently at him. "You mentioned we needed to talk," she said, gently prodding him.

Nathan chewed for a moment and asked, "How is the salad?"

"Fine," Elizabeth replied, realizing that he was not going to be rushed. She began to make small talk about her day at the dry cleaners.

The waiter arrived with the main course: sirloin steak, a baked potato, and steamed vegetables, complete with a lemon wedge and a sprig of parsley on the side. Nathan studied his plate as though admiring a work of art and waited for the waiter to remove the salad plates.

"It smells delicious," Nathan said, cutting into the steak and savoring the aroma.

Elizabeth took a small bite of potato. If Nathan was trying to get back at her for her indiscretions with Adam, he was going about it in a diabolical manner. The setting was romantic and the food was glorious, but the tension was palpable. Nathan seemed almost nervous, and Elizabeth noticed his jaw muscles twitch whenever he glanced at her and smiled.

At length he set his fork down. Dabbing the corners of his mouth with his cloth napkin, he sat up straight and tall, a determined expression on his face. "Elizabeth, there *is* something we need to talk about."

She looked at him in anticipation.

"We have been dating now for over a year. Thirteen months and three days, to be exact." A brief smile played across his face and he added, "I deal with numbers, after all." He dropped his gaze momentarily and continued. "We have had a lot of great times. I can't remember being happier in my life. But things change and we have to move on."

"Nathan, the hayride was just a casual—"

"I'm not talking about the hayride. I'm talking about...us." He reached into his pocket and pulled out a small box, covered in blue velvet and edged in silver trim. Placing it on the table, he slid the box toward her. "Go ahead, open it."

She lifted the lid and gasped in surprise. Inside was a ring with the largest diamond she had ever seen.

Nathan took the ring from the velvet box and held it toward her. "We have gone together long enough. It's time to take things to the next level. I have a good career...a home that will soon be paid for...stocks that are doing well." He paused to clear his throat. "But for all of that, there's something missing: someone to share it with. Elizabeth Baxter, will you marry me?"

Elizabeth hesitated, her eyes focused on the ring. She remembered her aunt's words from six days earlier: *You're a sensible girl, and your uncle and I are grateful that you're dating a sensible young man. Nathan has a good career and is a prominent citizen in the community. And he attends church with us. Nathan is an excellent prospect.*

Everything her aunt said was true. Nathan *was* an excellent prospect, and any young woman should be flattered by his attentions. In all honesty, Elizabeth did think of him as the man she would probably marry. Probably. And on one occasion she had even written *Elizabeth Roberts* on a piece of paper just to see what it looked like.

But there were several questions that begged answers. Did she love Nathan enough to spend the rest of her life with him? Was she ready to settle down, become a wife and homemaker, have a family, and leave her former life behind? Did she want to make the single most important decision of her life and consummate it at this moment with a simple *yes?*

Nathan moved the ring back and forth so the diamond glinted in the light. "Say you'll marry me, Elizabeth, and make me the happiest man alive." He looked at her expectantly.

Elizabeth lifted her gaze from the ring, stalling for time. "This is a big step, Nathan. Are you certain *you* want to take it?"

Nathan looked at her, puzzled. Indicating their surroundings with a sweep of his hand, he said, "That's what this is all about, Elizabeth. Of course I want to take it. And you should too. It's the perfect chance for you to quit Chop Suey's and not have to work another day of your life."

"Nathan, don't call him that. You know I don't like it. His name is Lee Yang."

"All right, all right. Let's not spoil the mood here." He dabbed his mouth with his napkin. "So what do you say?"

Arching an eyebrow, she said, "Do you really love me, or am I just some prize in a contest?"

He exhaled sharply. "Not that again."

She stared at him intently, allowing the question to linger in her eyes.

"You know how I feel," he said. "I'm crazy about you. And I want us to spend the rest of our lives together." He held the ring closer to her. "What do you say?"

Elizabeth sat back in her chair. "Nathan, we're not ready for this."

He swallowed hard. "But I thought we—"

"I'm not saying no, Nathan. I'm just saying we're not ready yet. At least, *I'm* not."

He placed the ring back in the case. "What will it take to make you ready?"

She smiled mysteriously. "That's for you to find out."

He drummed his fingers on the table. "Why do you always have to make things so complicated?"

"Do I?" she replied, suppressing a laugh. She enjoyed making him squirm.

He pocketed the case and motioned toward the waiter. "You'll come around to my way of thinking, Elizabeth Baxter. I just sprung this on you too fast. Think about all the things we've done together. Think about everything I can give you."

With that he flashed a thick wad of money and left a generous tip. Then he picked up the umbrella and escorted Elizabeth out to the car.

On the drive home they were quiet until they were well out of the city. Finally Nathan looked across at Elizabeth and said, "Julie's expecting us at her party. Do you still feel like going?"

"I promised her I'd come. Besides, everyone will be there."

Several more miles passed in silence before Nathan said, "By the way, just how do I go about finding out how to make you say yes?"

"That's for me to know and you to find out." Truth be told, Elizabeth didn't know the answer herself. She just knew something wasn't quite right. And until it was, she wasn't going to commit herself to marriage.

"Complicated!" Nathan groaned, shaking his head. "When we do get married—and I assure you we will—would you like a large wedding or should we just elope? Not that I'm trying to rush things, mind you." His grin shone eerily in the dashboard lights.

"When I *do* get married, it will be a very formal wedding. Aunt Lenora will turn it into the social event of the year."

"As it should be. Just make sure to give me enough notice so I can get a tuxedo tailored properly." He chuckled under his breath.

She glanced at him from the corner of her eye. "Out of curiosity, Nathan, when did you pick out the ring?"

"Actually, I've had it for a month. I was just waiting for the right time to give it to you."

"And what made you decide that today was the day?"

He looked across at her again. "Let's just say I finally came to my senses."

Elizabeth pursed her lips. She knew the timing had to do with a certain Adam Carlson. But she wasn't ready to confront Nathan with that fact. Or with its implications.

As they drove toward Reunion, she finally admitted to herself her attraction to Adam. But in all fairness to Nathan, she told herself, Adam was a soldier recently returned from overseas. He was strong and handsome, a modern-day hero who had laid his life on the line for her—for everyone. His attentions were enough to turn any girl's head.

But, she reminded herself, while Nathan lacked military mystique, he made up for it in business expertise. A heart murmur had kept him out of the war, but it hadn't stopped him from excelling in the world of finance and securing a prestigious position at the bank. Perhaps Nathan didn't sweep her off her feet, but he had many admirable qualities that would make for a happy and successful life together. As her aunt Lenora told her repeatedly: Marry Nathan and you will want for nothing.

So why did she find herself wanting...something more?

Ty sat behind the wheel of the red '34 Oldsmobile as it sped down Main Street, sending water cascading into the air. The rain was constant and the wipers labored to keep up. He peered through the liquid film that spread across the windshield in ever-changing patterns, obscuring his vision.

Adam sat in the passenger's seat, staring out the side window. Although he hadn't been able to accomplish everything he had wanted to by the time Ty came calling, he was ready for a break. Besides, his mother had practically shooed him out the door with a broom, like she did with the chickens when it was time to clean the front porch. "You've got this old jalopy running pretty good," he commented.

"You ain't seen nothing yet," Ty replied, stepping on the accelerator and forcing Adam deeper into the seat.

As they neared the end of Main Street, Ty suddenly spun the wheel, sending the car into a long skid. The tires hydroplaned over the pavement, and it seemed to Adam that the Olds had been transformed into a speedboat. He braced himself with his arms. "You trying to get us both killed?"

"It's a COD corner, don't you know?" Ty laughed, waiting until the last possible second before straightening the wheel.

"What's a COD corner?"

"Remember, I'm here to teach you some basics you're sadly lacking. COD stands for Come Over Darling. When you finally get up the nerve to ask a girl out, hopefully one you'll meet at

Julie's tonight, you'll need to know and master this move. It's one way to make sure your date ends up sitting right next to you."

"Learning about a COD corner won't matter much if I'm dead."

Ty laughed and yanked on the steering wheel at the next intersection, but he lost control of the car. It spun in a circle and skidded sideways before leaving the road, coming to a stop mere inches away from an ash tree on the boulevard. He let out his breath slowly and forced a grin. "See, nothing to it."

Adam scowled at his cousin. "Let's just get to the party in one piece. No more lessons on COD corners. Got it?"

"Spoilsport," Ty muttered, spinning the tires to get back onto the street.

Elizabeth felt exhausted by the time she and Nathan arrived at the party. The experience at the restaurant had been more emotionally draining than she realized. And defending her decision during the drive back had been equally taxing. Especially to herself.

She had just turned down a marriage proposal from the most eligible bachelor in town.

What an earful Lenora would give her if she ever found out. *What were you thinking?* She could hear her aunt's voice rising in pitch. *Are you willing to risk losing him for good?*

Elizabeth didn't have time to prepare an answer. Julie opened the front door just then and greeted her and Nathan enthusiastically. Sounds of laughter and talking came from inside the house.

"Happy birthday, Julie," Elizabeth said, holding out the present she had carefully wrapped. "We're finally here."

"It's about time," Julie said, searching her face for clues, inviting more information.

Nathan pulled a five-dollar bill from his pocket and handed it to her. "Happy birthday, Julie. Buy yourself something nice."

"Thanks, Nathan. That's very generous."

Nathan caught Elizabeth's eye and grinned. Elizabeth understood the message.

When they entered the living room, Elizabeth noticed Ty talking to several young women who were gathered in a group. Several young men were sitting on the sofa, near the appetizers. Everyone held a cup of punch. Then she saw Adam, visiting with Susan, and her fatigue disappeared. Being careful not to stare at him, she felt Nathan's hand clamp around her arm as Julie announced, "Look who finally arrived!"

Several people called out greetings, and Susan came over and embraced Elizabeth. "I'm glad you finally decided to grace us with your presence," she laughed.

As Elizabeth returned the embrace, she noticed Nathan eye Adam and nod stiffly.

Adam smiled in reply and set his glass aside. Picking up two full glasses of punch from the serving table, he offered them to Nathan and Elizabeth. "Allow me to be your waiter."

At the mention of *waiter*, Elizabeth thought of the experience at the restaurant again and heard her aunt Lenora's questions echo in her brain. Brushing the images aside, she accepted the glass and met Adam's eyes. "Thanks," she said.

Julie moved to the center of the room. "Now that everyone's here, game time!" she announced. "Wink!"

A murmur of anticipation went through the room. Everyone knew Wink.

It was a kissing game, one they'd played since they were teenagers. Chairs were arranged in a circle—one chair more than the number of young women participating. The young women sat down, and the young men arranged themselves behind each chair. The young man behind the vacant chair looked at the young women and winked at one of them. She then tried to spring from her chair and make it to the vacant one before being grabbed by the young man behind her. If she made it, no kiss was exchanged. But if he caught her, she had to kiss him. And often, depending on who was standing behind her, she didn't try very hard to escape.

Nathan guided Elizabeth to the seat directly in front of him and gently patted her shoulders. She understood the message: *You won't be escaping. Prepare for a boring game.*

As the game got underway, Elizabeth could feel Nathan's eyes on her, watching her intently. Several young men winked at her, but Nathan grabbed her each time, receiving a kiss for his efforts, to the accompaniment of raucous laughter and catcalls from the others.

Elizabeth laughed to show she was a good sport. But with Nathan's suffocating attentiveness, the game *was* becoming boring. She found herself frequently glancing at Adam, inviting a wink, ready to spring from the chair. But Adam didn't make eye contact, and she felt her disappointment grow. But what did she expect? The way she had reacted after the hayride when she learned of Nathan's arrival had sent Adam a message. And based on his behavior now, it was apparent Adam had received it.

From across the circle she noticed Ty wink at Julie, who managed to reach his chair successfully. Elizabeth laughed to herself when seconds later someone else winked at Julie and she was deliberately slow in responding, resulting in Ty easily grabbing her by the shoulders. Although Julie pretended to be upset at having to kiss Ty, Elizabeth wasn't fooled, and she glanced at Adam once more, hoping to catch his eye.

The game continued with young women changing seats in quick succession.

When the chair in front of Adam became vacant, he winked at Susan. The young man behind her lunged to grab her, and was successful, but also succeeded in knocking off her cat-eye glasses. They flew over her head and landed outside the circle of chairs.

Elizabeth heard Nathan chortle as Susan retrieved her glasses, inspected them for damage, and returned to her original seat, gracing her partner with a kiss. Then Elizabeth glanced across at Adam, and her heart practically leaped into her throat when she saw him look directly at her...and wink. She sprang forward as if shot from a cannon and landed in a heap on the chair in front of him. She settled herself and smiled innocently at Nathan, amused by his expression of disbelief and annoyance.

"Looks like she got away, Nathan," Ty called out.

Nathan attempted to laugh it off, but his clenched teeth and bulging jaw muscles gave his laugh a strained quality. Elizabeth knew that she was seated in front of the one person Nathan didn't want her near. If she was unsuccessful in escaping from the chair now, she and Adam would...Her heart beat faster at the prospect.

Shrugging his shoulders casually, Nathan winked at several young women in turn. He deliberately telegraphed his attempts so that no one made it to his chair. As a result, a kiss was exchanged each time, which elicited applause and catcalls.

Elizabeth could tell Nathan was biding his time and watching Adam from the corner of his eye, attempting to lure him into dropping his guard. She felt her pulse quicken as the suspense began to build. It was only a matter of time now.

Julie was still sitting on the chair in front of Ty. When she failed to escape his grasp and had to kiss him, it turned into a lengthy and passionate one. The room erupted in cheers and laughter.

Nathan made his move. Faking a wink one way, he turned and winked directly at Elizabeth. She had anticipated the wink and had already decided what she would do when it came. She remained seated, allowing Adam to gently grab her by the shoulders.

A murmur of anticipation went around the circle.

"You owe him a kiss, Elizabeth," Julie said, laughing.

Glancing in pretended helplessness at Nathan, whose taut jaw muscles gave his face a distorted expression, Elizabeth tilted her face up and kissed Adam on the lips.

In that moment the other people in the room disappeared. The laughter and catcalls faded. She was aware only of the sensation of his lips against hers. And it was everything she had anticipated.

Nathan was beside her in an instant. Taking her by the arm, he pulled her to her feet and turned to face Adam. Tension filled the air, and several young women exchanged nervous glances.

"Hey, everybody," Julie suddenly said. "Cake and ice cream in the dining room."

Elizabeth put her arm through Nathan's. "Come on," she said, realizing she had to defuse the situation.

Nathan glared at Adam a moment longer, then guided Elizabeth toward the dining room.

Elizabeth glanced over her shoulder at Adam and their eyes met. And then...she winked.

CHAPTER 12

THE RAIN CONTINUED off and on the next few days. The green hues of the pasture that surrounded the farm deepened in color, contrasting with the soil in the yard that was now a brownish gumbo.

On Saturday Adam went into town to get a few supplies at the Mercantile and to pick up his uniform at the dry cleaners. He discovered Elizabeth had left with Nathan, who, according to Julie, had talked Lee Yang into letting her off work early. Nathan wanted to surprise her by taking her to Helena to see the stage production of *Show Boat*. Adam was disappointed not to see Elizabeth, and Lee Yang's refusal to take any payment for the dry cleaning offered only a little consolation.

He did see Elizabeth at church on Sunday, but only from a distance, and he never had a chance to talk to her. Nathan hovered around her, and Adam couldn't think of an adequate excuse to intrude. It didn't seem appropriate to ask how they had enjoyed *Show Boat* or what they thought of Julie's birthday party, particularly the game of Wink.

The following day Adam was helping his father empty the rain barrel beside the front porch when a green Ford sedan pulled into the yard. Hector took one look and muttered, "I'd know that car anywhere. It's the Bible thumper."

"You mean Pastor Wight?" Adam glanced at the car. When he turned back, Hector had disappeared around the corner of the house. Adam shook his head at his father's religious skittishness. Drying off his hands, he walked to the front steps to greet the pastor.

Pastor Albert Wight climbed spryly out of the car and reached for his umbrella and a black leather attaché case. He was a thin, balding man with a genuine smile. His glasses, perched on the end of his long nose, gave him a scholarly appearance. Huddling under the umbrella, he made his way to the front porch and greeted Adam warmly.

Adam conducted him into the kitchen, where Maude was scrubbing dishes. Apologizing for not calling ahead, Pastor Wight explained the reason for his visit. He wanted to hold a special church service two Sundays from now, the theme being *sacrifice*. And in preparation for that, he wanted to interview Adam about his wartime experiences to help the members of the congregation better understand the nature of a sacrifice. Pulling a notepad and a pencil from his attaché case, he reviewed the questions he had prepared.

Adam had not spoken much about his experiences overseas. Some were too painful to talk about and others too mundane to mention. But when he listened to the pastor's questions, he realized they were general enough that he could respond without offending the congregation.

Maude made a pot of tea and set two cups on the table. She excused herself to attend to other household duties so the two men could talk alone.

Pastor Wight thanked her for the hospitality. With his pencil poised above his notepad, he asked the questions he had prepared, writing down Adam's responses word for word.

The process was slow, but it gave Adam time to consider his phrasing. Because it was a Sunday congregation, composed of civilians who knew little of wartime battle firsthand, he didn't want to shock sensibilities by relating graphic experiences. He kept his answers appropriate for the occasion.

After an hour of solid note taking, Pastor Wight put the notepad and the pencil back into his attaché case. Thanking Adam for his time and Maude for the tea, he got up to leave.

Adam and Maude walked him to the door. They stepped onto the front porch in time to see Hector climbing a ladder that was leaning against the side of the chicken coop. He was balancing a roll of tar paper on one shoulder.

"Hector Carlson," Maude called. "What on earth do you think you're doing?"

"The roof's started leaking and the setting hens are getting wet," Hector replied irritably, keeping his eyes fixed on each ascending rung of the ladder.

Adam stepped off the porch and held his hand out, testing the rain. "Dad, you'll fall and break your neck." He turned toward his mother. "Mom, talk some sense into that husband of yours."

Pastor Wight remained on the porch as Maude and Adam made their way toward the chicken coop. The clay gumbo clung to their shoes and made walking difficult.

Maude grabbed the ladder as though it might suddenly collapse. "Hec, get down from there right this minute."

Hector had reached the edge of the roof and was struggling to balance the roll of tar paper.

"Dad, let me help you," Adam said, moving toward his mother.

As Hector shifted his weight in an attempt to lift the tar paper onto the roof, his foot slipped, and he lost his balance. Grabbing onto the ladder so he *didn't* fall and break his neck, he let go of the tar paper.

Adam attempted to deflect it as it descended, but he was too far away. The roll of tar paper glanced off one of the rungs and struck Maude on her head and her shoulder. She cried out and fell to the ground.

"Mom!" Adam knelt beside her and cradled her head in his arms.

Pastor Wight made his way across the yard and bent over them, using his umbrella to shield Maude from the rain. "Good heavens, Maude," he said. "Are you all right?"

"My shoulder," she moaned.

Hector descended the ladder and knelt in the mud beside her. "You shouldn't have been standing under the ladder," he said, chiding her as he awkwardly brushed the hair from her face.

And you shouldn't have been climbing it, Adam thought, glancing accusingly at his father.

"Let's get her into the house," Hector said. "Then go into town and get Dr. Cosgrove."

"I'll go get him," said Pastor Wight. "Make Maude as

comfortable as possible, and I'll be back shortly with the doctor." He raced for his car and spun mud as he drove away.

Hector and Adam gently carried Maude into the house and laid her on the sofa, propping her up with cushions. She gritted her teeth and tried to mask the pain, but it was evident she was in agony. Adam got some ice from the icebox to make a cold compress, carefully applying it to his mother's injured shoulder.

Hector paced the floor, his hands behind his back, his chin on his chest.

Adam wanted to say something about the stupidity of trying to repair the roof in the rain. But judging by his father's solemn demeanor, he decided against it. His father was chastening himself sufficiently.

Dr. Benjamin Cosgrove, dressed in a tweed suit and carrying his black leather bag, came down the stairs from the bedroom, where he had directed they carry Maude. He adjusted his glasses and ran a hand through his graying hair.

"How is she, Doc?" Hector asked, sitting at the kitchen table with Pastor Wight and Adam, thumbing aimlessly through an agricultural pamphlet.

Setting the bag on the table, Dr. Cosgrove paused to stretch his back. "She's still in pain, but the shot I gave her is beginning to work."

"Thank the good Lord for that," Pastor Wight said, looking heavenward.

"How did you say the accident happened?" asked Dr. Cosgrove.

"A roll of tar paper fell off the roof of the chicken coop and hit her," Hector replied guiltily. "Is she badly hurt?"

"Her clavicle is definitely broken," Dr. Cosgrove replied. "That's the collarbone. And she has a large bruise on her forehead."

"But she's going to be all right?" Hector asked, staring down at the table.

"I'm prescribing three days of complete bed rest. And I mean *complete* bed rest. I'll come back on Friday morning and check on her. In the meantime, she needs to keep her movements to a minimum and not lift anything at all. After that, it will be four to six weeks of limited activity."

Hector shifted uncomfortably in his seat. "I know my wife. There's no way she's going to agree to three days' bed rest. She'll be up trying to cook meals and do the laundry by tomorrow."

"Mom can be a pretty determined woman," Adam added.

"I know," Dr. Cosgrove replied. "But you're going to have to see to it that she stays put."

Pastor Wight cleared his throat. "I have an idea. I'll call some of the ladies from the congregation to come and help out while Maude is convalescing. We'll arrange for meals to be brought in, the laundry to be done, and the housecleaning to be tended to. Surely that will set her mind at ease, and she'll agree to the bed rest."

Hector hesitated. "I don't want to be beholden to—"

Pastor Wight cut him off with a gesture of his hand. "Hector, this is for Maude's sake. It's the least we can do for one of our most faithful parishioners."

Hector glanced from Pastor Wight to Dr. Cosgrove to Adam. When all three looked at him encouragingly, he dropped his gaze and nodded.

"Good. It's settled," Dr. Cosgrove said, reaching into his leather bag and bringing out a small bottle. "I'm going to leave these. For pain. Give her two tablets, no closer than four hours apart."

Adam took the bottle. "What else can we do?"

"Let nature take its course. Most clavicles heal on their own, although she'll probably have a small bump along the fracture line after it knits back together."

"Will she need a cast?" Hector asked.

"No. A simple arm sling will do."

"And that's it?" Adam said.

"Sometimes surgery is required, but only if the bone fragments don't knit together. And once in a while the fragments overlap and create a shortening of the collarbone, which means surgery for sure. But I don't think that will be the case here. Especially if she follows doctor's orders."

Pastor Wight reached for the door and nodded to Dr. Cosgrove. "We'd better be going. You've got more patients awaiting you, I'm sure. And I've got some telephone calls to make." He shook Adam's hand and then extended his hand toward Hector. Hesitating briefly, Hector shuffled his feet and then reached for the pastor's hand.

Later that evening Adam and Hector sat at the kitchen table, eating a meal that had been hurriedly prepared and delivered by Alice. She had responded to a call from Pastor Wight and rushed over as quickly as possible, fussing over her sister until Maude finally fell asleep. Before hurrying home to tend to her own family, Alice also tidied up the house and set the table for the two men.

Now, seated across from his father, who had hardly said two words during the meal, Adam decided once more to risk raising the delicate subject of fixing up the farm. "Dad, I was just thinking how much it would cheer Mom up for her to see more improvements around here. After painting the barn, I'd like to tear down the old woodshed and build a storage shed. And as I mentioned before, I noticed the root cellar needs some attention before winter. In a few months I think we can have the place looking like new."

Hector's expression darkened, but he didn't respond.

"I thought about putting a fence around the garden to keep the animals out," Adam continued. "And I'd like to—"

"Stop right there," Hector said abruptly. "Your mother hasn't let me tell you this, but she's not here to prevent me now. It's time you knew what's going on."

Adam felt something tighten inside. It was a reference to the conversation they'd had at the dinner table last week. "Knew what?" he asked anxiously.

"She wasn't going to tell you until you'd been home a little longer. But there's no sense in you continuing to work so hard and planning ahead like this."

Adam looked at his father. "I don't understand."

Hector walked over to a small desk that sat in the corner of the room and opened the top drawer. He pulled out a ledger that held the record of the family's finances and opened it up. Extracting a single piece of paper from inside the ledger, he handed it to his son.

Adam took it and read the following:

Notice of Foreclosure, June 3, 1946

Dear Mr. & Mrs. Carlson:

As a result of your breach of our mortgage agreement, and as a result of your inaction concerning the three notices of nonpayment sent to you, this certified letter is to inform you that we are foreclosing on the mortgage. An auction date has been set for Friday, August 2, 1946, at 10:00 a.m.

As required by law, a legal notice will be published in the Reunion *Gazette*. It is our intent to exercise the rights described in the mortgage agreement in order to collect all money owing from this property as they become payable.

Sincerely,

Nathan Roberts

Reunion Savings and Loan

Adam looked up from the letter, stunned. "August second? That's less than a month away. Why didn't you tell me sooner?"

"Your mother didn't want to spoil your homecoming."

Adam glanced at the letter again. "How did this happen?" he asked, still reeling from the news.

Hector grimaced as he related the details. It was a common story, shared by thousands of farm families across the Midwest.

The 1930s had not been good years for the Carlsons. Successive years of relentless wind, no rain, blowing dust that piled up like snowdrifts, voracious grasshoppers that ate the paint right off the machinery, and hail that flattened what little the 'hoppers left behind had all combined to put the Carlsons on the verge of bankruptcy. In Hector's words, the farm was mortgaged to the top of the weather vane on the peak of the barn roof. Things began to improve in the 1940s. But because the bank had over-extended itself and had many unsecured loans on the books, a policy change was initiated; loans were called in, including the Carlson's. Money was needed for the war effort. And when the Carlsons couldn't make their loan payment...

"We had to go on credit to produce a crop year after year," Hector explained. "And when the bottom fell out of grain prices, we weren't able to make our mortgage payment. Jack Duncombe, who was the loan officer at the time, kept lending us more money in the belief that things would turn around and that we'd be able to repay everything." Hector grumbled bitterly. "But things didn't turn around. Leastways not for us. Just as the weather improved and it looked like we were finally in store for a bumper crop, Pearl Harbor happened."

"And I enlisted...leaving you shorthanded," Adam said, his voice barely above a whisper.

A low response rumbled in Hector's throat. "Although we were far in debt, a couple of good years of bumper crops would have helped us get our heads above water. But the bank tightened their lending policy. They fired Jack and hired Nathan Roberts in his place. Nathan set out to recover every last dime owed to the bank. As a result, we weren't able to replace our outdated machinery—everyone started going to newer and better tractors, which we couldn't afford, so I couldn't increase our yield...alone. So we fell further and further behind."

"Did you talk to Nathan and explain the situation? Did you ask him to reduce the amount of your monthly payments so they were more manageable? Did you—"

"All that and more. I told him we wouldn't have any money until after the harvest. He couldn't—or wouldn't—modify the terms of the loan. He sent us two notices, informing us that our monthly payments were delinquent. We made token payments, but it wasn't enough. So he sent us a third letter, demanding payment in full."

"But that doesn't make any sense. If you couldn't even make your monthly payments, how could you make the payment in full?"

"He wouldn't listen. He said his hands were tied. And that's when he sent us the notice of foreclosure. The bank is going to sell the farm and put the money toward the loan. It will help us clear the debt. But it also means...we lose everything."

"We can't let that happen," Adam said, setting his jaw firmly.

"We can't stop it," Hector replied. "What's done is done."

Adam studied his father. "That's it? You're just going to give up and let the bank sell the farm?"

Hector turned on him angrily. "You go away for four years, leaving me on my own, and then come back suddenly all concerned? I'm not going to waste any more time talking about it. Just don't tell your mother that I showed you the letter." He headed out the front door, slamming it behind him.

Adam slumped forward in his chair and fought his emotions. Feelings of anxiety over his mother's injury merged with what he had just learned from his father. A sense of dread, mingled with helplessness, came over him. Now he fully understood his father's resentment. Adam's enlistment had been more than an inconvenience. It had dealt the farm a fatal blow.

Anger rose up in him as he considered the irony of the situation. Here he had gone overseas and put his life in danger to keep his country free and the farm safe, while Nathan had remained at home and become a successful banker, enjoying the luxuries and security maintained by those willing to fight for their country. Adam had returned from the war virtually empty-handed, while Nathan controlled the purse strings attached to the lives of many people, including the Carlsons. The full weight of the law rested on Nathan's side, and he was dispassionately exercising the very rights Adam had fought to defend, using them to take the farm away. What the Nazis had been unable to do, Nathan was now going to accomplish with the impending foreclosure.

Adam's hand curled into a fist as he thought of the predicament. Nathan had the means, the position, and all the power. And he had Elizabeth! He could give her things Adam could never afford. And how could Adam compete with that?

Picking up the letter again, he bitterly studied it. August second! Was it possible? Had he actually gone overseas to fight for freedom, only to end up losing the farm? What had it all been for?

He remembered the question he had asked himself on the bus ride into Reunion following his discharge. Why had his life been spared when so many of his comrades had been killed? *For all the good I've done, I should have been killed in place of one of the others*, he thought miserably.

Suddenly, he sat bolt upright as if an invisible hand had just grabbed him by the shirt collar. There *was* a reason—and in that instant he knew what it was.

CHAPTER 13

TUESDAY MORNING ADAM drove into town, headed for the Reunion Savings and Loan Bank. Established in 1893, it was one of the first businesses in town and was housed in the red brick building on the corner of Main Street and Third Avenue.

Adam parked the pickup truck in front of the building and slowly climbed out. He wore his Sunday suit and a broad necktie that sported a fish being reeled in by a fisherman. Somehow it seemed appropriate for the occasion. Hesitating a moment to review his pitch, he strode toward the front door and stepped inside.

"May I help you?" asked the woman behind the front counter.

"I'd like to see Nathan Roberts."

"Do you have an appointment?"

Adam shook his head.

"It's all right, Doris," said Nathan, appearing in his office doorway. "Show Mr. Carlson in." Nathan disappeared inside the office, leaving the door ajar.

The woman hesitated slightly before conducting Adam toward the office. She waited for him to step inside and then discreetly closed the door behind him.

Nathan was seated behind his oak desk, which was completely bare, except for a thin notepad and a fountain pen. Several tall metal filing cabinets lined the far wall, and above one hung a photograph of Nathan and Elizabeth.

Pointing toward a chair, Nathan said, "Have a seat." He pressed his fingertips together and reclined back in his padded leather chair. "What can I do for you, Adam?"

Adam reached into his pocket, pulled out the letter of foreclosure, and placed it on the desk.

Nathan cut a glance at the paper and lifted his eyes back to

Adam. "I was wondering when I'd be seeing you about this. I've already talked to your father about it, you know."

"He told me he'd been in to see you. So I won't waste your time by rehashing everything. Let's cut right to the chase. What's the bottom line, Nathan? What can we do to save the farm?"

Nathan gave a slight shrug of his shoulders. "Pay out the mortgage."

Adam felt his frustration rise but remained outwardly calm. "You know we can't do that. If we could, we would have already. How can you expect us to do that? It's not reasonable."

"These are not reasonable times. Your father borrowed money to keep the farm afloat. He pledged his assets as security on the loan. It was a gamble, of course, in the hope that future earnings would offset the loan and he'd be able to pay it back. The loans were done when land values and crop prices were high. But when the markets crashed and the Depression deepened, land values plummeted. You know that. And since then, your dad hasn't been able to make much headway on the loan."

"I don't need a history lesson. I need options." He glared at Nathan, struggling to ignore the young man's smug expression.

"Adam, you and I go back a long ways. I'd help you if I could, but there are no options left. The loan has come due and we're not in a position to refinance the mortgage. We have to foreclose and sell the land so we can make up the difference. We're forced to take all of the assets pledged to the loan."

"But that means we'll literally lose everything. You can't do that to us, Nathan. We need more time. Now that I'm back, I can help with the harvest. We'll soon have some money to make payments on the loan."

"There have been some policy changes, Adam, and I'm under pressure to close out these old accounts. The bank has carried the Carlson holdings for too long. We have to cut our losses and move on. But the good news is, with land and grain prices becoming more favorable, the farm will have more value. Hopefully, the sale will result in enough money to pay off the outstanding loans and still leave some for your parents' retirement."

"What would my father do in retirement? Farm life is the only life he knows." He appealed to Nathan. "There has to be another way."

Nathan's expression didn't change. "Short of paying out the mortgage, there's no other way. We're putting up posters today advertising the foreclosure auction sale, scheduled, as stated in the letter, two Friday mornings from now, August second, at ten o'clock."

Adam sprang to his feet and leaned over the desk. "But you can't expect us to be ready to move out by then."

"I sent the letter back in June, Adam. It's now almost the end of July. But don't worry, you'll have a reasonable amount of time afterward to... well, you know."

Glancing at the picture of Nathan and Elizabeth on the wall, Adam wondered how much of Nathan's unyielding position related to their history and what had occurred at the shooting gallery and at the birthday party.

As if reading his thoughts, Nathan said, "It's business, Adam, nothing personal. You aren't the only ones we're foreclosing on. That's just how it is."

"You tell yourself whatever you need to, Nathan, in order to live with yourself. But I'll tell you this. To my parents and me, it's *very* personal." And with that he left the office, closing the door emphatically behind him.

Elizabeth arrived home early in the afternoon because there was a problem with the boiler and the shop had to close for repairs. Sunshine had returned to Big Sky Country, and she enjoyed the walk. As she stepped into the kitchen, she noticed that her aunt was wearing an apron and was bustling about the room. Bowls and utensils were scattered everywhere, and the sink was full of dishes. "Are we having company, Aunt Lenora?" she asked, glancing at the clutter.

Lenora motioned toward a large salad bowl. "Set that in the refrigerator, would you, dear? I want the lettuce to stay crisp."

Elizabeth placed a cloth over the bowl and put it in the refrigerator, pausing to let the cool air waft over her.

"I'm making dinner for the Carlsons," Lenora explained.

"The Carlsons? As in Hector and Maude?" *And Adam?*

Lenora nodded and put on a pair of oven mitts. She reached into the oven and brought out an apple pie, which she placed on the countertop to cool. "Pastor Wight called to say Maude had an accident. He's arranging for some women from the congregation to help out for a few days. "

"What kind of accident?"

"Apparently a heavy roll of tar paper fell from the roof of their chicken coop and struck her on the shoulder. It was her husband's fault."

"How badly was she hurt?"

"Bad enough to be bedridden."

Elizabeth frowned. "That's so unfortunate."

"What's unfortunate is that she ever married Hector Carlson. How she's put up with him for all these years is beyond me. That woman deserves a medal. Be a dear and slice the ham for me, would you?"

A cooked ham sat on a cutting board. Elizabeth reached for the carving knife and began to slice the ham. "What's the menu?" she asked, arranging the slices on a serving dish.

"It's a warm day, so I thought it best to prepare a meal that can be served cold. Potato salad, sliced ham, homemade rolls, and a green salad. And apple pie for dessert."

"Your famous homemade rolls and fresh apple pie. You've gone to a lot of work."

Lenora smiled in satisfaction. "Well, with Maude laid up, the least we can do is render Christian service. Not that Hector Carlson and his son can't take care of themselves for a few days while she is recuperating, mind you."

Elizabeth finished slicing the ham. "Can I do anything else to help?"

Lenora set a large picnic basket on the counter and began filling it. "You could be a dear and drive this out to the Carlsons."

Elizabeth felt something stir within her. "Okay," she said. She hadn't seen Adam since Julie's birthday party, where, for the second time, she kissed him. And even though it had been almost a week, she remembered the experience clearly.

Finishing up and closing the lid of the picnic basket, Lenora said, "I'd appreciate it. That way I can put the kitchen back together before your uncle gets home."

Her mind racing, Elizabeth hooked the basket under one arm and grabbed the car keys, only half aware of her aunt's list of instructions about how the food was to be served.

❧

Adam was standing on a ladder, tightening the hinges on the loft door of the barn in preparation for painting, when he noticed a dust trail snaking toward the farm. As a black Buick Roadmaster pulled in through the front gate and stopped in the yard, he slowly climbed down the ladder. Pocketing the wrench and brushing off his hands, he stared in surprise when he recognized the driver.

Elizabeth opened the door and got out, avoiding a large puddle nearby.

"You lost?" he asked.

"I'm looking for the Carlson residence," Elizabeth said with a teasing smile. "Am I at the right place?"

"That all depends. Who's asking?"

"Someone with a delicious dinner, including homemade rolls and fresh apple pie."

Adam grinned. "In that case, you're at the right place."

Elizabeth scanned the perimeter of the yard, her eyes moving from building to building. "So this is where you've been spending all your time."

He paused, awaiting her verdict.

She drew in a deep breath and closed her eyes, savoring the freshness of the air. Exhaling slowly, she looked directly at him. "It's lovely here, Adam."

He glanced around. *Lovely* wasn't the word he'd have used. *Lost* was more accurate. The faded buildings and sagging corrals showed signs of refurbishment, but there was still so much to be done. But for what? It was headed for the auction block. Still, he appreciated Elizabeth's appraisal, and her sincerity helped validate what he had accomplished so far, which, hopefully, would help the farm sell for more.

Her gaze stretched into the distance. "You have such a wonderful view. The mountains are so beautiful, and everything is so green." She surveyed the countryside a moment longer before reaching into the backseat for the picnic basket.

"Let me help you with that," Adam said, stepping around a mud puddle.

"What a gentleman."

As she held the picnic basket toward him, Adam reached for it and their hands touched. She didn't withdraw her hand immediately; neither did Adam. Following a lengthy pause, he took the basket and cracked the lid, peeking inside. "It looks delicious," he said.

"Actually, Aunt Lenora is the cook. I'm just the delivery girl."

"I hope it wasn't too much trouble for either of you. I never expected this much fuss made over us."

"No trouble at all," Elizabeth answered sincerely.

Adam turned and gestured toward the house. "Would you like to come in?"

"I should say hello to your mom, if she's up for a visit."

"She'd love to see you. Bed rest has been harder on her than the injury itself."

Adam led the way to the house, picking his way across the muddy yard. Elizabeth followed, walking carefully in his footsteps.

"Everything should go in the icebox," she said as they came into the kitchen. "It will keep until you're ready."

"Good, because we won't be eating for a while yet. Dad's taken the grain truck into town to get some work done on it."

Elizabeth unpacked the picnic basket and helped place the items in the icebox. Then she followed Adam upstairs to the bedroom at the far end of the hallway, waiting outside the door while he announced, "Mom, you have a visitor. Elizabeth Baxter brought dinner for us."

"Tell her to come in," Maude said.

Elizabeth stepped into the room and looked at Maude compassionately. "Hello, Mrs. Carlson. How are you feeling?"

Maude was sitting upright in the bed with several pillows propped behind her. She had a large purple bruise on her forehead, and she wore a sling over her shoulder, cradling her left arm. A large tin container sat beside her. Photographs of various sizes lay scattered around her on the bed.

Setting the photographs aside, Maude replied, "My shoulder aches and I'm confined to bed rest for three days, but otherwise I'm doing all right. Thank you, dear, for bringing dinner out to us. That's very kind of you."

"Aunt Lenora is the one who made the meal."

"Please tell her how grateful we are."

"I will." Elizabeth let her gaze wander out the open window. "I love the farm, Mrs. Carlson. It's so quiet and peaceful here."

A solemn expression crossed Maude's face. "The farm belonged to Adam's grandfather, Howard Carlson," she said, a catch in her throat. "After Hec and I were married, we moved in with Father and Mother Carlson. Adam has lived here all his life."

Except for four years overseas, Adam thought.

Elizabeth motioned toward the pile of photographs surrounding Maude. "It looks like you're organizing some family pictures."

Maude sighed. "I suppose every cloud has its silver lining. My confinement has given me time to organize this hodgepodge of photographs. For years I've been meaning to sort through them and put them in an album. And now I'm doing it. Memories are so precious, and sometimes they're all we're left with." Her hand trembled as she picked up the nearest photograph and handed it to Elizabeth. It showed a small boy wearing a cowboy hat and sitting beside a man on a tractor. "That's Adam when he was five, riding on a tractor with his father," Maude explained.

Elizabeth studied the photograph. "A cute little guy."

"Me or my dad?" Adam remarked, smiling at his own joke.

"Very funny," Elizabeth said, cutting him a narrow glance.

"And here he is—" Maude selected another photograph and read the handwriting on the back. "—at age seven."

The photograph showed a man and a boy standing beside a river, smiling broadly, each holding up a fish that dangled from a line.

"Dad had taken me fly fishing along the Missouri," Adam said. "I still remember landing that cutthroat."

"They were such buddies," Maude said softly, a faraway look in her eyes.

She dug out other photographs of Adam: baby pictures, school photographs, and ones showing him working around the farm. "There are so many good memories in here," Maude said, reclining against the pillows. "But that's enough for now. I'm sure you have better things to do than listen to an old woman prattle on about the past. It was so nice to have you here today," she said, squeezing Elizabeth's hand. "Come and see us again sometime."

Elizabeth nodded politely and followed Adam out of the room, lingering in the doorway to wave good-bye to Maude. Outside on the front porch, she paused and gazed around. "It really is lovely here, Adam. You told me you have big plans to fix the place up. It looks good already."

"*Had* big plans," Adam said, almost to himself.

Elizabeth eyed him inquisitively.

"It's nothing," Adam said, leaning against the railing.

"You're a terrible fibber," she said.

Adam smiled grimly. "You don't want to know."

She arched an eyebrow. "Try me."

As he had done on the evening walk with Elizabeth on the night of the hayride, he found himself opening up to her once more. He told her about the letter of foreclosure and the upcoming auction. And of his visit with Nathan. "We're going to lose everything," he said in conclusion.

"That's awful," Elizabeth gasped, pressing her hands to her lips.

"The bank has us over a barrel. And there's nothing Nathan can or will do."

"Maybe I could talk to him."

Adam clenched his jaw, determined never to give Nathan the satisfaction of having Elizabeth beg in his—Adam's—behalf. "Please don't. This is between Nathan and me. And besides, it's a done deal, I'm afraid," he said bitterly.

Scanning the farmyard once more, Elizabeth said, "I wish there was some way for you to keep the farm. It's been in your family for so long."

"It's been in debt so long," Adam muttered. "That's the problem."

She placed a hand gently on his shoulder. "I don't know what to say."

Adam looked into her eyes. "There's nothing to say. But thanks for listening. Just being able to talk about it with you has helped. I haven't even told Ty yet, and I'd appreciate it if you didn't say anything about this to anyone."

"Of course I won't." She narrowed her eyes in determination. "But I can do more than just listen. I may not know what to say, but my uncle Wil might. He's a chartered accountant. Maybe he can give you some advice."

"It's too late for that."

Elizabeth frowned. "Aren't you the fellow who went overseas and fought for what you believed in? And now you won't fight to save your own farm?"

"I tried, remember? Nathan wouldn't budge."

Crossing her arms and standing straight and tall, Elizabeth said, "The war wasn't won in a single battle. So why should the fight to save the farm be any different? Uncle Wil's in Helena on business, but he'll be back on Friday."

Adam studied her momentarily. "You realize that by helping me you're going against Nathan, don't you? I don't want you to get caught in the middle of this."

Glancing around the yard once more, Elizabeth said, "I just want you to be able to keep the farm, that's all."

Adam looked into her eyes and felt himself being drawn in. It would be so easy to get lost in them.

Elizabeth ran a hand down his arm and stepped away. "I've got to get back home or Aunt Lenora will think I'm stuck in the mud somewhere. Now don't forget to call Uncle Wil on Friday, okay?"

"Okay, Mother," he called after her.

Elizabeth laughed and got in the car. Driving slowly out of the yard to avoid a large mud puddle, she waved to him as she passed through the front gate.

He waved back and watched the car disappear in the distance, allowing his gaze to take in his surroundings. He exhaled slowly and glanced up at the loft door of the barn. Scaling the ladder with renewed energy, he retrieved the wrench from his back pocket and continued tightening the hinges of the door, buoyed by the first ray of hope he had experienced in days.

CHAPTER 14

ADAM HAD NOT told his father about his visit with Nathan at the bank or about the appointment he had set up with Wil Jackson. There was no use in needlessly getting his father's hopes up just yet. So he'd placed the telephone call to Jackson's accounting firm when Hector was out doing chores.

Now on Friday afternoon, as Adam stood in front of the red brick office building on Main Street, he adjusted his necktie before reaching for the brass door handle. The receptionist greeted him cheerfully and conducted him directly into Wil's office.

Wil was standing at a filing cabinet, poring over a file folder. He put the folder down and shook Adam's hand warmly. "It's a pleasure to see you again, Adam. You helped make the opening ceremony special. I couldn't have scripted it better myself."

"I was glad to help out, sir," Adam said.

Wil motioned him to have a seat, and they chatted for a few moments. At length Wil gestured toward Adam. "Now, what can I do for you, son?"

"Elizabeth suggested I talk to you. I hope it's not a bother."

"Elizabeth referred me?" he said, his eyes crinkling as he smiled. "Well, I hope I measure up. Why don't you tell me what this is all about?"

Adam did. In detail.

Wil drummed his fingers together as he listened, raising his eyebrows at the mention of the letter of foreclosure, frowning as Adam described his visit with Nathan, and murmuring as Adam indicated that the auction date was less than a month away.

When Adam finished his account, Wil exhaled sharply and smoothed down his moustache. "This puts me in an interesting position," he said at length. "Nathan is dating my niece, Elizabeth, and so understandably I have a vested interest in his welfare. On the other hand, you're a hero, Adam." When Adam protested, Wil raised a hand to cut him off. "Yes, you are. To me and to everyone else in this town. We'll never be able to repay you and the other veterans for what you did. Never. And I can't accept the fact that you'd go overseas and put your life on the line, only to return home and discover that the farm was lost to you. As I say, an interesting position."

Adam rose from his chair. "Maybe it's not fair to put you in the middle of—"

"Now, hold on, son," Wil said, motioning for him to be seated. "I'm not saying I can't help you. I'm just saying this is an interesting position."

"Is it a hopeless one?"

Wil ran a hand through his hair. "Not necessarily. There might be a way for you to save the farm and still appease the bank."

Adam eagerly leaned forward in his chair. "That would be wonderful."

Wil propped his elbows on his desk and looked directly at Adam. "What I'm about to tell you is strictly confidential. And off the record."

"Off the record?"

"Yes. This is not so much my giving you financial advice as it is telling you a story, albeit an informative one. So listen to the story and do with it what you will." He winked at Adam. "And I won't charge you a *penny* for my time."

He broke out laughing and Adam looked at him, perplexed.

"You'll see my little joke in a minute, son. During the Depression, farmers like your father had to go into debt to keep their operations running. Statistically, nearly three-fourths of all farmers needed credit in order to produce their crops. As crop prices declined, farmers weren't able to repay the loans, and so they went even further into debt. As they defaulted on loans and made fewer deposits, banks started to feel the pinch. Many small country banks went out of business. In order to survive, the larger banks had to reduce the amount of credit they made available to farmers. Loans were called in. This threw many farmers into foreclosure. Recognize the plot of the story so far?"

Adam nodded.

"Farm foreclosures became widespread," Wil continued. "At the height of the Great Depression, two hundred thousand farms underwent foreclosure."

Adam whistled under his breath.

"Now we get to the good part of the story. There was a group of farmers in Nebraska who decided to take matters into their own hands. About one hundred fifty of them showed up at a foreclosure auction being held at the farm of a family by the name of Von Bonn. The family couldn't repay their loan, so the bank was holding an auction to recover what money they could. The bank expected to make three or four thousand dollars. Anyway, as the auctioneer began with a piece of equipment, one of the local farmers opened up with a bid of five cents. When an outsider tried to raise the bid, he was encouraged in a rather physical manner to withdraw his bid. No one else bid on the piece of equipment and so it went for five cents. Item after item went for ridiculously low bids. When the auction was finally over, the bank had made a grand total of five dollars and thirty-five cents. A far cry from the four thousand dollars they had hoped to make."

"So what happened?"

"The idea of the penny auction, as they called it, spread like wildfire. Farmers began attending public auctions as a group and crowding around the auctioneer, intimidating rival bidders. In some cases they set up roadblocks or changed signposts so the public couldn't attend. They would place outlandishly low bids on everything. If someone tried to raise the bid, they were met with ridicule and sometimes even outright violence from the crowd. By using this strategy, many farmers managed to block foreclosure sales. The bank often ended up making mere pennies on foreclosure sales when they expected to make hundreds if not thousands of dollars."

"Didn't the government do anything to help out?"

"They passed the Federal Farm Bankruptcy Act, but it wasn't very effective. Following that, Congress passed the Farm Mortgage Moratorium Act, which is in its third renewal by the way, and has done a little better. It has allowed some farmers to maintain their holdings even though foreclosures have occurred."

"But they still had to go through foreclosure proceedings first?"

"Yes, and of course that would go on their record. Still, with so little money being raised, the banks were forced to reconsider foreclosures. They became more willing to work out a deal to ensure they didn't end up with mere pennies applied against the outstanding balances. They discovered that small but regular payments beat five dollars and thirty-five cents. And in the end, most of the banks were able to keep afloat."

"So perhaps Nathan would—"

Wil cut him off. "Now, I can't comment on that, son. I'm just relating a story today." He got up as an indication that the meeting was over. "I haven't dispensed any financial advice, so I won't bill you a penny." Leading Adam to the door, he added, "It was nice talking to you, son. Good luck."

Adam was hardly aware of making his way back to the truck. He climbed in and unrolled the windows to create a cross breeze. Loosening his tie, he leaned against the steering wheel, his mind churning. Ideas began to form in his brain.

He started the truck and drove away, heading out of town to the Hansen farm. He needed to talk to his cousin immediately, and he hoped Ty would like his idea.

He wasn't disappointed.

Nor was he disappointed when he returned home and talked to his mother. He explained that he knew about the letter of foreclosure and informed her of the idea he'd shared with Ty. She liked it too and agreed not to tell Hector. They both realized he would never agree to it. Accepting help from the women of the congregation during Maude's convalescence was hard enough on him. Something on the scale Adam was contemplating would lead to civil war within the Carlson home. And Adam, for one, had had enough of war to last a lifetime.

CHAPTER 15

As THE DATE of the foreclosure auction approached, Hector became increasingly moody. He was more critical than usual about the farm and of life in general. The wheat wasn't maturing fast enough, and the chickens weren't giving enough eggs. The cows had less cream in their milk, and the beet greens from the garden were as tough as shoe leather. Maude could hardly do anything right, and Adam, who seemed to be away a lot, even less so.

Maude, now released from bed rest, did her best to soften each negative observation with a positive one. She reassured him, consoled him, and did everything short of telling him about Adam's idea. Their whole life together, she said, had been based on the struggle to survive, to turn the farm into a successful operation. They would somehow see this through too. But Hector did not seem convinced, and for the first time ever, she saw him resigned to impending defeat.

On the morning of the auction she sat beside him on the front porch, noticing how he looked like someone condemned to watch his own execution. He continually swept the perimeter of the farm with his eyes as if trying to memorize each detail. Low sounds occasionally escaped his throat as though he was carrying on a conversation with himself.

Well before the appointed hour of ten o'clock, Ty and his father, Sid, arrived, followed by a large contingent of local farmers. Pickup trucks and wagons rolled into the yard, one after the other, sending up a dust trail that hung in the air like a funeral pall.

Ty went to join Adam, who stood out in the yard, greeting the arrivals and directing everyone toward the front of the barn, where the auction was to take place.

Sid made his way toward the house. "Well," he said, joining Hector and Maude on the front porch. "Ready for the big day?"

Hector glared up at his brother-in-law. "How do you get ready for something like this?"

"Now, Hec," Maude gently said.

Alf Whitehead, who had driven the truck when Adam and Elizabeth had gone on the hayride, interrupted them. "Morning, Hec, Maude. I'm sure sorry about all this."

Hector cut him a surly look but didn't reply.

"I'm the auctioneer today," Alf continued. "And I'm going to get you the best prices I can."

"Thanks, Alf," Maude said, putting on a brave smile. "We appreciate it."

A blue four-door Chevrolet sedan, with whitewall tires and shiny chrome hubcaps, pulled into the yard. Hector rose from his chair and made his way toward the car. "This isn't your place yet," he said as Nathan got out of the vehicle. "So get on back where you came from."

"You know better than that, Mr. Carlson," Nathan replied. "I have every right to be here. This is a *public* auction, and the bank is officiating here today."

Hector took a menacing step toward him, but Adam stepped between the two men. "It's okay, Dad," he said.

"It's *not* okay," Hector growled.

"Nathan," Alf Whitehead said, joining them. "I'm going to set up over at the barn. Why don't you help me?"

Nathan squared his shoulders and followed Alf. Hector returned to the front porch and sat down in a huff.

By ten o'clock the farmyard was crowded. Alf Whitehead hardly had room to turn. Men were bunched in groups on his right and on his left. There was even a group of men behind him.

"Let's get started, gentlemen," he said, glancing at the auction sheet on the oat bin that served as his table. "First item up for bid is a team-driven hay rake, in good condition, newly painted. What am I bid for it? Let's start the bid out at ten dollars."

A silence fell over the group.

"Ten dollars!" Hector gasped from his place on the porch. "I thought Alf said he'd get us the best prices he could. He should have at least started out at sixty."

"Who'll start us out at ten dollars for this excellent piece of equipment, gentlemen?" Alf said. Following a sustained silence, he cleared his throat. "Okay, let's drop it to five dollars. Who will give me five?"

He looked out over the sea of expressionless faces. When no offers came, he turned to Nathan, who glared at the men.

"Let's be reasonable, gentlemen," Nathan said. "Five dollars is a ridiculous bid for a piece of equipment like this. It's worth twenty times that much."

"Five dollars," Alf repeated. "Do I hear five?"

A man in the middle of the group raised his hand and said, "I'll give you five—" But that's as far as he got. Ty was beside him in an instant and clenched the man's arm firmly from behind, whispering, "You were saying?"

The man's face went red and he dropped out of the bidding.

"Okay, let's move to the second item on the list," Alf said. "A six-row cultivator. Horse-drawn, but it could be pulled behind a tractor. All metal construction, in good condition. What am I bid for it? Let's start at five dollars."

No one responded.

From his place on the porch, Hector looked at the crowd in bewilderment. Such a good turnout usually meant keen interest and fierce bidding. But it wasn't happening. Which meant the auction would raise little money to appease the bank. "What's going on?" he muttered. "The cultivator's worth a hundred dollars." He turned to Maude, who smiled supportively and reached for his hand.

Alf perused the crowd, waiting for a response. None came, so he repeated the asking price. When still nothing came, he turned toward Nathan. "No one's bidding. You want me to lower the bid?"

"Lower it to what?" Nathan replied fiercely. "Five *cents?*"

"Now you're talking," Sid called out. "I bid one cent."

"One cent!" Nathan and Hector both said at the same time.

"I'll bid two," said another man in the crowd.

Sid cut the man a narrow look and said, "All right, three. But that's my final offer. Take it or leave it."

"We'll leave it," Nathan said.

"Actually, we have to take it," Alf said. "Three bids are a legal auction." He addressed the crowd again. "Okay, we have a bid of three cents. Do I hear four?"

No one replied.

"Going once," Alf said. "Going twice. Sold to Sid Hansen for three cents."

Nathan held up a hand. "Wait, you can't do this. Three cents is absurd."

Hector jumped to his feet and climbed down the steps. Three cents was beyond absurd. And bid by his own brother-in-law! It was...he couldn't think of an adequate word to describe his outrage. But he was going to give Sid and the entire crowd a piece of his mind anyway.

Adam met him before he reached the crowd. "Stay out of it, Dad," Adam said.

Hector tried to push him aside. "I'll do no such thing. I'm going to—"

Ty appeared and blocked his way. "You need to go sit down and relax, Uncle. You're looking a little flushed."

When Hector tried to get past him, several more men stepped forward to block his path. "Get out of my way!" Hector sputtered. "All of you."

The group of men pressed forward, sweeping Hector back toward the porch.

"Keep him here, Mom," Adam said, stepping through the crowd.

Maude grabbed her husband's arm. "Hector, do what Adam says. Please."

Hector attempted to push through the group of men, but they closed ranks and kept him on the porch. Fuming and grumbling, he slumped in his chair and glared at each man in turn.

Alf called for a bid on the next item. A seed drill. It went for two cents. The item after that also went for two cents, and the next one for one cent. Item after item began to receive bids now. The tractor went for six cents, and the harrows for one cent, the wagon for three cents, the land and the outbuildings for eighteen cents, and the farmhouse for a grand total of twelve cents.

On and on it went, and the longer it continued, the angrier Nathan and Hector both became. Nathan regarded the auction as an illegal attempt to block the sale of the farm, and Hector saw it as an ultimate betrayal by his friends and neighbors, who were shamelessly picking his bones clean. According to Hector's calculations, the auction had raised a grand total of four dollars and some loose change. That wouldn't pay for the auctioneer's fee, let alone put any money toward the amount owed to the bank. He was going to lose everything and have nothing to show for it.

Nathan turned on the crowd and wagged a finger at them. "I know what you're trying to do. But it won't work. I'll return with the sheriff and hold a fair and open auction."

"We have one hundred fifty witnesses who'll say this was a legal auction, Nathan," Ty said. "Bids were called for and bids were received. Isn't that right, Alf?"

"That's right," Alf replied.

Nathan drew himself up a little taller. "You can't seriously believe you can get away with this."

"If you try to dispute it," Adam said, "we'll take it to court. Imagine the time and expense that will entail. Not to mention the publicity."

When Nathan hesitated, Adam softened his tone. "Look, Nathan. All we're asking for is a chance to pay back the loan at a rate we can afford. Aren't regular monthly payments, small though they may be, better than what little money you have raised today?"

Sid stepped up to Nathan. "Most of us are in hock up to our eyeballs. What you've seen today is a united front. We're all determined to pay back what we owe, but you have to work with us so we can do it. Foreclosure isn't the answer. Cooperation is."

A murmur of agreement went through the crowd.

Nathan clenched his jaws. "You don't understand. It's not up to me. I don't set policy; I just implement it."

"But you can help modify it," Adam said. "The pendulum has swung too far the other way. We've got to get back to middle ground."

This was met with another murmur of agreement.

"You've known us all your life, Nathan," Sid said. "We belong to the same community and attend the same church. If one of our own won't help us, what hope do any of us have?"

"When you got stuck in a snowdrift on the county line road last winter," one of the farmers piped in, "who came with his team of horses and pulled you out?"

"And when you got a flat tire out at our place," said another farmer, "who took the tire into town to get it patched and then put it back on for you?"

"You see, that's what friends and neighbors do for each other," Sid said. "You found yourself beholden to others, and now we find ourselves beholden to you."

Nathan dropped his gaze and stared at the ground. "I can't make any promises. And I can't guarantee the bank will accept what happened here today. But I will speak to the board of directors."

Hands reached out and patted him on the back as he turned and made his way through the crowd. With a final look at the group of determined faces, he climbed into his car and drove away.

A shout erupted from the crowd, and men began shaking hands.

"Four dollars and some loose change!" Ty shouted, embracing Adam. "Now that's what I call a successful auction."

Hector and Maude got to their feet and made their way through the crowd. The noise gradually subsided, and all eyes turned to follow them. Hector approached Adam, his expression solemn and unreadable. "So everyone here was in on it?"

Adam nodded as a ripple of laughter went through the crowd.

Hector fixed his gaze back on his son. "And you couldn't let me in on it?"

Adam wanted to say, *You're too proud, Dad. You'd have never asked for help. This was the only way.* Instead, he simply shrugged and waited for his father's rebuke. Maude took hold of her husband's arm, silently appealing to him not to make a scene.

Hector continued to stare at his son. His expression suddenly softened, and his eyes glistened as he gestured toward the crowd in disbelief and simply said, "How?"

Ty motioned toward Adam. "Let's just say your son has been very busy, Uncle. He organized the whole thing."

Maude embraced Adam and buried her face against him.

Sid clapped a hand on Hector's shoulder. "Sometimes it takes something like this, Hec, to remind us that we're all in this together. I think you've seen today the kind of friends and neighbors you truly have."

Hector scratched his chin and glanced at Adam. "And family."

"And by the way, Hec," Sid continued. "I bought that cultivator for three cents. I'll sell it back to you for five."

Hector grunted and put an arm around Sid. "We'll see about that. Come into the house and we'll negotiate over coffee."

CHAPTER 16

ELIZABETH GLANCED OUT the window of Yang's Dry Cleaners. Main Street seemed uncommonly deserted for a Friday. People usually came into town to stock up on groceries and supplies for the weekend, but only a few cars were parked along the curb.

She went to the spotting table and applied cleaning solution to a soiled garment, gently working it in with a soft brush. She glanced up at the clock and puffed out her cheeks. "It should be over by now," she said.

Julie was standing at the garment rack, hanging up a dress. "You mean our shift?"

"No, the auction. I wonder how it went."

The auction was no secret, since there were posters up all over town. She and Julie had discussed it at work through the week. Even Lee Yang, who normally didn't say much, had expressed his hope that the bank would be more lenient to his business than it had been to the Carlson's, should the dry cleaners ever fall on hard times. "Mr. Roberts serious man," he had said. "He all business, business. Try to make jokes, but he not really funny. Not even when he call me Chop Suey."

During their conversations Elizabeth had wondered if she had done the right thing in encouraging Adam to talk to her uncle. But the more she thought about it, the more certain she became. Although Adam was a seasoned war veteran, he was in need of help, and she was in a position to see that he received it. Besides, there was a vulnerability about him that touched her.

She had looked for him at church on Sunday, to try and get a sense of how things were progressing, but he hadn't been there. Nor had he or Ty come to the barbecue at Susan's house on Wednesday, although most everyone else was there. As a result she came close to picking up the phone and calling him but decided against it.

When she talked to her uncle Wil, he told her of their conversation in his office, but he really had nothing more to report. He could only speculate. "In this case," he told her, "your guess is as good as mine. Probably better. Women's intuition and all that."

Now, as she stood at the spotting table, Elizabeth shook her head, perplexed. Women's intuition, indeed!

Julie hung up another freshly pressed dress. "Just ask Nathan about the auction when you see him. Or wait and read about it in tomorrow's *Gazette."* She smoothed down the fabric with her hand. "Or you can drive out after work and ask Adam yourself."

Elizabeth maintained a neutral expression. "Why would I do that?"

"Because you're dying to find out about it."

"I'm not dying. I'm just *curious."*

"Dying," Julie chirped, breezing over to the steam press.

"Who dying?" asked Lee Yang, carrying a box of supplies in from the boiler room.

"Me," said Julie. "It's like an oven in here."

Lee Yang shrugged. "Heat good for you. Clean your system."

Julie rolled her eyes and waited until Lee Yang went into the back room again. "So are you going to admit it?" she asked Elizabeth.

"Admit what?"

"That you're interested in Adam Carlson."

Elizabeth did a dramatic double take. "What? Do you have heat stroke or something?"

"Don't play innocent with me, Elizabeth Baxter. I've seen the way you two look at each other."

"When?"

"Where do I begin? At my birthday party, for example."

Elizabeth avoided making eye contact. "We didn't look at each other any more than we looked at anyone else. There were lots of people there."

"Oh, you looked at each other, all right. Especially when you kissed."

"It was just a game, Julie. The kiss didn't mean anything."

"Try telling that to Nathan. I thought there was going to be a fight."

"He's just possessive. You know that."

"And I know what I saw between you and Adam."

Elizabeth turned over the garment she was spot cleaning and rubbed on the other side of the stain. "Well, I don't care what you say. I wasn't *looking* at him."

"And the expression on your face when he left the party! You watched Ty and him go and practically moped around the rest of the evening."

"I did not."

Julie positioned a garment on the bottom pad of the steam press. "Do you know why you're being so defensive?"

"I'm not being defensive."

"Yes, you are. And it's because you know I'm right." Julie softened her tone. "Just call him. Or drive out after work and see him."

"I'm not going to drive out and *see* him. And that's final." She turned away, signaling the end of the conversation.

Elizabeth drove slowly down the turnoff to the Carlson farm. The farmyard was deserted except for the familiar pickup truck parked beside the house. She stopped the Roadmaster in the middle of the farmyard and shut off the engine, waiting to see if her arrival had been noticed. But no face appeared in the kitchen window, and no one emerged from the screen door. The yard was quiet.

She started toward the house, telling herself that her first inquiry would be concerning Maude's health. After that she'd ask about the auction. She was halfway there when a whinny caught her attention.

A white horse stood in the corral, rubbing its shoulder against the top railing. Glancing around, she slowly approached the horse, speaking softly as she proceeded. "Hey, boy," she said. "How are you doing?"

"That's Snowflake," came a voice from the barn door.

141

She turned to see Adam walking toward her.

"Snowflake," Elizabeth said. "He's beautiful."

"Got him as a yearling when I was in high school. And the bay right behind him is Babe, a Morgan." As if wanting to be noticed, Babe stepped out from behind Snowflake and peered toward them. "Step into the corral and I'll introduce you."

As he opened the gate for her, her foot slipped in the soft ground. He reached out and took her hand. "Hold on," he said.

Elizabeth held his hand firmly and didn't let go immediately when they were beside the bay horse.

Stroking Babe's forelock, Adam said, "Babe is as gentle as his name suggests. Go ahead, touch him."

Elizabeth released Adam's hand and gently ran her fingers through the wiry mane.

"By the way," Adam said, "I'll never be able to thank you and your uncle Wil for your help."

This was the lead-in she'd been hoping for. "How did the auction go?" she asked.

Adam grinned. "We raised a grand total of four dollars and sixteen cents."

Elizabeth's eyes widened. "Four dollars and sixteen cents? That's terrible."

"Actually, it's great."

Elizabeth blinked in confusion. "I don't understand."

"A group of us united together to keep the bidding down, forcing the bank to reconsider foreclosing on us."

"So you get to keep the farm?"

"We're not out of the woods yet, but hopefully things will work out. Nathan left in a more cooperative frame of mind than when he arrived." He paused and looked into her eyes. "I owe you a lot, Elizabeth. Thank you."

As he reached out to touch her hand, Babe snorted and nudged him impatiently, as if to redirect Adam's attention.

Adam laughed and patted Babe on the neck. "Someone's feeling excluded." He turned to Elizabeth. "Would you like to go for a ride? I've been meaning to exercise the horses anyway."

Shifting indecisively, she said, "But I'm wearing a dress."

"Tuck it between your knees and the saddle. Italian women do it all the time. You'll be fine."

She still appeared doubtful. "I've never ridden a Morgan before."

"Well, like they say, there's a first time for everything."

Hesitating for only a moment, Elizabeth said, "We won't ride very far, right?"

He pointed toward the far end of the pasture. "Just to those cottonwoods by the river. Some great fishing down there."

"I've never been fishing."

"You'll have to try it some time. I find it very relaxing." He motioned toward the barn. "I'll get the gear."

Elizabeth watched as Adam saddled up the two horses, giving a final tug to both cinches to make sure they were tight.

"Climb into the saddle on Babe's left side," he said, "and I'll adjust the stirrups."

Elizabeth placed a foot in the stirrup and tried to swing up into the saddle, but she only made it partway. Her second attempt was also unsuccessful.

Adam boosted her up into the saddle, enjoying the sensation of his hands around her waist. "Hold the reins loosely and don't make any sudden moves," he said, adjusting the stirrup on the left side before moving around to the right.

She glanced around. "We won't go fast, right?"

"No, we'll start out with a walk," he replied, swinging effortlessly into the saddle. Easing Snowflake through the corral gate, he glanced back at Elizabeth, who sat straight and rigid, looking uncertain. "Gently nudge Babe and say 'Gee up,'" he said.

Hesitantly, Elizabeth urged the horse forward. Her eyes widened in alarm as Babe responded, stepping out into the yard and falling in behind Snowflake.

"You're doing great," Adam said, winking at her and turning back around. "Now, all you have to—"

A brown blur suddenly flashed by him, and he looked in disbelief as Elizabeth urged Babe into a gallop and sat expertly in the saddle as her mount vaulted a sawhorse. "Last one to the trees is a rotten egg!" she shouted over her shoulder as she raced across the pasture, her hair streaming behind her in the breeze.

"Elizabeth Baxter!" he muttered under his breath.

Digging his heels into Snowflake, he took off after her. She was already partway across the pasture and seemed determined to increase the distance between them. Despite the fact that Snowflake was a larger horse, Adam was unable to close the gap. Elizabeth had dismounted and was waiting for him when he reined up.

"Something must have spooked my horse," she said, smiling at him innocently. "But never fear, Prince Charming has come to the rescue." She gently patted Babe on the neck and let the horse nuzzle against her.

Adam arched an eyebrow. "Prince Charming, huh?"

"On a white steed, no less."

Climbing down to join her, he said, "I thought you said you didn't know how to ride a horse."

Elizabeth smiled guiltily. "I said I'd never ridden a *Morgan* before. Actually, Uncle Wil owns part interest in a ranch east of Great Falls. I've ridden Palominos and Arabians since I was a little girl."

Adam cut her a look of pretended disapproval. "And I suppose you have been fishing too and caught a trophy trout that's mounted on a wall somewhere."

"No, that part was true. I've never been fishing before."

"Actually, you have."

Elizabeth wrinkled her forehead. "When?"

"Back at the corral when I swallowed your story…hook, line, and sinker."

Sunlight danced lazily on the water, shimmering in rhythm to the listless current, as they tied the horses in the shade and walked down to the river. Cottonwoods and willows bordered the river, pressing down to the water's edge and creating an atmosphere of seclusion.

"It's so beautiful here," Elizabeth said.

Especially now, Adam thought as he glanced at her from the corner of his eye. "There's a nice grassy spot down this trail," he said, pointing to his left. "The river bends, creating a large pool. It used to be Ty's and my swimming hole. Our old Tarzan rope swing is still there. Some kids have discovered the place, I noticed, because there's a small raft sitting abandoned on the shore."

"Come on, I'll race you there," she said, rushing ahead.

"What is it with you and races?" he said, addressing the empty space beside him.

Elizabeth was already running through the tall grass that lined the trail. She flitted in and out of the trees like the shadow of a bird soaring overhead. Pausing briefly, she poked her head from behind a tree farther down the trail. The sunlight caught the reflection in her eyes, highlighting their color. The breeze lifted her hair gently away from her shoulders, and she smiled impishly.

Jolted into action, he took off after her.

She laughed and continued down the trail, her dress billowing like wings.

Adam followed in pursuit, but she disappeared around a bend in the path. When he finally burst into the grassy clearing, she was nowhere to be seen. He scanned the area, puzzled, before noticing her on the raft, struggling to keep her balance as she used a long pole to push off from the shore.

"You'd better get back here before you fall in," he called to her.

She looked at him in playful defiance. "Make me."

Adam leaned against a nearby cottonwood tree and considered the situation. He noticed a few rocks lying half buried in the grass. Prying up a rock about the size of a cantaloupe, he passed it ominously back and forth between his hands. "I sailed across the Atlantic on an army transport ship," he said. "We had to travel a zigzag course to avoid torpedoes." He drew back his arm. "You'd better start zigzagging!"

He launched the rock. It landed near the raft, sending a column of water cascading into the air. The splash reached her, and she squealed in complaint, almost losing her balance as she tried to maneuver the raft out of range.

A second rock landed even closer.

"You're getting me all wet!" she protested.

Another rock sent a wave of water coursing over the raft. She squealed again and dropped the pole in an attempt to protect herself. "Look what you made me do!" she exclaimed loudly, eyeing the pole in dismay as it floated out of reach.

Adam picked up an even larger rock and balanced it carefully. "We could call a truce."

"Yes, truce, truce!"

He dropped the rock and dusted off his hands. "See, safe passage. You're free to dock, Captain."

Elizabeth looked at the pole bobbing in the water, just out of reach. "So how do I get into the harbor?"

"I've got an idea...but you won't like it."

"Paddle with my hands, right?"

"No, but you might get a little more wet."

Before she could inquire further, he picked up the large rock and sent it sailing through the air. It landed with a splash, and Elizabeth screamed as the spray drenched her.

"I thought we had a truce!" she cried.

Adam held up his hands to show he posed no further threat. "I told you that you might not like it. But you can reach the pole now."

The ripples had washed the pole toward her. She bent down carefully, keeping her head up to maintain her balance, her fingers groping for the pole. "Just a little more to your left," Adam said. "And down another inch or two."

The raft tipped slightly under her weight, and she leaned the other way to compensate. The raft responded by tilting the opposite direction as she overcorrected. Adam watched helplessly as her attempts to stabilize the raft only made the situation worse. Before long the raft was seesawing wildly as though riding a stormy sea. As her cries for help turned into a sustained scream, the raft listed and pitched her overboard.

Her wail was muffled as she disappeared beneath the surface of the water. She came up almost instantly, coughing and gasping. The water was only waist deep, however, so she was able to stand up. "My dress is completely soaked!" she gasped, folding her arms across herself for modesty's sake.

Adam burst out laughing. She scowled at him, and he bit his lip in an effort to regain his composure. But he couldn't maintain it and laughed again. "Here, give me your hand," he said, reaching for her.

She waded awkwardly toward him, the mud rising from the bottom and swirling with each step. "Don't look!" she said.

He turned his head and pulled on her hand but lost his grip. With a squeal, she fell backward in the water and fought to keep from going under again.

"You did that on purpose," she protested.

"Honest, I didn't," Adam replied sincerely. "Your hands are slippery." He reached out and turned his head away once more.

"I'm glad you find this so amusing."

"I don't." He failed to stifle a chuckle. "Okay, I do. It's funny when you think about it."

"Then *don't* think about it. Just help me."

As he extended his hand again, she grabbed him firmly by the wrist and yanked, catching him off-balance. He gasped in surprise and plunged headfirst into the water.

"You're right," she said, laughing in triumph as he resurfaced. "It *is* pretty funny."

"What a dirty trick!" he sputtered, wiping the water from his eyes.

"That's what you get for laughing at me."

He bent down and scooped up a handful of mud. "And this is what *you* get for laughing at me."

Her laughter faded and she eyed him narrowly. "You wouldn't dare."

The mud sailed through the air and splattered against the front of her dress. She looked at him in disbelief and bent down to retrieve a handful of mud herself. She threw it and hit him on the shoulder.

"Mud fight!" he cried, scooping more mud from the bottom.

Mud flew back and forth furiously, turning the water into a soupy mix. Finally, Elizabeth threw herself at Adam in an effort to force his head underwater, but it was like trying to bend an iron bar. He merely laughed and rubbed a gob of mud on the end of her nose.

She relented and backed away, looking up into his face. He returned her gaze, smiling gently. He stared into her eyes, hearing unspoken words, reading unexpressed emotions. Moving toward him, slowly at first and finally in a rush, Elizabeth wrapped her arms around his neck, and he pulled her against him. They kissed passionately, desperately, consumed with the overpowering feelings of the moment. Adam ran his fingers through her hair, and she moaned and clung to him.

Finally parting lips, they held each other close, caressing one another. Then Adam lifted her into his arms and carried her to the shore, setting her down on the grassy bank. She reclined in the grass and spread her dress out to dry in the sun. Adam bent over her, propping himself on one elbow. She looked up into his face, and they kissed long and passionately once more.

At length Elizabeth pulled away and placed a hand to Adam's lips. "Adam, we need to slow down. I—I need some time to think."

"About what?"

"About us. About Nathan."

He stroked her hair tenderly. "I don't want to push you, Elizabeth. I just thought what you and I shared meant—" He broke off. "I know what I felt. I was hoping you felt the same thing."

"I did. I do. But it's not that simple, Adam."

Adam cleared his throat. "I know. But let me ask you a question. And answer honestly. Don't try and spare my feelings...or Nathan's, for that matter. How do you feel—truly feel—when you're with him, compared to how you feel being here with me?"

She turned back toward him and put a hand to his face, tracing the outline of his lips with her fingers. "The day I kissed you at the shooting gallery, I felt something—" She touched her heart. "—here. And when we ditched the hayride and danced alone at the pavilion, I knew then I was falling in love with you. Our kiss at Julie's party only convinced me all the more."

"So why would you have any doubts about us now?"

"I've tried to tell myself my feelings for you are nothing more than a schoolgirl crush, that my future is with Nathan. But being here with you today…"

Adam kissed her lightly on the cheek.

They sat up, and she put her arms through his and leaned against his shoulder, her body beginning to tremble. "Oh, Adam, I can't do this right now. I have to talk to Nathan first. I have to consider his feelings too." Tears formed in her eyes and ran down her cheeks.

He wiped them gently with the back of his hand. "I understand, Elizabeth. I honestly do. And I accept your decision." He looked at her tenderly. "If you follow your head and marry Nathan, you'll never want for material things, we both know that." He held her hand toward him and touched her finger as if she were wearing a diamond ring. "You'll live like a princess." Then he pretended to rotate the ring so the diamond disappeared under her finger. "If you follow your heart and marry me, you'll be giving up a lot of those things. But this I promise you: I'll work until the day I die to make you happy. I love you, Elizabeth."

Adam's words rang in her ears during the subdued ride back to the farm. She hardly felt Babe's hooves plodding through the pasture, nor did she hear the song of the western meadowlark from its perch on a nearby fence post. And during the drive into Reunion, Adam's words continued to echo in her mind. She was oblivious to the sounds of the gravel popping against the floorboards of the

Buick Roadmaster and to the trail of dust that rose behind her like the giant tail of a kite.

Her mind was far away, her heart troubled.

She thought of Nathan's proposal at the restaurant. He had presented her with the diamond ring over an expensive meal. She had been dressed up, with her hair neatly styled and her makeup just right. The location could not have been more perfect. It was a storybook setting, and any girl should have felt fortunate to be the center of such extravagance.

Then her thoughts turned to her experience with Adam on the riverbank. She had sat there with mud clinging to her dress, her hair unkempt, her makeup smeared. The location could not have been more unpretentious or the situation more unlikely. The contrast between the two experiences was marked, and each typified the life she would lead, depending on her choice. On the surface, the choice seemed like a simple one to make. And yet, all things considered, it was complicated. There were people involved—people she cared about—and there were strings attached. Feelings were going to be hurt...and hearts broken.

She was still torn with uncertainty when she arrived home and found Nathan sitting on the couch in the living room, having tea with her aunt Lenora.

CHAPTER 17

ADAM WENT THROUGH the motions of doing the evening chores, trying unsuccessfully to distract himself. He went from one unfinished task to another. Finally giving up, he went into the house.

Maude was sitting at the kitchen table, putting the finishing touches on the photo album she had started organizing during her three days of convalescence. Hector sat beside her, poring over an agricultural magazine and talking about some new equipment the farm could use in order to increase yield.

"Son," Maude said, looking up from her work. "Can I fix you something to eat?"

"I'm not hungry."

"With all you did today, you should be famished."

Hector looked up from his magazine. "Just how did you manage to organize the auction without me knowing about it, anyway?"

So far there had been little family time to discuss the success of the auction. With people coming and going throughout the day and telephone calls from people calling to hear the details of the penny auction, there hadn't been an idle moment. And, of course, there was Elizabeth's arrival, the horse ride, and the experience down at the river.

At his father's question Adam smiled. He knew very well how he had organized the penny auction. He and Ty had spent the preceding week visiting all of the farms in the area, talking to friends and neighbors, and placing telephone calls to acquaintances in neighboring counties. But instead of relating this to his father now, he simply said, "I did it with a lot of help from a lot of people."

"I don't know how we'll ever be able to thank everyone," Maude said, getting up from the table and embracing him. "Or you."

Adam looked over her shoulder at his father. Hector was a man of few words, particularly when it involved paying compliments. He held Adam's gaze before clearing his throat and turning back to his magazine.

"We owe everyone our undying gratitude," Maude said, almost reverently.

And I owe one person, in particular, my undying love, Adam said to himself as the thought of Elizabeth caused an invisible hand to grip his heart. To change the subject, he looked at the photograph Maude was placing in the album. It was a picture of his parents on their wedding day, standing beside a modest two-layer cake.

"How many years have you been married now?" he asked.

"Twenty-seven," Hector replied, setting the magazine aside.

Shaking her head, Maude said, "Thirty-one years, in May."

"How did you two meet?"

"Too long ago to remember," Hector muttered.

"Actually, it seems like only yesterday," Maude replied.

Hector coughed.

"It was on a street corner, one block from Main Street," Maude continued. "My sister, Alice, and I were on our way downtown to get some groceries when we happened to meet her husband—your uncle Sid—and his friend, a handsome young man named Hector Carlson, coming up the street. I'd seen Hec around town, of course, but he was several years older than me. He hardly looked at me when Sid introduced us. Sid told me later that your father thought I was just a young girl. 'Young girl, nothing,' Sid told him. 'She's nineteen.' And with that information, Hector Carlson came calling the very next day."

Adam looked at his father in surprise. "Really?"

Hector became busy with the magazine again.

"He courted me like a gentleman," Maude said. "Sid once told me that when your father learned I was nineteen, he said, 'Sid, that's the woman I'm going to marry.'"

"You did?" Adam said, directing the question at his father.

"Sid's a storyteller," Hector said. "You can't believe a word he says."

Adam smiled thinly. "It must be true or you wouldn't be so touchy about it."

"Oh, it's true," Maude affirmed. "Your father admitted it to me himself."

Adam tried to visualize his father as a young man in love. He gave up when it proved too difficult. But one fact remained: his father had known Maude was the woman for him, and he had gone and done something about it, courting her like a gentleman.

Adam stared at the floor as questions began swirling in his brain. How could he court Elizabeth when she was so torn? Had he gone too far in telling her how he felt about her? Was he guilty of a gross impropriety when she already had a boyfriend? What kind of man weaseled his way into another couple's relationship, anyway?

Maude resumed her work on the album, and Hector continued reading, commenting on a new type of drop seeder that was featured in an article.

Adam looked at his parents—now engaged in activities that belied the terrible stress and strain they had experienced earlier that morning—and thought how ironic life could be. On a day that should have been filled with rejoicing and gratitude, *he* was the one now experiencing terrible stress and strain.

Excusing himself, he went out to gather eggs. A cheerless activity.

His thoughts remained on Elizabeth and their experience at the river. There were so many more things he had wanted to say to her, but in the end he had let her drive away, not knowing if or when he would see her again or under what circumstances it might occur.

She was back in her world now, he realized, which included Nathan, who might overwhelm her with gifts, sweep her off her feet with promises, and insulate her from further contact. Adam realized he might never have a chance to talk to her again. Perhaps he had lost her for good, if he'd ever really had her at all.

His emotions seethed, and he dropped an egg. It splattered on the floor and released its yellowy-white contents. Scooping up the remains, he threw it out in the yard for the crows and the barnyard cats to fight over.

When he finished the chores, he sat on the front porch as the evening descended. The sun dipped below the jagged horizon, and from somewhere in the distance, crickets sawed contentedly away. The occasional hoot of an owl harmonized with them, and a breeze rustled the buffalo grass, creating soft background accompaniment. The dimness hid the farm's blemishes, and the scene might have been one on a postcard, extolling the serenity of life on the Great Plains.

Finally he went upstairs to bed. But he tossed and turned all night and kept seeing the cracked egg on the floor, releasing its contents. Breaking an egg while gathering them had happened many times over the years. There was always a certain amount of loss in the process. That was to be expected. But there was something about *this* broken egg that wouldn't leave his head. It seemed like an omen, a harbinger of broken dreams and shattered plans.

Saturday morning arrived, announced by the cry of the rooster. Adam rolled out of bed, feeling tired and restless. He got dressed and went through the routine of chores mechanically, numbly. Dew glistened in the meadow as the sun slowly climbed the morning sky, shortening the shadows. Wisps of clouds hung above the Rocky Mountains like a film of gossamer, gradually disappearing in the growing heat. Neither the beauty nor tranquility of the setting served to lift his spirits, as it usually did.

He was in the barn, fixing a feed box, when he heard a vehicle pull in through the front gate. At first he thought it might be Ty, coming to talk about the success of the penny auction or perhaps wanting to drive into town for a game of pool at Herb's Pool Hall.

He would almost welcome the distraction, even though he was falling behind in his work.

Glancing out the window, he felt the blood rush to his head. A black Buick Roadmaster sat in the yard. He was through the door in an instant, brushing himself off and smoothing down his hair.

As Elizabeth climbed out of the car, Adam walked toward her. He stopped a few feet away and stood in uncertainty. There was a pause as they stared at each other. Suddenly Elizabeth broke into a smile and rushed toward him. They threw their arms around each other, and he twirled her in a circle. They kissed tenderly, and he led her over to a bale of hay near the barn so they could sit in the shade.

"I thought I'd lost you, Elizabeth," he said, embracing her. "I've never been so miserable in my life." He kissed her again and placed his head against hers. "You were still undecided when you left here," he said, gently stroking her hair. "What helped you make up your mind?"

Elizabeth nestled against him, her breath coming in short bursts. "All the way home I thought of what you said about following my head or following my heart. I wasn't sure what you really meant until I walked in and saw Nathan, dressed in his suit, wearing a silk necktie, having tea with Aunt Lenora. He was so...proper. Not a hair out of place, fingernails neatly trimmed. He looked at me in shock when he saw my appearance: mud on my dress and my hair, my makeup smeared. You remember how I looked."

"Beautiful," Adam whispered in her ear.

She nudged him playfully in the ribs. "I did not."

"Yes, you did. To me."

"Well, I didn't to Nathan. I saw disapproval in his eyes—almost disgust—and he wouldn't let me near him for fear of getting mud on his suit. A small thing, I know. But I realized that I didn't love him the way I love you."

They shared another kiss.

At length Elizabeth continued. "Nathan and I spoke alone in

the front parlor. He was already upset about the auction, but he became even more upset when I told him about you and me. He tried for an hour to change my mind. Finally I asked him if he could see *us* riding horses together or having a mud fight in the river. He looked at me in disbelief." Elizabeth paused and clasped her hands. "I asked him to look into my eyes and tell me that he would devote his life to loving me and making me happy. I asked him to tell me that he loved me...passionately. And he couldn't do it. He just kept staring at my muddy dress and hair with disapproval written all over his face. I realized that if I married him, I would have everything and nothing at the same time." She paused and looked off into the distance, remembering. "But as upset as he was about losing me, I had the feeling he was more upset about losing me to *you*. It was like the shooting competition or the community dance all over again."

"Like I once told you, Nathan and I go back a long ways. We competed against each other for a spot on the basketball team. Raced against each other in track and field. You know, high school competitiveness."

Elizabeth arched an eyebrow. "So this is a competition? To the victor go the spoils?"

Adam kissed her passionately. When they finally parted, he said, "Does that answer your question?"

She smiled and tilted her face back up to his. "I don't know. Let me ask once more."

"I love an inquisitive mind," he said, kissing her again.

Snowflake whinnied from the corral, causing them to look up and laugh.

"Someone's feeling left out," Elizabeth said.

Adam smiled and then became serious. "How did your aunt take it?"

"After Nathan left, Aunt Lenora started in. She kept telling me that I was giving up a secure future, that Nathan would be able to provide me with things that—"

"—I never could," Adam said, dropping his voice to a whisper.

Elizabeth said, "When Uncle Wil got home and heard everything, he reminded Aunt Lenora that when they were courting, her mother hadn't approved of him either. He was working as a stock clerk at the time and was so strapped for money that he didn't have two nickels to rub together. Her mother had warned her about marrying poor. 'You'll be living from hand to mouth,' she had said, 'and what kind of life is that?' But Uncle Wil also reminded Aunt Lenora that things had worked out. He had gone to college and studied accounting. The early years had been lean, he said, but in the long run, it had brought them closer together as they struggled to build his business."

"Your uncle Wil actually spoke up for me? But with the uncertainty of the farm and all..."

"Aunt Lenora's arguments ended when Uncle Wil took her hand and said, 'What would have happened, Lenora, had you listened to your mother and not married me?'"

Adam whistled under his breath and took Elizabeth's hand. "And I wonder what would have happened had you listened to Nathan and agreed to marry him."

"You're Prince Charming, right? You'd have come for me. On your white steed."

Adam dropped his gaze guiltily. "But I didn't come, Elizabeth. You had to make the choice on your own."

She rested her head against his shoulder. "And I made it. Here I am."

He kissed her forehead. "I meant it yesterday when I said I'll spend the rest of my life making you happy. And that's a promise."

She snuggled closer to him and sighed contentedly.

Adam fell silent for a moment. Finally he said, "Sometimes two people meet and they know—they just know—they're meant for each other. It doesn't take years or even months for them to fall in love. It can happen in one magical instant. The night we danced together in the pavilion, just the two of us, and I looked into your eyes—that was the instant for me. It was like I was looking into the eyes of someone I had known and loved all my life. And every moment I've been around you since then has only deepened that conviction. I love you, Elizabeth Baxter. Passionately. And if you'll let me, I want to spend the rest of my life with you."

Tears formed in Elizabeth's eyes.

Adam looked at her in concern. "Did I say something wrong?"

Sniffing back more tears, she answered, "No, you said everything right. I love you and want to spend the rest of my life with you too."

He gently wiped her tears, and they kissed once more. Finally, he whispered, "Elizabeth, will you marry me?"

Without hesitation she replied, "Yes!"

This time when they kissed, it was even more meaningful. They were committing to a lifetime together, to charting their course as husband and wife.

As they parted lips and embraced one another, Adam said, "Let's get married right away."

"We need to give our families a little time to get used to...us. Besides, the preparations will take some time, especially when Aunt Lenora gets involved. I'll need until at least October."

"We'll be done with the harvest by then, so that will work out well." He stroked Elizabeth's cheek. "So where do we go from here?"

"We can begin by attending church together tomorrow. You can pick me up just before ten. That will be a good way to start. Aunt Lenora firmly believes in church attendance."

"I hope she still feels that way after the service."

Elizabeth let out a sigh. "I know it will be awkward for us to be seen together at first, but—"

"No, I don't mean it like that. Pastor Wight is using his interview with me for his sermon tomorrow."

Elizabeth stared up into his face. "So you're giving the sermon...indirectly. That *will* impress Aunt Lenora."

"You'd better reserve judgment until after the service. I'm actually quite nervous about it."

"It will be a wonderful meeting," she said, squeezing his hand in encouragement. "Then you can bring me home and stay for Sunday dinner. Afterward, you can talk to Uncle Wil."

"I suppose we need to have *the talk,* don't we?"

"Mostly to appease Aunt Lenora. You won't have any trouble with Uncle Wil."

Adam shuddered. "I know I have to do it. But being around your aunt and uncle so soon...sitting in Nathan's chair...taking Nathan's place..."

"Don't even try to take Nathan's place. I'm in love with someone else, remember?"

Adam leaned over and kissed the top of her head. "I'll keep reminding myself of that fact when I'm seated across the dining room table from your aunt, enduring her scrutiny."

"It won't be that bad," she replied. "And you'll doubly impress her if you wear your uniform."

"I guess I should wear it, since I'll be entering enemy territory for Sunday dinner," he said, receiving a playful swat on the arm.

"What will your parents think?" Elizabeth asked.

"Mom will be overjoyed. She really likes you. And Dad? Well, as I'm sure you know from living in this town, Hector Carlson is...Hector Carlson. He'll be happy for us too. He just won't show it, that's all."

He suddenly got to his feet and pulled Elizabeth up beside him. "Let's drive into Great Falls and look at rings."

"Adam, wait. There's something else you need to know." She gazed at him searchingly, almost apologetically.

"You're not having second thoughts, are you?" he asked teasingly. When she didn't smile, he grew solemn. "What is it?"

"After I told Nathan about us, he pointed at me angrily and told me to give you a message. *All bets are off.* That's how he said it."

"So that means he's not going to help after all," Adam said, digging at the ground with the toe of his boot. "It's not right to turn a business issue into a personal one."

"They're one and the same for Nathan. I can see that now."

Adam was silent for a moment. "What are we going to do?" he asked at length. "Who can we appeal to?"

"The bank president."

"I don't even know who he is."

"Uncle Wil does. Let's ask Uncle Wil to go over your books and find out where the farm is financially. Perhaps he can advise us on a plan that will satisfy both parties."

Adam looked doubtful. "Won't that put him in the middle between Nathan and me?"

"I think you'll find that Uncle Wil's in our corner now."

Considering the situation momentarily, Adam said, "I'll bring the farm ledger and the bank statements when I come tomorrow. Meanwhile—" He grabbed Elizabeth and swung her around. "—let's drive into Great Falls and look at rings."

"Now?"

"Right now."

Her feet lit back down, and a slight frown creased her forehead. "But diamonds are expensive."

Adam was not to be deterred. "I want everyone to know you're spoken for." *One guy in particular.*

CHAPTER 18

THE TRIP INTO GREAT Falls was surreal. The truck was like a magic carpet, floating through the clouds, and neither Adam nor Elizabeth were aware of anything but each other. They spoke excitedly of the future, making plans and basking in each other's company.

Adam drove to Halton's, the largest jewelry store in the city, and parked alongside the curb. A sign in the window stated: HALTON'S: THE JEWELRY STORE THAT OFFERS MORE. Adam read the words excitedly and hurried around to open Elizabeth's door. Hand in hand they went inside.

The proprietor, a balding man with a noticeably large gold ring on his left hand, greeted them warmly. "How may I help you?" he asked.

"We'd like to look at engagement rings," Adam said.

"Of course. Let me show you our most popular line. Right this way, please."

He conducted them to the front counter. It was filled with rows of exquisite diamond rings, each set in an open velvet box. A series of small lights illuminated the interior of the counter, causing the diamonds to sparkle.

Pointing to the first ring, he said, "Here we have the classic four-prong diamond ring in fourteen karat gold. Next to it is the star diamond engagement ring, in eighteen-karat white gold. And then we have..." He continued down the row, naming the rings and explaining the features that made each one special or unique.

Adam glanced at the price tags. A light-headed sensation washed over him, and he realized the rings were impossibly expensive. "They're all really nice," he said. "Can we look at some other styles?"

The proprietor nodded and led the way to another counter.

Adam's hopes rose when he saw it contained rows of gold

bands, each with a small diamond. But his hopes fell abruptly when he glanced at the price tags. It was frustrating to come into the store to pick out a ring worthy of his love for Elizabeth, only to be jolted back to reality by the cost. He lamented that finances had a way of bursting lovers' bubbles quickly.

Looking at the proprietor, Adam swallowed. "What other styles do you have?"

The proprietor conducted them toward a smaller counter that contained silver bands, each with a diamond chip.

Once again Adam noted the price tags and felt his spirits sink. Glancing at Elizabeth, he asked, "What do you think?"

"They're all so beautiful," she replied.

Adam drew the proprietor aside as Elizabeth continued to browse. "Do you have a credit plan?" he asked. "You know, so we can take a ring now and pay for it over time?"

The proprietor shook his head. "Not a credit plan, but we do have an *installment* plan."

"How does it work?"

"You put down a deposit and make payments as you can. We keep the ring here, locked up safely. When it's paid for in full, it's yours."

"There's no way to get it sooner?"

"I'm afraid not. But at least it guarantees the ring of your choice. No one else can buy it in the meantime."

Adam ran a hand through his hair. "How much is the down payment?"

"Thirty percent."

Adam didn't need to feel his wallet or check his bank statements to know he didn't have enough money. Everything had gone into fixing up the farm, and he was stretched to the limit. "Look, I'm entitled to some benefits under the GI Bill. I don't have the money yet, but it's coming. Can you set aside a ring for us until then?"

The proprietor shook his head. "Not without a down payment, I'm afraid."

Adam dropped his gaze and nodded in defeat. Putting on a brave smile, he walked over and stood beside Elizabeth.

"Oh, Adam," she said. "There are so many to choose from. I don't know where to start." She walked past the other counters again, pausing to examine their contents. "I just can't decide. Can I have more time to think about it?"

"Sure." He knew the relief was evident in his voice.

"It's all so exciting and overwhelming right now. I just don't want to feel rushed. Besides, half the fun is in the shopping."

Adam turned to the proprietor. "Thanks for your help, but I guess we're going to do some more looking around."

"Of course. Selecting the perfect ring takes time," he said, winking at Elizabeth. "You want to make sure you're completely satisfied."

Adam noticed the wink and felt his cheeks burn. It was obvious the man knew Elizabeth was letting Adam off the hook. The rings were simply too expensive for Adam to buy, and everyone in the room knew it.

Taking Elizabeth by the hand, Adam escorted her toward the door, unable to make eye contact with the proprietor as they exited. He walked in silence beside Elizabeth as they headed for the truck, glancing back at the sign in the jewelry store window. HALTON'S: THE JEWELRY STORE THAT OFFERS MORE.

It offers more all right, he thought bitterly, as he started the truck and backed away from the curb. *But only to those who can afford it.*

He was subdued on the drive home.

The magic carpet ride was over, and the truck labored noisily along, seeming to hit every pothole in the road. The engine protested as the truck climbed the hills and coughed in respite as it descended them. The scenery became a blur. The occasional vehicle passed by, but mostly the road remained deserted. The hum of the tires harmonized with Judy Garland singing "Over the Rainbow" on the radio, and the bittersweet strains epitomized the somber mood.

Adam fixed his eyes straight ahead. Today had been a roller-coaster ride of emotions. As high as the ups had been, the downs were equally low. But now the two were merging, and he wasn't sure what he felt anymore, other than numbness coupled with a sense of failure.

It was Elizabeth who first broke the silence. "Adam, I just want you to know that I don't need a ring. At least, not for a while."

"But it just won't seem real otherwise."

She bit her lip hesitantly. "I have some money saved up and—"

"You're not buying your own engagement ring, Elizabeth." He was silent for a moment and then looked at her apologetically. "I'm sorry. It's just that so much of my money has gone into fixing up the farm."

Elizabeth laid her head on his shoulder. "It's okay. A ring will come in its own time." She reached up and kissed him on the cheek.

"Hey, don't distract me," he said, managing a half smile. "I'm driving."

She kissed him once more.

Waves of frustration continued to sweep over him, washing him along in their wake. The engagement would seem less official if he couldn't buy her a ring. But how could he afford it? He'd have to save for years to buy her the ring she deserved. And he couldn't wait that long.

"Adam," she said softly, "I'd rather be engaged to you without a ring than to anyone else in the world with one."

"Nathan could give you a diamond the size of your fist," he lamented.

"Yes, he could," she replied, nudging him playfully. "And look where that got him."

Adam smiled. "You're just saying that to make me feel better."

"I'll prove it to you," she replied, smothering his face with kisses.

Her hair blocked his vision momentarily, and he fought to see the road ahead. "You're going to cause an accident!"

"Then you'd better shape up, soldier. Your bottom lip is

practically dragging on the road. You're so busy being upset about what we don't have that you're forgetting what we do have."

"And that is...?"

"Each other. And right now that's enough for me."

CHAPTER 19

SUNDAY MORNING DAWNED bright and clear.

Following chores, Adam appeared in his mother's bedroom doorway, wearing his uniform and carrying his service cap under his arm. A breeze wafted in through her open window, billowing the curtains gently.

Maude was sitting at her vanity, brushing her hair. She looked up at him and smiled. "You look so handsome, son."

Hector came down the hallway from the bathroom and eyed Adam up and down. "Looks like you're ready to go," he said.

Maude set the hairbrush aside. "I'm so looking forward to Pastor Wight's sermon today. It would be nice if we were *all* there to hear it." She glanced at her husband. "It is *our son* that is being quoted today."

Hector waved his hand dismissively. "Someone's got to tend to the farm."

Maude rolled her eyes. "That's just an excuse and you know it. I'm not asking you to be *baptized* into the church, Hec. I'm talking about coming with us to support your son."

Hector glanced at Adam but addressed Maude. "The congregation will do just fine without me."

Maude sighed and turned her gaze back to Adam. "When you go to the Jacksons' for dinner, son, remember to thank Lenora for the meal she sent last week. Tell her how much we enjoyed everything."

Hector raised both eyebrows. "The Jacksons? As in Wil and Lenora?"

"And Elizabeth," Maude added, smiling at Adam. He had told her yesterday of his feelings for Elizabeth but had not yet told his father.

"When did you become such good acquaintance of theirs?"

Hector muttered. "Wil's not too bad, but Lenora is one fuss-budget of a woman."

Adam winced as the reality of entering Lenora Jackson's world caused something to tighten in the pit of his stomach.

Maude patted his hand. "You'll be fine, son." She looked patiently at her husband. "Adam is taking Elizabeth to church. And afterward he's going to the Jacksons' for Sunday dinner."

Adam tugged at his collar. "I guess I'd better get going. You'll be fine riding with Uncle Sid and Aunt Alice?"

"Of course. They should be here any minute." She stood up and glanced out the bedroom window. "Good luck with everything today, son. My prayers are with you."

"Thanks. I can use all the prayers I can get." Adam looked over at his father. "How about you, Dad? Are your prayers with me, too?"

"My *thoughts* are with you," Hector replied.

That's an improvement, Adam wanted to say, but didn't.

The pickup truck glistened in the morning sun. Adam had washed and scrubbed the truck, attempting to restore some of its former sheen, which lay buried beneath oxidized layers of paint.

He drove slowly into town so the truck wouldn't get dusty. The three-mile trip seemed to last forever, but the nearer he got, the more nervous he became. Not even the Andrews Sisters' upbeat "Boogie Woogie Bugle Boy" on the radio eased his tension. He looked at the bouquet of wildflowers he'd picked from his mother's flower garden and wished they were long-stemmed roses instead. He also glanced at the ledger and box of bank statements, old receipts, and other documents he'd brought along for Wil to pore over. So much was riding on this visit. It would be a day of outcomes...one way or the other.

He pulled up in front of the Jackson house and drew in a deep breath. Then, climbing out of the truck, he put on his service cap and tugged at his uniform. Leaving the ledger and documents in the truck, he grabbed the bouquet and approached the front door. He lifted the brass knocker and gave three metallic raps.

As he tweaked the angle of his service cap, he thought about who might answer the door. If it was Mr. Jackson, he could thank him profusely for his counsel and advice. If it was Mrs. Jackson, he could compliment her on how nice she looked. You could never go wrong there. If it was Elizabeth—

The door swung open before he could finish his tactical plans.

It was Elizabeth. She wore a yellow cotton dress that brought out the green in her eyes. Her auburn hair hung loosely down to her shoulders and captured the morning radiance. She wore red lipstick that accentuated her delicate mouth, and a subtle fragrance of perfume enveloped her. "Come in," she said, gesturing toward the foyer.

"I brought you these," he said, handing the bouquet to her.

"Thank you. They look beautiful."

"So do you," he said, uncertain whether to hug her or kiss her here in her home.

She did both, ending his dilemma. "I'll take these into the kitchen and put them in a vase. Would you like to sit down?"

"No, I'm okay here."

He surveyed the interior while he waited. It was evident at first glance that the Jacksons lived a different lifestyle than did he and his parents. The furnishings were elegant, as though they had come straight from a fashionable catalogue. A large vase sat on an antique corner table near the crushed velvet couch, and several ornate paintings hung on the wall. The curtains looked expensive, and plush carpeting ran throughout the house. Oak trim stood out against the light-colored plaster walls, and brass doorknobs and hinges sparkled in the sunlight. Obviously business had been better for accountants than farmers.

Adam was examining some jade and porcelain ornaments when Elizabeth came back from the kitchen. "As you can tell, my aunt is a woman of simple tastes," she said.

They shared a laugh until Lenora came into the room and greeted him with a stiff but cordial, "Hello."

"Hello," Adam replied, removing his service cap. "You have a lovely home, Mrs. Jackson."

"Thank you," Lenora replied with cultivated politeness. "Elizabeth tells me that Pastor Wight is basing his sermon today on some of your wartime experiences."

"Yes, I—"

"It's gratifying to see young people finding a place in their lives for the church, don't you think?"

"Well, it—"

"And it's wonderful to cherish Christian principles, don't you agree?"

Adam nodded, giving up the attempt to reply.

Wil came down the hallway and extended his hand. "Hello, Adam. You're the subject of the sermon today, I hear. I'm looking forward to that." He lowered his voice. "Between you and me, Pastor Wight's sermons can get a little dry sometimes."

"Wilbur Jackson!" Lenora protested. "That's no way to speak of the Lord's anointed."

Wil winked at Adam and reached for the door. "We'd better not keep the good pastor waiting. Are you two riding with us?"

Adam wasn't sure how to respond.

"I'll go with Adam," Elizabeth said.

"We'll save you a place," Lenora said. "I like to sit front and center, as you know. I get such a kink in my neck if I sit on the side."

"Front and center," Elizabeth repeated, as Wil took Lenora by the arm and led her toward the Buick Roadmaster parked in the driveway.

Elizabeth closed the front door, and Adam extended his arm, escorting her toward the truck. Halfway down the sidewalk, she slid her hand into his. Adam's hand automatically closed around hers, and a tingle of excitement raced through him as if they had just completed an electrical circuit.

"The church is only two blocks away, Adam. Why don't we walk? It's such a beautiful day."

"Sure." He could handle two blocks of bliss.

As they headed toward the church, Elizabeth said, "So was entering *enemy territory* as bad as you thought it would be?"

Adam exhaled slowly. "Actually, no. Your aunt was very civil."

"She can be that, all right. It would be *unchristian* to be otherwise."

"Thank goodness for that. I need all the allies I can get."

She bumped against him on purpose. "Am I an *ally?*"

"You're more than that, Elizabeth."

She arched an eyebrow. "What, then? And you'd better make it good, buster."

Adam leaned toward her and whispered, "You're my future."

Elizabeth squeezed his hand. "That is the correct answer."

Pastor Albert Wight stood at the front door of the church, greeting the parishioners as they arrived. "Good morning, Elizabeth," he said. "You certainly look nice." Turning to Adam, he pumped his hand vigorously. "Thanks again for helping me out with today's sermon. I truly appreciate it."

"You're welcome," Adam replied.

He looked at Adam earnestly. "Your mother just arrived with Sid and Alice. She's looking much better. That was a terrible accident. She could have been seriously injured, if not..." He left the sentence unfinished.

"Thanks for all you did in arranging the meals and everything."

"My pleasure." He turned his attention back to Elizabeth. "Where's Nathan?" he asked, glancing around expectantly.

Elizabeth gave a slight shrug of her shoulders. "I don't know."

Pastor Wight looked from her to Adam and smiled in comprehension. "Well, I'm sure he'll be along. The meeting is about to start. Why don't you go in and get seated?"

Eunice Murphy was playing the prelude music in droning,

sustained tones as they entered the chapel. The light from the stained glass windows cast a radiant glow through the room. Adam spotted Lenora, who motioned to them.

Adam followed Elizabeth up the aisle and let his eyes wander over the crowd. He saw his uncle Sid and aunt Alice and their family, along with his mother, sitting in their usual place in the center section. He waved to them, and Ty waved back, shaking his head in chagrin. Adam winked in reply and sat down beside Elizabeth.

A short time later Adam felt a pair of eyes on him, boring into the back of his head like twin bayonets. He turned and saw Nathan sitting along the far wall, glaring at him. Elizabeth slipped her hand into his just then and slid closer, obliterating his awareness of Nathan.

A few minutes later Pastor Wight approached the podium and nodded at Eunice, who ended the prelude music with a dramatic flourish. "Welcome to worship service," he began, adjusting his glasses and leaning into the microphone. "We'll begin our service by singing 'Onward Christian Soldiers.'"

As the congregation sang, Adam felt a rush of emotion. Phrases from the hymn seemed to jump out at him, taking on new meaning. *Onward Christian soldiers, marching as to war...on to victory...leads against the foe...like a mighty army...we are not divided, all one body we.* Adam found it almost overpowering, and he struggled to find his voice.

Following the hymn, Pastor Wight offered an invocation. Then he conducted several items of church business. Adam found it difficult to concentrate on the service. Sitting beside Elizabeth and holding hands with her was a major distraction. His attention kept wandering as he continually snuck sideways glances at her. Hopefully God would understand.

At the conclusion of the business Pastor Wight looked down at the congregation. "The theme of our service today is *sacrifice.* I interviewed First Lieutenant Adam Carlson, recently returned from overseas, and I will be quoting him extensively for my sermon. He is in attendance today, as a matter of fact. Adam, would you please stand and be recognized?"

Adam stood self-consciously and turned so the congregation could see him. As he looked around the chapel, he started in surprise. His father was sitting on the back pew, dressed casually, but his hair was neatly combed and he had shaved. A lump formed in Adam's throat, and he sat down in disbelief. This was the first time he could ever remember his father attending church. He tried to get his mother's attention but was unable to communicate the news to her.

Pastor Wight unfolded his notes and put on his glasses. "First Lieutenant Carlson says: 'My story begins in the summer of nineteen forty-two. Some friends and I were talking one day about enlisting. We'd heard from others who'd already signed up about what they were doing, and it sounded like a great adventure. At the time, though, none of them were involved in any actual fighting. And so we enlisted, wide-eyed and ready to take on the world.'"

How naïve we were, Adam thought, shifting in his seat on the bench.

"'Several of us traveled to the recruiting center and enlisted in the infantry. We thought we'd be living like college buddies and having ourselves quite the time. But they put us in separate units, and I never saw any of them alive again. We kept in touch as best we could at first, but one by one, they were killed or reported missing in action.'"

A hush fell over the room. "'After Basic Training, one thousand of us sailed overseas on an army transport ship. It took five days to cross the Atlantic, zigzagging our way to avoid the German submarines.'"

Adam squeezed Elizabeth's hand at the memory of their day down at the river and her experience on the raft. She squeezed his hand in reply. Hard.

"'For most of us it was our first time on a ship, and we were excited about an ocean voyage. But it didn't turn out to be the cruise we had anticipated. Most of us got seasick. I don't know about anyone else, but I know one soldier who knelt down and kissed the docks when we finally arrived in Naples.'"

A light laugh rippled through the congregation.

"'We were brought in as replacements for the Fifth Army. As we advanced north, the terrain became mountainous, with peaks rising several thousand feet in elevation. Adding to that challenge was the weather. It turned cold and wet. It rained every day, and the rivers became swollen and dangerous. In those conditions it was impossible to keep our feet dry. We all got trench foot. I remember thinking of my mother darning socks at the kitchen table at night and wishing she could reach out and hand me a warm, dry pair.'"

Pastor Wight paused to turn a page.

"'Despite the difficult conditions, we were able to push the Germans back two hundred miles. In a four-week period we took Rome and then moved on toward Florence. I found myself in the thick of the fighting for what was to become the Morgan Line, and I remember keeping my head low as the bullets flew around us like flies on a dead cow.'"

Adam saw Elizabeth and Lenora wince. If they only knew how he was sparing the congregation the truth about how bad it *really* had been. It was infinitely worse than words could ever convey. To have your comrades drop beside you, singled out by a sniper's bullet. To hear the wounded and dying calling to God. Or to their mothers. That was the part that had bothered him the most. Grown men whimpering for their mothers like a child who awakens in the night, frightened and confused. War had done that to them. How could you measure that sacrifice?

Adam closed his eyes and fought the images that always remained on the horizon of his memory. They threatened to overpower him, and he wondered for the thousandth time how he had survived when so many of his comrades had not. That, he decided, was the hardest part to understand. He was guilty by association—association with the living.

"'Wherever we went, it seemed we had to dig in. The foxholes were cold and damp, and they were often flooded in the spring. Sickness was common, and food rations were often scarce. Blankets and other bedding were comforts we frequently had to go without. But we knew what we were fighting for, and so we persevered, pushing the enemy steadily out of Italy.'"

Pastor Wight lifted his eyes from the paper to get control of his emotions. "'I don't want to dredge up the horrors of the past,'" he continued reading, "'and I'm not trying to shock anybody in an effort to win praise or sympathy. I just want to encourage everybody to get on with their lives. To be better friends and neighbors. And to remember God and all He stands for. He is good on His word. I'm a living witness of that. The world would be a better place if we followed His teachings. There would be no more war. No more hatred. No more conflict. That's the world I pray for—a world where everyone can get along with each other.'"

Adam looked directly back at Nathan, who dropped his gaze and stared at the back of the pew.

Pastor Wight looked toward the ceiling and uttered a heartfelt *Amen* before gazing out over the congregation. "I would just like to add to what First Lieutenant Carlson said. Besides remembering those who sacrificed their lives for our freedom, we must not forget the greatest sacrifice of all. The Lord Jesus gave His life for us. He died that we might live. We need to keep Him in mind and not let the temptations of the devil overpower us. We must let Jesus's sacrifice motivate us. We must walk in the light of His love and help make the world the place that First Lieutenant Adam Carlson and the rest of us pray for. Amen."

As the closing hymn was announced, Adam noticed movement from the corner of his eye and turned in time to see his father slip out of the side door of the chapel.

During the hymn Lenora looked over at Adam and tilted her head in approval, and Elizabeth squeezed his hand three times, conveying her love. Adam felt a sense of overwhelming peace wash over him. For the moment God was in His heaven, and all was right with the world.

CHAPTER 20

THE TABLE WAS elegantly set with a lace tablecloth, fine china, long-stemmed crystal glasses, polished silverware, napkins in ivory holders, and two ornate candlesticks spaced equally apart with new candles in them. This was Lenora's world, and Adam felt his throat go dry as he prepared to enter it. Elizabeth smiled at him reassuringly, and he felt some of the tension leave.

"Adam, you can sit there across from Elizabeth," Lenora said.

Adam held the chair for Elizabeth.

Wil was halfway seated when Lenora flashed him a look. He quickly straightened back up and reached for her chair. "You're making me look bad, Adam," he said, grinning guiltily.

"Or you're making Adam look good," Elizabeth said.

Lenora directed the pretense of a scowl at her husband. "I'm glad someone around here is a gentleman."

Wil shook his head. "Now see what you've started, Adam. I'm going to have to be on my best behavior the rest of the day."

Elizabeth looked at Adam, who seemed about to apologize. "He's only teasing," she said, laughing.

Adam was struck by the irony of the moment. Here he was, a farm boy from a modest background, sitting in this lovely home, at a table more elegant than he'd ever been seated, being held up as a model of decorum to the mayor of Reunion. And all because he had helped Elizabeth be seated. If such a small thing could make him a paragon of civility, how little of a breach of etiquette would it take to topple him from his pedestal?

Wil motioned toward his niece. "Would you say grace, Elizabeth?"

Elizabeth bowed her head and offered a short, sincere prayer, expressing gratitude for the food, their freedom, and their blessings.

"Help yourselves, everyone," Lenora said. "Don't be bashful, Adam. Take all you want."

Adam wondered if she meant it or if this was a gentle reminder not to exceed polite portions. He watched Wil for his cue. The mayor undid his napkin and placed it on his lap. Adam followed suit. Wil then filled his plate up generously, and Adam did the same, piling up the potatoes, pouring on the gravy, taking two servings of vegetables and three slices of roast beef.

Waiting for the women to begin eating, Adam took a bite. "This is delicious," he said.

Lenora looked pleased. She held her fork precisely and took small bites. Wil noticed her stylized manner and rolled his eyes, causing Elizabeth to stifle a giggle.

As the meal progressed, Adam's secret wish that he wouldn't need to make conversation was granted. Between Wil's stories and Lenora's views on the town, the country, and the entire world, little was required of him. Until Lenora looked at him and made a direct comment, inviting a response.

"I enjoyed your contribution to the service today," she said.

"Thank you," he replied. "The music was inspiring, and the company was exceptional." He winked at Elizabeth.

Wil noticed but said nothing.

Lenora noticed too and asked, "Do you plan to make regular church attendance a part of your life?"

The correct answer was yes, of course. Adam knew that any other answer would end his chances of ever being around Elizabeth with Lenora's approval, however slight it might be. But he answered honestly, without pretext. "I admit I didn't attend church much before the war. Somehow in my youth, it didn't seem important. But in Italy I got back in touch with God. We all did. I made a deal with Him. He kept His end of the bargain, and I intend to keep mine."

"What deal did you make, if you don't mind my asking?" Lenora inquired.

"I don't mind," Adam said. "Just hope it doesn't spoil your appetites."

Lenora tilted her head as if giving royal consent. "Please continue."

"We were on rekky patrol one day and—"

"*Rekky* patrol?"

"Reconnaissance patrol. We were trying to pinpoint the German's position. We didn't want to walk into an ambush, you see. Anyway, three of us were crawling through a field, making our way forward, when I heard a soft thud close by. I wondered if a bird had fallen out of the sky, it sounded just like that. But I couldn't see anything...except for a hole in the mud where something had just landed. Suddenly there was this muffled explosion, and I was hit in the face with flying mud and debris. Turns out it was a German grenade. But because it had embedded itself in the mud, I was spared the full force of the shrapnel. The mud did enough damage, though. I was knocked unconscious. My two comrades managed to get me back to our unit, and when I finally came to, I couldn't see. Every time I blinked, it felt like someone was rubbing my eyes with pieces of broken glass."

Lenora dabbed her forehead with her napkin.

"Sorry," Adam said. "I didn't mean to upset you."

"No, no, it's fine," Wil said, anxious to hear more. "Please go on."

Adam glanced at Lenora, who nodded solemnly.

"I was taken to an army hospital. They removed my eyes from their sockets to get as much debris out as they could."

Once again Lenora's napkin whisked across her forehead. She looked down at the food on her plate, her appetite now completely gone.

"They put my eyes back in and bandaged them up. I lay in a bed for six weeks, not knowing if I'd ever see again. That was when I remembered some of the things I'd been taught in church. I began to pray, and I made a deal with God. If He would restore my sight, I'd start going to church again. Well, long, lonely days followed, and I kept repeating my deal with Him, adding new details almost hourly. By the end of the six weeks, I'd practically committed to become a Benedictine monk."

Wil chuckled humorlessly.

"The day finally arrived for the bandages to come off. I can't tell you how frightened I was. I'd had plenty of time to think about what I'd do if I couldn't see again, and I had almost reconciled myself to that fate. But as luck—no, as God—would have it, I *could* see. The images were blurry at first, but they got clearer as the days went by. My sight returned to as good, if not better, than it was before the war. It was a miracle. God kept His part of the deal, and I intend to keep mine."

Lenora raised her eyes heavenward, and for a moment, Adam thought she was going to shout, "Hallelujah, praise the Lord!" But she maintained her composure, placed her napkin beside the plate, and allowed silence to dignify the moment.

Wil finally broke the solemn mood. "So, Adam, what are your plans, now that you're back?"

"Well, sir, after considering various options, and in light of recent developments, I've decided to stick with farming. I'm going to register at the agricultural college in Bozeman this winter and learn how to make our farm productive again. Maybe even buy up more land in time to increase our yield."

Lenora expressed surprise. "Isn't it expensive to go to agricultural college?"

"Under the terms of the GI Bill, my tuition and fees will be paid," Adam replied. "Up to five hundred dollars a year."

Wil whistled under his breath. "For that amount, you could go to Harvard."

"But Bozeman's good too," Elizabeth added. "Where would we be without farmers, right?"

Wil rapped on the table with his knuckles. "Hear, hear."

Lenora dabbed her mouth with her napkin and pushed away from the table. "I'll clear the dishes," she said.

Adam rose to his feet, but Lenora motioned for him to sit back down. He complied, watching her gather a few plates and leave the room. He looked at Elizabeth, who reached across the table and took his hand, squeezing it several times.

Recognizing the cue, Adam cleared his throat. "Sir, I was wondering if I could talk to you for a minute."

Wil set his napkin aside and said, "Certainly. Let's go into the den."

After the two men left, Elizabeth worked at clearing the table. She carried the dishes to the sink and began to wash them absent-mindedly, all the while stealing glances down the hallway.

Lenora worked in silence for a moment, wiping down the countertop, but kept glancing at her niece. "Elizabeth, is this what I think it is?"

Elizabeth shrugged innocently and continued washing the dishes.

"Good heavens, Elizabeth, you've got me sitting here on pins and needles."

Drawing in a deep breath, Elizabeth told her everything.

A look of concern crept into Lenora's countenance. "Elizabeth, you can't be serious. Land sakes, you just ended things with Nathan. You and Adam haven't even known each other that long."

"We know each other well enough to know we're in love."

"In love!" Lenora said this as though biting into something bitter. "You thought you were in love with Nathan. It's too soon, I tell you. You have to give yourself more time. Marriage is such a big step."

"We went through this the other night, Aunt Lenora," Elizabeth said. "Let's not rehash it again. I love Adam Carlson. He's the man I want to marry and spend the rest of my life with."

"Living on a...farm?" Lenora scowled and turned on Elizabeth. "A wedding isn't something you just rush into. You have to book the church, discuss the decorations, send out invitations, select a wedding dress." She took Elizabeth by the hand. "What about rings? Has he bought a diamond yet?"

"We went and looked at them...to get ideas. But, no, he hasn't bought a ring yet."

"He can't afford it, can he?"

"It's not that, Aunt Lenora. I told him I don't need an engagement ring yet. We'll get one when we're ready."

Lenora didn't reply. She busied herself with the leftovers, scraping them into a bowl and placing them in the refrigerator.

Elizabeth went over to her aunt and put her arms around her. "We're giving ourselves enough time, Aunt Lenora. Saturday, October fifth."

Lenora's eyes widened in horror. "That's only two months!"

"Yes. And all those details you mentioned? We'll work them out one by one. Just like you and Uncle Wil did. Just like every other engaged couple has done."

Lenora's shoulders slumped in disappointment. "I was hoping you and Nathan—" She shook her head.

"Aunt Lenora, you want me to be happy, don't you?"

"Of course I do, dear."

Elizabeth glanced down the hallway. "Inside the den is the person who truly makes me happy. Adam Carlson is the man I'm going to marry."

Wil listened with interest as Adam recounted the details concerning the penny auction. He chuckled to learn the grand total raised was four dollars and sixteen cents. "You brought in less than the Von Bonn auction in Nebraska. Congratulations. I think you'll find the bank more than willing to work with you now. They can see the handwriting on the wall."

"I'm not so sure," Adam replied. "After Elizabeth broke up with Nathan, he told her to pass along a message to me. 'All bets are off,' he said. Obviously, I won't be getting any help from him now. And I don't want the bank to find a legal loophole and come after the farm again."

"I understand," Wil said. "Especially when there are alternatives."

"Elizabeth suggested I have you look at the farm's records. Help us come up with an equitable plan that we could present to the bank president. Bypass Nathan altogether. I've got the records out in the truck. Would you consider going over them, sir?"

Wil stroked his chin. "Another referral from my niece, I see."

"She has a lot of faith in you, sir. So do I."

Appearing pleased with the compliment, Wil said, "I'll take a look at things and see where you stand financially. There's got to be a way for you to keep the farm and allow the bank to recover its investment."

"That would be greatly appreciated."

Wil paused briefly and studied Adam. "Glad to help out. Now with that matter out of the way, anything else on your mind?"

Adam cleared his throat. "Actually, I wanted to talk to you about your niece."

Wil sat back in his chair and smiled knowingly.

"I love Elizabeth," Adam continued, "and I'd like to ask your permission to marry her. I know this seems sudden, but I promise I'll spend the rest of my life providing for her and making her happy."

Studying Adam a moment longer, Wil said, "When Elizabeth ended things with Nathan the other night, I knew you and I would soon be having this conversation. And frankly, between you and me, I never felt that Nathan was the right one for Elizabeth. Their relationship was one of availability, if you know what I mean. There were never any sparks between them. Not like I saw between you and Elizabeth today." He lowered his voice further. "But just for the record, you'll have your work cut out for you. Elizabeth is one headstrong woman. Like her aunt."

Adam chuckled. "Elizabeth *does* have a mind of her own."

Wil leaned forward in his chair and twisted the ends of his moustache. "I remember how nervous I was when I asked Lenora's father for her hand in marriage. I was afraid he'd give me a rough time. And he did. He raked me over the coals, I can tell you. He wanted to know how I was going to provide his daughter with the lifestyle to which she had become accustomed. I felt that it was unfair to expect a young man just starting out to achieve what had taken the bride-to-be's parents a lifetime to accomplish, and I said so. That didn't go over well. But when I looked him respectfully in the eyes and told him that I loved his daughter and she loved me, and that I would care for her and always put her needs above my own, he relented and gave his permission." With that, Wil reached out and shook Adam's hand. "Like I give mine today. You have my blessing."

"Thank you, sir," Adam replied, exhaling in relief.

Wil began relating stories about his and Lenora's own early years of marriage and the struggles they had faced. Adam felt himself relax further as Wil reminisced, convinced that he and Wil would get along fine over the years. He wasn't so sure about his relationship with Lenora, however. That would come in time...if at all.

At length Wil got out of his chair. "I suppose we should go see the women. Lenora will want to know where we've gone. But don't tell her what we actually talked about. When she asks, I'll tell her that I raked *you* over the coals and lectured you on how to treat my niece—the whole ball of wax." Then he slapped Adam on the back and reached for the door.

They were hardly to the kitchen before Lenora blurted out, "My word, Wil Jackson. What took so long in there?"

Wil stretched himself a little taller. "We were having a man-to-man talk."

"I know all about it. Elizabeth told me everything."

Elizabeth looked at Adam and shrugged guiltily.

Lenora stepped closer to Wil. "And?"

Wil nodded affirmatively at Elizabeth, who rushed forward and embraced him. Then she went to Adam and looped her arm through his.

Regarding them for a moment, Lenora excused herself and disappeared into her bedroom. Elizabeth watched her leave and glanced anxiously at Adam. But Lenora wasn't gone long. She reappeared moments later carrying a small envelope that had yellowed over the years, the corners of which were slightly dog-eared. "This is something I've kept locked in the cedar chest, Elizabeth, where inquisitive young girls wouldn't find it," she said. "I've been trying to decide when to give it to you. I think the time has arrived."

"What is it?"

"Open it and see."

Everyone gathered around as Elizabeth lifted the flap. As she tipped the contents into her hand, two rings fell out: an engagement ring and a matching wedding band. The engagement ring had a modest diamond in the center, with two smaller ones on either side, delicately held in their settings. The wedding band contained four smaller diamonds and bore witness of quality and craftsmanship.

Elizabeth looked at her aunt in surprise. "Whose wedding rings?"

"They belonged to your mother. When she was involved in that terrible car accident, she regained consciousness long enough to take these rings off her finger and give them to me to hold in trust for you." Lenora embraced her niece, her eyes moist. "And now they're yours."

Tears ran down Elizabeth's cheeks. "Oh, Aunt Lenora."

Lenora sniffed back her own tears and looked over at Adam. "I know you probably have your heart set on buying Elizabeth a diamond ring, and I'm not trying to interfere. But it would mean a great deal to us if you'd allow her to wear her mother's wedding rings."

Elizabeth looked at Adam hopefully.

Conflicting emotions tore at him, but only for an instant. He took the engagement ring and gently slipped it onto Elizabeth's finger. It fit perfectly. Gently wiping her tears, Adam put the wedding band back into the envelope and placed it in his pocket.

Elizabeth held out her hand to admire the ring. The diamond glistened, seeming to capture the magic of the occasion.

Wil headed for the wine cupboard. "This calls for a celebration."

Elizabeth embraced Lenora. "Thank you," she whispered, sniffing back her tears.

Moments later four glasses were lifted into the air in a toast.

"To the happy couple," Wil said.

"To the happy couple," Lenora repeated, a catch in her voice.

Adam and Elizabeth touched their glasses together. "To us," they said in unison.

CHAPTER 21

ONCE THEY COULD pry themselves away from Wil and Lenora, who reminisced at length about their courtship, interspersed with concerns about the wedding details, Adam drove Elizabeth out to the farm. "Let's have some fun," he said, as they neared the turn-off. "Instead of bursting in and making the big announcement, let's make a little game of it. See how long it takes my parents—Mom especially—to notice the engagement ring."

"And you think *I'm* a tease," Elizabeth said, laughing.

Adam parked in the yard and escorted Elizabeth into the house.

Maude was sitting at the kitchen table, darning a sock. Hector sat beside her, repairing the handle on the egg basket. When they saw Adam and Elizabeth, they both got to their feet.

"What a nice surprise," Maude said, embracing Elizabeth warmly.

"Dad, this is Elizabeth Baxter," Adam said.

"Hello," Hector said, running a hand through his hair.

"Hi," Elizabeth replied, tilting her head to the side and smiling. She held her left hand out so the ring was clearly visible, but Adam knew the gesture was lost on his father. Hector wouldn't have noticed the ring had it been the size of a chicken's egg.

"Let's go into the living room," Maude said. "We can visit in there."

The photo album Maude had worked on during her convalescence lay on the coffee table. Elizabeth gestured toward it and said, "Did you finish your project?"

"Finally," Maude replied. "It was a labor of love, and I enjoyed the walk down memory lane. But three days of it was enough. The walls began to close in on me. I, for one, was ready to get back in the saddle."

At the mention of *saddle*, Elizabeth shot Adam a glance. He smiled in return, remembering their horseback ride, and then stifled a laugh when Elizabeth sat on the couch beside him and placed her hands on her lap, the ring plainly visible. The last rays of sunlight streamed through the open window, and the ring glistened as though reluctant to let the light of this day fade. Neither of his parents noticed it, however, not even when Elizabeth made a sweeping gesture with her hand and said, "It's so homey here. I love it."

"Thank you, dear," Maude said. "I love it too. I remember the times when all the relatives used to come here for Sunday dinner or Thanksgiving. The kitchen would be bustling with women putting the finishing touches on the meal, under Mother Carlson's direction, while the men gathered here in the living room to swap stories. It *was* homey."

"It was crowded," Hector said.

"But those were such good times," Maude continued. "Laughter used to fill the house, and the children kept things lively. Adam was a going concern back then, I can tell you. I had to keep an eye on him all the time. He was into this and into that, and before I could turn around, he was into something else."

Elizabeth nodded in agreement. "I can just imagine."

"Oh, you have no idea. He ran me ragged, but I wouldn't trade those days for anything. They're gone now, of course. Mother and Father Carlson have both passed on, and some moved away because of the Depression. The get-togethers have become fewer and farther between."

She turned to Adam and smiled wistfully. "And my little boy is all grown up." Catching herself, she said, "But enough of that. Tell us about you, dear. What's the latest news in your life? How are things at the dry cleaners?"

Adam coughed into his hand to stifle a laugh. The latest news, indeed!

Elizabeth looked away from Adam so she could maintain her composure. "The funniest thing happened at work the other day," she said. "A customer brought in a sweater to be dry-cleaned. He said his car had stalled and he'd spilled something down the front of himself when he lifted the battery out to examine it. Afterward, he took off his sweater and left it on the front seat. When he finally brought the sweater into the shop and opened it up, it fell apart in his hands. It was nothing but strings of ragged fabric. It turns out he'd spilled battery acid on himself. So Lee Yang began teasing him, saying times must be good for him to bring in rags to be dry-cleaned."

Even Hector smiled at the notion.

Adam looked proudly at Elizabeth. Her presence added lightness to the mood, and it was refreshing to have his father on his best behavior. The game of seeing how long it took his parents to notice the ring added to the enjoyment, but if they didn't notice it soon, he was going to come right out and tell them. He stifled a laugh when Elizabeth deliberately rubbed her nose in such a way that the ring was conspicuous.

"You must have all kinds of stories from work," Maude said. "Your aunt and uncle must enjoy listening to them."

"She's making up for all the grief she caused them over the years," Adam said.

"Oh, Adam," Maude said in protest. "She did no such thing."

Adam furrowed his brow. "This young lady is mischief with a capital M," he said, taking Elizabeth's hands in his so the ring was visible. "These hands have caused more trouble than you can imagine."

Maude looked apologetically at Elizabeth. "Adam is such a tease."

"She's a trouble-maker, I tell you," Adam continued, hardly able to keep from laughing. "And she's got the hands to prove it. Just look at them. What do you think, Dad?"

He looked at his father for a reaction. Hector glanced at her hands and simply shrugged.

"How about you, Mom? Aren't these the hands of—"

He never had a chance to finish. Maude suddenly gasped and took Elizabeth's hand in hers. "A ring!" she said, looking up into Elizabeth's eyes. When Elizabeth's smile confirmed Maude's suspicions, Maude exhaled sharply. "Look, Hec," she cried, tilting Elizabeth's hand toward him.

"What about it?" Hector muttered.

Maude turned Elizabeth's hand so the ring was pointing directly at him. "It's a diamond ring!"

The expression on Hector's face remained unchanged as he looked at Adam. "You're...engaged?"

Adam couldn't hold it back any longer. He burst out laughing. "That's what we came to tell you!"

Maude slid over and embraced Elizabeth, stealing another peek at the diamond ring.

"Where did you come up with the money for a ring like that?" Hector asked, shaking Adam's hand noncommittally, as if worried that a piece of farm machinery might have suddenly made its way to Alf Whitehead's auction business.

"It belonged to my mother," Elizabeth said.

"Have you set a wedding date?" Maude asked.

"Saturday, October fifth," Adam replied, cutting a glance at his father. "After the harvest."

"We're so happy for you. Aren't we, Hec?"

Hector forced a smile.

Maude gave Elizabeth another congratulatory embrace. "We'll need to get together with your aunt and uncle to discuss wedding arrangements."

Hector suddenly got up from the chair. "I just remembered that I left the door of the root cellar open. I best go close it before a skunk gets in."

"I'll help," Adam said.

He followed his father outside. Once they reached the root cellar, Adam said, "So, Dad, you didn't say much. What do you think?"

"About what?"

"About my engagement, of course."

Hector sniffed into the back of his sleeve. "Reckon it had to happen sooner or later."

Adam stared at his father. "That's not really an answer."

"If you want to get married and leave, that's up to you."

"I am going to leave, Dad, but not until after the harvest. I'm going to go to the agricultural college in Bozeman and learn all I can about how to make the farm operational again. Then I'm coming back, and together we're going to rebuild the farm."

Hector seemed taken by surprise. He paused to gaze at the mountains silhouetted against the fading skyline. "When I married your mother, I had plans. Big plans. Ones that didn't include this farm. We were going to move to California. I had a business opportunity there. A good one. I could have given your mother a good life. But then my dad—your Grandpa Carlson—got sick. I had a choice to make. Let the farm go under or stay and work to try and make it all mean something, like it did to my father and to his father before him."

"And like it does to my father and to his son now."

A smile flickered across Hector's face. He shut and latched the door of the root cellar. "We best get back or your mother will send out a search party," he said, placing a hand on Adam's shoulder.

As they walked toward the house, Adam was overcome by the realization that their relationship could be reborn and live again, like a phoenix rising from the ashes. Forgiveness and reconciliation were possible if you were patient, you worked for it, and you prayed to receive it with all your heart. And now, as they walked toward the house, he received his father's love gratefully. With all his heart.

CHAPTER 22

ADAM WINCED AS he nicked himself while shaving. He set the straight razor down and reached for a piece of tissue paper. Sticking the paper on the cut, he watched a crimson dot appear in the center. When the blood clotted sufficiently, he contorted his face to draw the skin tight and continued shaving. He tried to keep his mind on what he was doing so he didn't accidentally cut himself again. But it was difficult, considering what was about to happen.

It was Wednesday evening, and he and his parents were going to the Jackson home. It was the first official meeting between the two families, supposedly to work out the wedding details. But he saw it as an acid test to determine if the two families were compatible.

Adam finished shaving and rinsed his face with warm water. He dried his face on a towel and slapped some Old Spice on his cheeks, grimacing as it burned and soothed at the same time. He looked at himself in the mirror, aware of the tension etched in his face. Even someone with a crystal ball would be hard pressed to predict the outcome of this evening.

He squirted some Brylcreem on his hands and rubbed it in his hair. As he combed fastidiously, he wished he could control the outcome of the evening with the same ease.

❧

Wil glanced at his wife overtop his newspaper. "If you dust the furniture any more, there won't be any finish left," he said.

Lenora frowned. "I'm just trying to make things presentable."

"They were presentable yesterday. And the day before that. How much more presentable can they get?"

"For heaven's sake, Wil Jackson. I just want the place to look half decent for our company."

Wil folded the newspaper back to the next page. "The Carlsons wouldn't want you to go to all this bother."

"I just want to make a good impression."

Wil grunted under his breath and returned to his paper.

Lenora fussed a few minutes longer. "I like Maude. She's a fine woman. But that Hector! He's another story."

Wil kept his eyes on his newspaper. "You just have to take Hec with a grain of salt."

"But he's so surly and obstinate."

Wil wisely chose not to say anything.

"It's just our luck to have *him* in the family."

Elizabeth came into the room, and the conversation stopped abruptly as Lenora returned to her dusting and Wil remained behind the newspaper. Elizabeth looked from one to the other and shrugged, heading into the kitchen to check on the refreshments.

Hector stood beside the bedroom dresser, attempting to knot his necktie. "I don't see why we have to go," he complained.

Maude looked at herself in the full-length mirror. "Because we have to discuss the upcoming wedding. It's not intended to be a personal inconvenience directed at you."

"But why do I have to go? You women will be making all the decisions anyway."

Maude turned to look at her profile. "To show your support."

Hector yanked his necktie off in frustration. "But Lenora Jackson's going to be there."

"She happens to live there." Maude picked up the necktie and tied it for him. She folded down his collar and helped him into his suit jacket.

"Of all the women Adam had to fall for, why did he have to pick someone related to *her?*"

Maude smoothed down the front of his shirt. "Because that someone happens to be Elizabeth Baxter, the young woman our son is going to marry."

Adam knocked on the bedroom door. "We'd better hurry. We don't want to keep them waiting."

"Heaven forbid," Hector muttered.

Adam turned on his father. "Dad, I want you on your best behavior tonight."

"We're *all* going to be on our best behavior and put our best foot forward," Maude said.

Adam took a giant step forward. "Here's my best foot."

Outside, Hector reached for the door handle on the truck. "My best foot's going to be the one on the gas pedal when we're driving home from the Jackson's."

When the doorbell rang, Lenora quickly put the dust cloth away and swept the room with a final glance.

"I'll get it," Elizabeth called.

Wil gave Lenora a warning glance, reminding her to be on her best behavior. She waved her hand dismissively, offended at the insinuation that she'd be anything but the perfect hostess.

Elizabeth opened the door and said, "Come in."

Adam allowed his parents to step in ahead of him and then embraced Elizabeth. "You look beautiful," he whispered.

Elizabeth smiled at the compliment and turned and embraced Maude. "I'm so glad you could come, Mrs. Carlson."

"Thanks, dear," Maude said. "You *do* look beautiful. Just like a blushing bride-to-be."

Elizabeth turned toward Hector. She was uncertain whether to hug him or shake his hand.

Hector removed his hat and nodded at her. His eyes scanned the perimeter of the room and settled on Wil, who had risen from his chair, and then to Lenora, who smiled cordially, the corner of her mouth twitching slightly.

Wil approached Adam and slapped him on the back. Then he reached out and shook Hector's hand vigorously.

Lenora greeted Maude like a long-lost friend. "We're glad to have you visit our *humble* home." She turned to Hector, willing her smile to remain in place. "How nice to see you."

Hector nodded.

"Why doesn't everyone have a seat here in the living room," Lenora said. "Elizabeth and I will get the refreshments."

Elizabeth squeezed Adam's hand and whispered, "So far, so good," before going into the kitchen.

Adam joined his parents on the sofa.

The mood lightened as Wil began talking about the weather and then broadened the conversation to include local and national news. Hector didn't have much to contribute until Wil brought up the subject of rising grain prices. This got a reaction. Hector mumbled a few responses to show his encouragement of the economy in general and the state of agriculture in particular.

Lenora and Elizabeth returned with the refreshments, and everyone became busy with the fruit punch and slices of coffee cake.

After a few moments, Wil said, "A wedding is an occasion for celebration, isn't it?"

Hector shifted in his seat.

Maude understood her husband's discomfort. She knew he was worried about the finances of the wedding, coming so soon on the heels of the foreclosure auction. Money was scarce, it was true, but she had been saving the egg money for months and had a modest stash put away. Hopefully it would be enough for them to carry their part of the financial commitment. She'd tell Hector about it later when it was too late for him to suggest spending it to fix the farm or buy a new piece of equipment.

Lenora set her cup aside and dabbed the corners of her mouth with a napkin. "Weddings certainly bring families together, don't they?"

Maude nodded in agreement. "And we're so happy to have Elizabeth as part of ours."

Elizabeth waited for her aunt to reply in kind regarding Adam, but it never came. Instead, Lenora charged into the matter of wedding details. "Weddings are so much more elaborate than when Wil and I were married," she said. "The wedding dresses are much fancier and..."

She spoke at length, outlining her vision of the entire wedding ceremony. *Suggestions only*, she kept reassuring the others, but no one believed her. She expressed her opinion as to how the responsibilities should be divided: the Carlsons could take care of the invitations; the Jacksons could take care of the decorations and the wedding reception, including the banquet and dance.

Adam and Elizabeth exchanged glances.

"Naturally, Pastor Wight will perform the wedding ceremony," Lenora continued. "Isn't it convenient, Maude, that we both attend the same church?"

Maude smiled good-naturedly, remembering her own wedding ceremony, which, of necessity, had been simple and inexpensive. It was clear, however, that Lenora had a different vision of what the wedding should entail.

Hector became increasingly restless and began pulling at his collar as if his necktie was choking him. Maude glanced at him from the corner of her eye and hoped he wasn't going to cause a scene.

Elizabeth noticed it too and decided it was time to set the situation straight. "Aunt Lenora," she said. "Adam and I appreciate all your ideas."

Lenora beamed.

She took Adam's hand. "But we're going to do things differently."

"What in heaven's name do you mean?"

Elizabeth described a simpler version of the grandiose one Lenora had presented. The more she talked, the more Lenora's countenance fell.

Hector, on the other hand, stopped tugging at his collar.

"That's how we want it," Elizabeth concluded. "And we'll be just as married as those who have a Hollywood wedding."

Lenora appeared desperate, and Wil watched her with interest.

It was obvious she and Elizabeth were not on the same page, which surprised him since they actually thought very much alike on such matters. His niece was being conservative, if not downright Spartan, and he had his suspicions why. But it was Elizabeth and Adam's decision, and if they wanted a simple, straightforward ceremony, so be it.

Lenora tried to hide the bitterness she felt toward the Carlsons, blaming their humble station in life for the reduction in pomp and circumstance. It was evident Elizabeth was downplaying her own wedding because of a perceived lack of funds on the Carlsons' part. But no matter. Lenora and Wil would finance the entire wedding if need be. They had the means to make the wedding the social event of the year, and Lenora would be there to supervise every last detail.

Elizabeth listened to her aunt's generous offer to pay for catering, hire a band, import the liquor, and so on. Then she kindly but firmly declined, causing Lenora to slump in her chair in disappointment.

Hector smiled inwardly as he witnessed Lenora's defeat. The wedding was going to be short, simple, and, more importantly, inexpensive. "Well, we best get home for chores," he said, with an almost cheerful tone in his voice.

Lenora solemnly ushered the Carlsons to the door.

As she and Elizabeth said good-bye to Maude and Hector, Wil pulled Adam off to the side. "I've gone over the farm records," he whispered, pulling an envelope from his pocket and handing it to Adam. "This is an overview of your assets and a repayment proposal to give to the bank. It's addressed to Harold Brown, the president. Drop it off tomorrow."

"Thanks," Adam replied, shaking Wil's hand warmly. "First thing in the morning." He approached Elizabeth and discreetly showed her the envelope. She smiled in comprehension and embraced him. "Good luck," she whispered in his ear.

Following a last round of good-byes, Lenora closed the door

and immediately announced, "I'm going to bed." She promptly left the room.

Wil lingered for a moment. "Elizabeth, it's your decision, you know that. And we'll respect your wishes. But if you and Adam change your mind, we'll throw the biggest—"

"Thanks, Uncle Wil, but we won't change our mind." She embraced him firmly. "I saw the envelope. Thanks so much for your help."

Wil returned her embrace. "That's what family does for each other." Stroking her cheek affectionately, he turned and left the room.

Elizabeth shut off the lights for the evening and made her way down the hallway, pausing outside her aunt and uncle's bedroom doorway, listening briefly to the whispered conversation within. Biting her lip, she slipped into her bedroom and closed the door.

It did not take an ornate, elaborate wedding to make a good marriage, she knew. She was still reminding herself of that fact as she finally drifted off to sleep.

CHAPTER 23

ALTHOUGH THE WEDDING was to be a simple ceremony, there were still many details to be arranged. Elizabeth and Lenora worked frantically to select a wedding dress, along with a bridesmaid dress for Julie, and have them fitted; order a wedding cake; coordinate the date with Pastor Wight; make arrangements for the decorations; plan the wedding ceremony itself...the details seemed endless.

Elizabeth had to keep reining in her aunt, who continually made new *suggestions*. And nothing caused more friction between them than the guest list. Imagine, Lenora fretted, the mayor's niece getting married and the entire town *not* being invited. What would the ladies in her social circle think if they didn't receive an invitation?

This caused Elizabeth to half-heartedly wish that she and Adam could simply elope. Adam would be more than willing, she knew. But she also knew that the wedding was not their day alone. Others had a vested interest in the proceedings, and it wouldn't be fair to shortchange them.

As the days passed quickly, Elizabeth found herself on the brink of exhaustion. She continued to work at the dry cleaners by day and do all the wedding preparations by evening. But battling her aunt in most of the arrangements every step of the way took the biggest toll.

She knew her aunt loved her and was attempting to show that love by making the wedding as grandiose as possible. But her aunt's love-inspired interference was more difficult to deal with than her outright objection would have been.

Adam came in late one evening from threshing to find his mother sitting at the kitchen table, huddled over a pile of envelopes. "How's it coming, Mom?" he asked, pausing to stretch his back.

"This is the last of the invitations," she said.

She had worked alone addressing the wedding invitations intended for their side of the family. Adam and Hector were too busy with the harvest to help out. Lunch was eaten in the fields, and the evening meals were served at the kitchen counter because the table resembled a post office mail room during Christmas rush. Egg money had covered the cost of the invitations, which were on simple card stock, printed at the local newspaper office. But money was needed to go toward things other than postage, so Maude had delivered as many as she could.

Hector put up with the messy kitchen because he was in an uncharacteristically tolerant mood. The harvest was going well, and he'd just received a letter from the bank agreeing to refinance the mortgage. It was signed by Harold Brown, president of the bank, and read:

Mortgage Renewal Agreement, September 12, 1946

Dear Mr. & Mrs. Carlson:

After a careful review of the matter, we are pleased to inform you that we will be renewing your Mortgage Agreement. Please come in at your earliest convenience to sign the forms. We look forward to continuing to serve you in the future.

Sincerely,

Harold Brown, President

Reunion Savings and Loan

Now, as Adam thumbed through the last of the envelopes, he said, "Elizabeth and I will deliver these when I go to see her tomorrow night."

"Doesn't she have her own invitations to do?"

Adam smiled thinly. "Mrs. Jackson has already mailed them out." He put a hand on his mother's shoulder. "Thanks for all your hard work, Mom."

She stroked his hand. "You're worth it. Now go get cleaned up, and I'll fix you and your father something to eat."

Maude remained at the table for a moment, staring at the pile of remaining envelopes.

Mrs. Jackson has already mailed them out.

The words echoed in her head. It would have been easy to feel sorry for herself and lament the fact that she couldn't afford the simple luxury of postage except for a few selected envelopes. But there was no time for self-pity. There was still so much to do.

She went to the counter and cut several slices of bread. As she reached in the cupboard for the butter dish, her hand brushed a glass jar that was hidden behind several containers of bottled fruit. The egg money. A glance at the jar told her there was little remaining inside.

She was determined to honor their part of the financial commitment. If need be, she would pawn her grandmother's cameo brooch until money from the harvest mercifully began arriving.

She was grateful Adam wouldn't need a new suit for the wedding. He had decided to be married in his uniform. The only thing left to buy was a necktie for Ty, the best man. A new dress for herself was out of the question; her Sunday one would suffice. And Hector's old suit could be resurrected from the closet. It would have to be pressed, but that was cheaper than buying a new suit—one he probably wouldn't wear again until his own funeral.

She smiled grimly at the thought as she made two sandwiches and set them on the table. On that eventful day Hector would undoubtedly roll over in his grave and complain about having to wear his suit. Again.

Two days before the wedding Adam and Elizabeth drove up to Castle Hill, a rise to the north of Reunion. Nightfall had enveloped the town, and the air was filled with the earthy aroma of fields bursting in ripening abundance. A light rain earlier in the day now lent a damp fragrance to the atmosphere.

As Adam turned off the engine, lights began to go out here and there in town. Snuggling closer to Elizabeth, Adam looked out over Reunion. Many times he had envisioned this scene while fighting in Italy. How much more breathtaking it was with Elizabeth seated beside him.

"When Ty and I were kids, our two families used to come up here at Easter time," Adam said. "We'd roll colored eggs down the hill and see whose could go the farthest." Chuckling, he added, "That is, those Ty and I didn't throw at each other or break over each other's head first."

"What a pair you two must have been."

"And over there is a drop-off, with a thicket at the bottom." Adam pointed to his left. "Every year our families would get together and pick huckleberries by the bucketful. You've never tasted huckleberry syrup until you've tasted Mom's."

"It sounds delicious."

"Mom says they haven't picked berries together since the start of the war."

Elizabeth studied the fading landscape. "A lot of things have changed."

Adam murmured in agreement. Many traditions had been interrupted, others completely broken. But that didn't mean they couldn't be reestablished. Next year Elizabeth and he would invite their parents and the Hansens to pick huckleberries with them. And afterward they would have a barbecue of Montana beef and celebrate the harvest.

With that determination he looked up at the sky as if making a solemn vow. The evening was clear and crisp, and the North Star glistened above the Pointers. He felt happier than he had ever been. The longing he felt in Italy when he would gaze at the night sky and think of home seemed a lifetime ago.

He leaned over and kissed Elizabeth, long and passionately, and the world around him disappeared. The only thing he was aware of was the moment: the softness of her lips, the warmth of her body, the sensation of her breath on his cheek. He brushed back her hair with his fingers and followed it down her neck, tracing the outline of her ear with his finger.

When they finally parted lips, Adam held her close and whispered, "Well, Miss Baxter, any final concerns about becoming *Mrs. Carlson?*"

Elizabeth arched an eyebrow. "Actually, yes."

Adam pulled away from her in surprise. "Oh?"

"Just one."

"And that is...?"

"I was talking to Julie yesterday about the bridesmaid's dress, and she said something that didn't register at the time. But the more I've thought about it, the more suspicious I've become."

"What did she say?"

"Actually, she didn't come right out and say it. It was something she implied."

Adam frowned. "What was it?"

"She and Ty are going to kidnap me after the wedding ceremony."

"You mean...they're planning a shivaree?"

A *shivaree* was a time-honored tradition of separating the bride and groom after the wedding, whisking the bride away, and driving around for an hour or two until the abductors were certain the groom was unbearably hot and bothered. Then they would return the bride and wish the newlyweds a happy honeymoon. Sustained echoes of laughter usually followed, as the groom spun gravel in his anxiousness to get on the road with his new bride.

Adam scowled. "Betrayed by the best man and maid of honor!" He looked earnestly at Elizabeth. "Well, it isn't going to happen, Elizabeth. Tomorrow at the wedding rehearsal, I'm going to give

Ty a piece of my mind. And whatever else I do at the wedding ceremony, I'm not letting go of your hand all night long."

To emphasize his determination, he took her by the hand and clasped it gently but firmly.

CHAPTER 24

THE MEMBERS OF both families arrived at the church at three o'clock the following day for the wedding rehearsal. Also in attendance were Ty, the best man; Julie, the maid of honor; Pastor Wight, the officiator; and Eunice Murphy, the organist.

It had been agreed everyone would dress casually, since it was only a walk-through. Hector, who normally would have shown up in his bib overalls and work boots to discourage Pastor Wight from trying to proselytize him, wore a pair of clean jeans and a cotton shirt. The pastor's gesture in organizing the women to help out during Maude's convalescence had obviously had more of an impact than Hector would openly admit.

Lenora wore a new dress purchased in Great Falls especially for this occasion. She bristled with nervous energy, making a series of suggestions to those assembled in the foyer of the church. Hector escaped to the water fountain, which was down the hall and out of earshot.

As Lenora continued her suggestions, Ty came up behind Adam, who was standing with Elizabeth off to one side, and clamped him into a headlock. "I've got him, Elizabeth. You don't need to worry about him backing out at the last minute."

Elizabeth put a restraining hand on Ty's muscular arm. "Don't rough him up too much. He needs to be in shape for the wedding."

"You mean for the honeymoon," Ty said, grinning wickedly.

Julie winked at Elizabeth, who suddenly got busy with a loose thread on her dress.

"Hey, relax," said Adam. "I promise I won't get cold feet."

Ty leaned close and whispered, "Just remember, we know where you live, and we'll hunt you down like a yellow dog if you do."

"Just make sure you take care of *your* part."

"I'll take care of the ring, if that's what you mean. I promise not to lose it like I once did at my friend's wedding."

There was a moment of stunned silence, and Ty burst out laughing.

Elizabeth slowly shook her head. "I still think we're taking a big risk letting him be in charge of the ring tomorrow."

"O ye of little faith," Ty replied.

Pastor Wight motioned toward the company. "Please come into the chapel, everyone. We'll get the rehearsal started."

As they filed in, Adam nudged Ty firmly. "By the way, I'm on to you."

Ty showed his puzzlement. "What do you mean?"

"There's no way I'm letting go of Elizabeth's hand tomorrow night, so you'd better give up on the idea of a shivaree."

Feigning innocence, Ty said, "I don't know what you're talking about."

"Nice try," Elizabeth said.

"You've got it all wrong. As best man, it's my job to make sure you two *get* married, not separate you. Isn't that right, Julie?"

Julie had joined them in time to overhear the conversation. "What a distrustful mind you have, Adam Carlson."

Adam looked at them suspiciously. "So you're telling me there's no shivaree planned for tomorrow night?"

Ty raised his hand as though being sworn in for testimony. "Would I lie to you?"

"Yes!" Adam and Elizabeth both said at the same time.

"I'm wounded," Ty said, placing a hand over his heart.

Elizabeth opened her mouth to reply, but Pastor Wight interrupted. "Adam and Elizabeth, if you would sit on the front pew, with Ty and Julie on either side. We'll have the parents and the rest of the wedding party sit in the second row."

When everyone was seated, Pastor Wight referred to his notes and leaned into the microphone. He described the ceremony and explained the procedure. His voice echoed through the spacious chapel as he outlined everyone's duties. He concluded by saying, "Let's practice the ceremony to that point."

Everyone rose and moved to their designated positions.

Pastor Wight nodded to Eunice Murphy, who began the processional music. With a further nod to those in attendance, the rehearsal went according to plan. Once Maude, Hector, and Lenora made their way down the aisle and were seated, Pastor Wight cued the organist, who began playing Mendelssohn's "Wedding March." As directed, Lenora stood up as a signal to everyone else. And Wil, with Elizabeth holding his arm, began the walk down the aisle.

Wil had trouble with the foot order, but Elizabeth coached him. *Right, left, pause. Right, left, pause.* Wil fell into the rhythm and negotiated his way up the aisle, beaming proudly with every step. When he and Elizabeth reached the front of the chapel, she released his arm and took Adam's outstretched arm, in turn. Wil took his place in the second row.

Satisfied that everything was in order to this point, Pastor Wight called for a break while he went to consult with Eunice about the music for the balance of the ceremony.

During the delay Ty approached Julie and whispered something to her. She listened and broke out in a grin as Ty slipped out of the chapel. He was gone for a few minutes. When he returned, he rejoined Julie and nudged her with his elbow. She nodded in reply.

Pastor Wight returned to the podium and thumbed through his papers. "I'll begin the ceremony tomorrow with some initial remarks and the giving away of the bride," he said. "The wedding vows will take place at this point. I'll then make the concluding pronouncement and—" He stopped and smiled down at Adam and Elizabeth. "I'll save the rest for tomorrow. We don't want to get ahead of ourselves, now, do we?"

Light laughter rippled through the chapel.

As everyone stood up to leave, a church assistant stuck his head in through the side door. "Pastor Wight, there's a telephone call for Adam Carlson. It's Susan Godfrey."

Adam and Elizabeth exchanged glances. Susan was taking the photographs at the wedding. Perhaps there was a question or some problem. Still, Adam was surprised Susan would ask for him and not for Elizabeth.

Excusing himself, Adam followed the assistant to the pastor's office and picked up the phone. "Hello?"

"Hi, Adam. This is Susan. Listen, I have something to tell you."

Adam was certain she was going to say, "Something's come up and I can't take the wedding photographs, after all." Instead, she said, "I just want to tell you not to worry about a shivaree tomorrow night."

"What?"

"There isn't going to be one."

An uneasy feeling began to grow in the pit of Adam's stomach. "That's what Ty said too. But I don't believe him. Actually, I don't trust the whole bunch of you. I'm going to be holding on to Elizabeth's hand like we're glued together."

Susan chuckled. "And knowing you, you'll do it too...and spoil all the fun."

"I wouldn't exactly call a shivaree *fun*. Especially for the bride and groom."

"Oh, I think Elizabeth will enjoy it."

Adam wrinkled his brow. "I thought you said there isn't going to be a shivaree."

"No, I said there isn't going to be a shivaree *tomorrow night.*"

Adam blinked in confusion. "Look, Susan. If you're thinking about following us on the honeymoon—"

"Don't worry about the honeymoon. Nobody's going to follow you and short-sheet the bed or anything like that."

"Then what are you getting at?"

"The shivaree is *today.*"

"What?"

"You're not holding Elizabeth's hand, in case you haven't noticed."

And then the phone went dead.

Adam dropped the receiver and hurried toward the front foyer, where he found his parents chatting with Wil and Lenora. "Where's Elizabeth?" he asked anxiously.

"She went out back with Ty and Julie," Maude answered. "They said they had something to show her."

Adam winced in exasperation. "That's where Ty parked his car."

"What's going on?" Hector asked.

"They've kidnapped Elizabeth. The phone call was a trick to separate us."

"Are we talking about a shivaree?" Wil said. "I thought they did that on the wedding day."

"They knew we were on to them, so they decided to do it a day early."

Wil chuckled. "Our friends tried to give us a shivaree when we got married."

"And they would have succeeded too," Lenora added indignantly, "if I hadn't kicked Alf Whitehead in the shin."

Adam started for the door. "I'm going to find Elizabeth."

"Save your energy, son," Wil called after him. "They're probably miles away by now. They'll bring her back when they've had their fun."

Adam scowled and stood in indecision, but Hector just grunted and brushed past, muttering something about *all that nonsense.*

Wil took Lenora by the arm and suggested they all go home in case Elizabeth was dropped off at one place or the other.

Scowling again, Adam followed his parents down the sidewalk. As he climbed into the truck, he began thinking about what he was going to do to Ty when he got his hands on him. His cousin was going to pay for this.

When they had led her through the back door of the church and out into the parking lot, Elizabeth asked, "So what did you want to show me?"

"Happy shivaree!" Julie said, as she and Ty grabbed her by the arms and hurried her toward the red Oldsmobile. They crammed her into the backseat, and Julie slid in beside her. Ty climbed in behind the wheel and started the engine.

"A shivaree is supposed to happen *after* the wedding," Elizabeth laughed.

"And it would have," said Ty, "if someone hadn't let the cat out of the bag." He glanced at Julie in the rearview mirror.

"Me?" Julie replied defensively.

"It's okay," Ty said, revving the engine. "It actually worked out better. By moving it up a day, we're not so rushed."

"And it's for your own good, Elizabeth," Julie said. "You'll see."

"Sure I will," Elizabeth said sarcastically.

Ty sped out of the parking lot and headed toward Main Street.

"So where are you taking me?" Elizabeth asked.

Ty glanced at her in the rearview mirror. "First, we have to pick up Susan."

"She's in on it, too?"

"I slipped out during the rehearsal and talked to her on the telephone," Ty said. "I got her to call back and ask for Adam."

Elizabeth's eyes grew wide in realization. "So when Adam went to the telephone..."

"I think she gets the picture," Ty said, sharing a laugh with his accomplice.

Folding her arms in resignation, Elizabeth asked, "After we pick up Susan, then what?"

"We cruise around and make up the contract."

"What contract?"

"The marriage contract," Julie said, picking up a stenographer's notepad and a pencil. "Adam has to sign it before he gets you back."

"You'll thank us in the end," Ty added.

Elizabeth exhaled slowly and decided to be a good sport about it. Besides, resistance might cause them to drive farther and keep her away longer, and she could only imagine how Adam was feeling now that he'd undoubtedly discovered her absence.

She came back to the moment as she felt the car slowing. Susan was already standing in front of her house. With a single motion, she opened the car door and bounded into the front seat. Seconds later the car was back up to speed, heading down the street.

"Nice job, Susan," Ty said.

"Did I time it about right?"

"Perfectly."

"Now, down to business," Julie said, wetting the tip of the pencil on her tongue. She began scratching on the notepad, verbalizing what she was writing: "I, Adam Carlson, do hereby agree to the following terms." She paused, waiting for suggestions.

"I promise to take out the trash every week without being asked," Ty offered.

Julie wrote down Ty's suggestion, much to Elizabeth's delight.

"I promise to do the dishes at least twice during the workweek and every Sunday," Susan added as Julie's pencil moved rapidly over the notepad.

Ty snapped his fingers. "Here's a good one. I promise to keep the garden weeded and the lawn cut."

"And I will serve my wife breakfast in bed on holidays," Susan suggested.

"I like it," Elizabeth said. "This contract is a great idea."

At the end of Main Street Ty turned and proceeded out of town, into the country. They continued to throw out ideas, laughing hysterically as the list became more outrageous, growing to resemble a legal document promoting slavery.

Ty was busy looking in the rearview mirror as they crested a rise in the road.

No one saw the cattle.

Someone had left a gate open, and six Hereford steers, searching for greener pastures, were crossing the road with all the speed of a lazy stream moving against its own backwater.

Too late Susan cried out a warning.

Ty whipped around in time to see that a collision was imminent. He instinctively hit the brakes, but the tires refused to bite or maneuver in the gravel.

Julie screamed as the Olds bore down on the cattle with the precision of an assassin's bullet.

An unearthly *thud...thud...thud* caused some sparrows, perched on an adjacent barbed-wire fence, to scatter. Animal bodies bounced down the road like gigantic tumbleweeds. The car, its front end now unrecognizable, fishtailed wildly and rolled in the thick, loose gravel on the side of the road.

Once...twice.

It came to rest, upside down in the ditch. The trailing clouds of dust closed over the scene like a stage curtain, signaling the end of an act.

Silence returned, and a few sparrows ventured back to reclaim their perch on the fence.

CHAPTER 25

ADAM CAME IN from feeding the chickens. "Elizabeth call yet?" he asked anxiously.

Maude stood at the kitchen counter, making dinner and enjoying Perry Como singing "Till the End of Time" on the radio. She glanced up from her work. "Not yet, dear. But I'm sure it won't be long now."

Adam muttered under his breath and went over to the sink to get a drink of water. He glanced at his father, who adjusted his reading spectacles and glanced over the figures in the ledger. Footing their share of the wedding expenses, Adam knew, coupled with the business of running the farm, was financially draining on his parents. Literally. The ledger contained little wiggle room until the harvest money actually arrived, and there were few contingencies for matters of the heart and their attendant expenses.

Rocking back and forth on his heels, Adam looked at the clock above the kitchen table. It was five-thirty. An hour and a half since the kidnapping.

He began pacing back and forth until Hector finally looked up from the ledger and muttered, "You're going to wear a hole in the floor."

"What's taking so long?" Adam asked, more to himself. He forced himself to stand still. For thirty seconds. Then he began pacing back and forth again.

Hector opened his mouth to make another comment when the telephone rang.

"I'll get it!" Adam said, scooping up the receiver and almost shouting, "Hello?"

Wil's voice came on the other end. He spoke so fast that Adam could hardly understand him. As Adam listened, he became overwhelmed by the sheer rapidity of the mayor's words. He did catch the words *accident...Elizabeth...hospital* before dropping the phone.

Maude looked at him in alarm. "Son, what is it?"

Adam stared wildly around the room, trying to focus his thoughts. A desperate sound rumbled in his throat, and he placed his hands against his head as though trying to suppress a headache.

"What's the matter?" Hector said, staring at Adam as though his son was having a seizure.

Adam shook his head, trying to clear his brain. "There's been an accident. Elizabeth's been taken to the hospital. I've got to go." He hurried toward the front door.

"We'll go with you," Maude said, removing her apron. Hector followed close behind.

Moments later they climbed into the pickup truck, and Adam started the motor, grinding the gears in his anxiousness. He popped the clutch and the truck lurched forward, roaring out of the yard and speeding down the gravel road toward town, leaving a trail of dust in its wake.

Hurrying ahead of his parents, Adam burst through the hospital doors. Lenora was hunched in a chair in the waiting room, crying into a handkerchief. Wil was pacing the floor, hands clasped behind his back, his head bowed.

"How is Elizabeth?" Adam asked anxiously, staring from one to the other.

Lenora let out a loud sob and shook as though she had the chills.

Wil drew him off to one side. "We don't know yet. Dr. Cosgrove's with her right now. We'll just have to wait and see."

Maude and Hector came into the waiting room moments later and went directly to Adam. He bit his lip and slowly shook his head, pain and confusion vying for expression. Lenora let out a sorrowful cry, and Maude hurried over to her, placing a hand on her shoulder. The last of Lenora's emotional restraint gave out, and she began sobbing uncontrollably. Maude stood beside her, sharing her sorrow.

Adam turned to Wil. "How did it happen?" He was still unable to get his mind around the details.

Wil cleared his throat. "As best as I know, Ty was driving and—"

"Is my nephew all right?" Maude said.

Wil shrugged helplessly.

"What about Sid and Alice?" Maude pressed. "Have they been contacted yet?"

As though on cue they came through the front doors and hurried toward the waiting group. Alice embraced Maude and clung to her, worry and anxiety etched in her countenance. Sid nodded grimly at Hector and then, with Alice, asked the same questions Maude and the others had already asked. Every one had questions. No one had answers.

Julie's mother and Susan's parents arrived a short time later and gathered with the others, getting what information was available.

Everyone huddled in groups and began the vigil. The talking lessened and finally stopped altogether as they faced their dread and grief privately.

When Dr. Benjamin Cosgrove finally came out of the emergency room, Adam sprang to his feet as everyone descended upon the doctor at once, firing questions from all sides.

"Julie has three broken ribs and severe bruising on her arms and forehead," he said, removing his glasses and rubbing his eyes wearily. "But, miraculously, she is going to be okay." Julie's mother covered her face with her hands, overcome with relief.

"What about our daughter?" Susan's mother asked, clutching her husband's hand firmly.

"She has some abrasions on her arms and legs, and she has a sprained right ankle," Dr. Cosgrove replied. "She has bruising too, but considering what she's been through, it's a miracle she wasn't hurt worse."

"And Elizabeth?" Adam asked, his voice a hoarse whisper. "What about her?"

Dr. Cosgrove looked at Adam and exhaled slowly. "Elizabeth's condition is worse. We have her heavily sedated at the moment, both to reduce movement and for pain. We've started her on a transfusion, because she lost a lot of blood."

Lenora's knees buckled, and Wil and Hector both reached for her, supporting her on either side.

"We're monitoring her vital signs and checking for any swelling on the brain," Dr. Cosgrove continued. "Her heart rate is strong, and she's breathing steadily on her own. That's the *good* news."

Adam steeled himself for what was coming next.

"The bad news is that she has suffered deep cutaneous wounds to the left side of her face and neck. Flying glass cut her. I've cleaned the lacerations and taken the splinters from them. And her left ear—"

Adam stared at him expectantly.

"—was completely severed in the accident."

Lenora's head fell back against Wil's shoulder as if she had fainted.

Adam realized he hadn't breathed during the explanation of Elizabeth's condition. A light-headed sensation came over him, and he began breathing rapidly, waiting for the room to stop spinning. He felt his mother loop her arm through his and squeeze supportively.

"I've sutured and bandaged the area, and the bleeding is under control," Dr. Cosgrove added.

Wil swallowed hard. "Will there be...scars?"

Adam stopped breathing again.

"I tried to preserve as much skin on her face and neck as possible to ensure maximum blood flow. That's crucial to proper healing. I'll remove the sutures in a few days to reduce the chances of scarring."

Lenora whimpered.

"I'm encouraged that there doesn't seem to be nerve or muscle damage to her face," Dr. Cosgrove said, "so there shouldn't be any sunken scars when she heals. The biggest job now is to make sure the wounds don't become infected."

"What about her ear?" Lenora asked through her tears.

"We're looking at reconstructive surgery, I'm afraid."

Adam balled his hands into fists as he contemplated what his *friends* had just taken away from Elizabeth and him by their idiotic prank. He became aware of someone brushing against his arm and realized that his father was standing directly beside him.

"What about Ty?" Alice asked anxiously, taking a hold of her husband's arm. "You haven't said anything about our son."

Dr. Cosgrove's expression darkened. "I'm sorry to have to tell you this. He didn't make it."

A stunned silence followed, and then Alice slumped to the floor and Sid cried out and buried his face in his hands. Maude and Hector rushed forward and helped Alice into a chair. Then Maude leaned over her sister and embraced her firmly, their tears mingling together.

Adam stared blankly at Dr. Cosgrove, stung by the devastating news. Ty...*gone?* It wasn't possible. And yet there was no mistaking the doctor's words. They echoed inside Adam's head until they became a cacophony of indistinguishable noises.

Dr. Cosgrove looked apologetically at Sid. "I'm so sorry. I did all I could."

Sid pulled a handkerchief from his back pocket and wiped his eyes, mumbling a response.

Placing a hand on the tall man's heaving shoulders, Dr. Cosgrove said, "Why don't you take Alice home and have her lie down? She needs to get some rest. You both do."

"We'll go with you and do what we can to help out," Maude volunteered, motioning toward her husband. Hector stepped over and assisted Alice to her feet.

"Your father will come back for you later, son," Maude said to Adam. "Are you going to be all right?"

Adam nodded sullenly.

"I'll give him a ride home," Wil said. "Stay with Sid and Alice as long as you need to."

"Thank you," Maude replied. "And please give our love to Elizabeth."

She and Hector supported Alice on each arm and headed toward the front door. Sid followed, wiping his eyes and sniffing into his handkerchief. "We're going to get through this, Alice," Maude said, her voice breaking. "We just have to trust in the Lord."

Adam watched them leave and then slumped into a chair beside Lenora. His emotions were involved in an intense civil war. He had just lost his cousin. And yet his cousin was the person responsible for Elizabeth's present condition.

He began praying for a miracle. One similar to the miracle he'd received while hospitalized in Italy, when the German grenade had blown debris into his eyes and he had lain with his face heavily bandaged for six weeks, not knowing whether he'd ever see again.

But this time he needed a miracle of *emotional* healing. He needed to be able to skim off the anger, which had risen to the surface, and find the calmness beneath—the calmness that would help him know what to say to Elizabeth.

Adam turned to the doctor. "Can we see Elizabeth?"

Dr. Cosgrove considered the question. "She *is* sedated, so obviously she won't be able to respond. Just keep your voices down and your comments positive. Agreed?"

"Yes," Lenora replied, her voice trembling.

As Adam followed Wil and Lenora down the hallway, he noticed Susan in a nearby room, being attended to by a nurse. He paused in the doorway. Susan's arms and legs were bandaged, and her right ankle was wrapped in a tension bandage and elevated. When she saw Adam, her eyes immediately filled with tears. She began stammering words of apology, made indistinguishable by her sobbing.

Anger choked a response, and Adam simply stared at her,

remembering her earlier telephone call. The nurse hurriedly closed the door, and Adam proceeded down the hallway.

As he walked to catch up to Wil and Lenora, the door to another room suddenly opened, and an orderly stepped out and proceeded down the hallway. Julie lay inside, accompanied by a nurse who was taking her pulse. Julie's ribs were wrapped, and she was in obvious pain. Adam stopped and glared at her.

It took a moment for Julie to notice him. Several long seconds passed, and Julie's chin began to tremble. "It was only meant in fun, Adam," she moaned. "It wasn't supposed to turn out like this. I'd never do anything to hurt Elizabeth. You know that." Her chest heaved, and the nurse let go of her wrist and looked up in frustration.

Adam turned and walked away.

Elizabeth was hooked up to an intravenous tube that branched upward, connected to several bottles. The empty bottle, from the blood transfusion she'd received, hung from a metal stand nearby.

Adam came up behind Wil and Lenora, careful to negotiate his way around the equipment. The three of them crowded around her, and no one spoke for several moments. The entire series of events still seemed dreamlike—nightmarish—and not until Adam saw Elizabeth did it become real. The accident *had* occurred, and the wedding *was* going to be postponed.

Elizabeth's head was heavily bandaged to keep pressure on her left ear, and light gauze bandages covered the sutures on her face and neck. She lay so still that Adam studied the sheet over her chest, looking for the rise and fall to make certain she was still breathing.

Sniffing back tears, Lenora bent over her niece's prostrate form. With trembling fingers she gently stroked a strand of Elizabeth's hair that protruded from the bandages. Speaking softly, Lenora told her how much she was loved and that everyone's prayers were with her.

Wil stood beside her, offering the same reassurances.

Adam found himself on the outside, looking in. Elizabeth was much more than a niece to them, he knew, and he gave them a few moments of privacy. He stepped back, moved by the tender scene. How much *he* wanted to touch Elizabeth and tell her the feelings of his heart.

He got his wish a short time later when Wil touched Lenora and motioned toward the door. She lingered a few moments longer and wiped her eyes and nose in her handkerchief, which had become saturated with this day's tears. Then she moved away and made room for Adam.

Wil patted him on the shoulder. "We'll wait outside. Give you some time alone."

Adam nodded and waited until the door shut. Once he was alone with Elizabeth, he took her hand and gently kissed it. "How are you doing, darling?" he asked, not as a question but as a statement of deep concern.

He waited, hoping for a response. None came.

"I just want you to know that I'm here." His chin began to quiver, and he paused to collect his emotions. "I shouldn't have let go of your hand, not even for one minute." He gripped her hand gently, but determinedly. "I should have insisted you come to the phone with me. I should have—" He broke off, remembering Dr. Cosgrove's instructions about keeping his comments positive.

"You're going to get better, Elizabeth. We're still going to get married. You're not going to get rid of me this easily." He forced a smile. "You're still going to have to put up with me for a long time. We're going to have a wonderful life together, darling. This won't stop us. You'll see."

His body began to shake as he fought to hold back the tears. But it was a losing cause. He finally opened up and let his emotions out. The tears came, slowly at first and then in a torrent. He buried his face in the blankets and cried until there were no tears left.

Finally, his strength spent, he wiped his eyes and kissed her hand again. "Bet you didn't know you were marrying such a cry-baby, did you?"

He tried laughing at his own joke, wishing she would respond by arching an eyebrow at him like she often did. But there was still no response.

The silence deepened into a solemn vigil until Wil and Lenora appeared in the doorway some time later. "Would you like to go now, Adam?" Wil asked.

Adam shook his head. "I'm going to stay."

"All night? You need to get some rest. There's nothing you can do for her right now."

"I just want to be here with her. I'll call Dad in the morning for a ride."

"I'll be here bright and early so you can go home and get some sleep," Lenora said.

Adam merely nodded.

Lenora took Elizabeth's hand. "We'll see you first thing in the morning, dear." Her voice broke, and Wil gently led her from the room, pausing briefly to look back at Elizabeth before closing the door.

Adam pulled a chair beside the bed. "I'm here, Elizabeth," he whispered, pressing his forehead against her hand. "Hurry and come back to me."

CHAPTER 26

SUNLIGHT WAS PEERING into the room when Elizabeth woke to pain down the left side of her face and neck. She looked around the room and struggled to focus her eyes. The sparse furnishings, the walls, and the curtains were unfamiliar. Then she noticed a figure asleep in the chair by the side of the bed. It took her a moment to recognize Adam.

She tried to call to him but found that it hurt to move her jaw. Lifting her hand, she felt thick bandages wrapped around her head. She shifted in an effort to find relief.

Her movement woke Adam. He looked up sleepily, and his eyes widened when he saw that she was conscious. "Hi, darling. You're awake," he said, pressing the call button to signal a nurse.

"H–hi," she said, surprised at the effort it took to speak that one syllable.

"How are you feeling?"

"Where...am...I?"

Adam took her hand. "You're in the hospital. Do you remember anything?"

She looked up at the ceiling, trying to force the memory. "We were...driving...out of town..."

"Ty and Julie took you from the rehearsal."

"We hit...something."

"Yes, there was a car accident."

She trembled, and he gently stroked her hand. "Oh, Adam." Her voice broke. "I'm so...sorry."

He gently kissed her hand. "It's not your fault. There's nothing to be sorry about."

"I was...supposed to be...Mrs. Adam Carlson. But now—"

"And you still will be, darling." He pressed her hand. "You can't get out of it this easily."

She tried to smile in reply but winced in pain.

"Just lie still, Elizabeth."

She closed her eyes for a moment. When the pain subsided, she looked at Adam. "Tell me."

"Tell you what, darling?"

"About the others. How are they?"

A shadow passed across his face, and she knew the news couldn't be good.

"Susan has bumps and bruises, but she'll be all right. Julie got banged up pretty good. She has broken ribs, but she's going to be okay too."

Elizabeth exhaled weakly in relief. "What about Ty?"

Adam dropped his eyes. "He didn't make it."

Elizabeth blinked, trying to absorb the news. "What?"

"He was killed in the accident."

Tears filled Elizabeth's eyes, but she fought to control herself. It hurt too much to cry aloud and contort her face in grief. She had to weep silently.

"Poor Ty," she said, her voice soft and full of pain. "Poor, poor Ty. What will we...ever do...without him?"

Adam clenched his teeth so hard that his jaw muscles bulged, and she watched a wave of love and anger and grief pass over his face.

"When is...the funeral?" Elizabeth asked.

"We'll talk about it later. Just try to relax, darling."

She managed a weak nod and looked back up at the ceiling, searching the textured plaster for answers.

Moments later a nurse bustled into the room. "Well, look who's awake," she said, examining the intravenous bottle and the tube that led to Elizabeth's arm. "How are you doing?" Without waiting for a reply, she turned to Adam. "I need to check her vital signs and look at her bandages. Would you mind leaving the room? I'll call you when I'm finished."

Adam slowly released Elizabeth's hand.

Elizabeth sensed his hesitation and whispered, "Go ahead, Adam. It'll just take a minute. But then...hurry back."

"I will."

She smiled at him weakly and watched him leave. So much had changed in an instant. One minute she had been laughing and drafting a silly marriage contract with her friends, and the next minute...

A sob rose in her chest, and her vision blurred. She tried to distract herself by thinking about other things. Childhood memories...good friends...loving family. But she was unable to find consolation in any of them. Everything was overshadowed by the heartbreaking realization that this was supposed to have been the happiest day of her life. Her wedding day.

In the waiting area Adam found it impossible to sit down. He paced back and forth, his hands clasped behind his back.

Dr. Cosgrove came in a short time later and approached him.

Adam stopped pacing. "How bad is Elizabeth hurt...really?"

"Naturally, I'm concerned about the lacerations on her face and neck. The edges of the wounds were ragged and irregular, and there was some tissue damage underneath. I closed the wounds in layers, placing some stitches underneath the skin to hold the deeper tissues together. I repaired the muscle layer and approximated the skin edges to maintain proper skin tension. That should minimize scarring. But right now the big concern is infection. We'll have to keep her on antibiotics for a while."

"Will she be able to go home soon?"

"Providing there are no complications, *relatively* soon."

Adam nodded gratefully.

Dr. Cosgrove looked at him sympathetically. "I wish I had more answers for you, Adam. The truth is, it's wait-and-see time now."

Elizabeth was asleep when Lenora returned, so Adam reluctantly agreed to go home and get some rest. He called his father for a ride, and Hector came a short time later. Following a query about Elizabeth's condition, he and Adam drove to the farm in silence, lost in their own thoughts.

Adam showered and changed into fresh clothes, while Hector made some toast and oatmeal for breakfast.

"Mom not home?" Adam asked, coming into the kitchen.

"She stayed overnight at Sid and Alice's, to help with the funeral arrangements. She'll be home later today."

Adam sat at the table with his father but had no appetite. He only picked at his food, prompting Hector to look up from his own bowl of oatmeal and say, "You've got to keep up your strength."

"I'm going out to do the chores," Adam replied, hoping the distraction would offer some relief.

As he gathered the eggs, a thought worked its way into his brain and stirred his emotions. Today was to have been his wedding day. Now, instead, his bride lay in a hospital bed, going through agonies that paralleled his own wartime hospital experience.

Sadness deeper than anything he'd ever known overcame him. His hands trembled and he dropped an egg, its yellow center seeping out through the cracked shell. Tears blinded him as he kicked straw over the broken egg. Stepping outside, he leaned against the side of the chicken coop, but the freshness of the morning air and the feel of the sun on his face did little to displace the emptiness he felt within. Exhaling in resignation, he finished gathering the eggs and took them into the house.

He went out to the barn to clean the stalls. The aroma of the straw made him think of the hayride. He smiled at the memory of ditching the ride and walking around town with Elizabeth, talking for hours. His smile broadened as he reminisced about ending up at the pavilion and sharing the dance with her. He laughed aloud at the memory of his awkward attempt to twirl

Elizabeth, practically dropping her on the cement. He was grateful they'd had the dance pavilion to themselves. That's where it had started—the evening he and Elizabeth had danced together. It was there that he had recognized his feelings for her.

He allowed other memories to surface chronologically until the image of Elizabeth lying in the hospital bed surfaced. Then the emptiness returned. He slid to the floor and slumped against the stall. Burying his face in his hands, he found relief in tears, his body convulsing in bitterness and grief.

Elizabeth shifted from side to side and moaned softly as Lenora sat beside her, speaking words of consolation. It had been almost four hours since her last dose of pain medication, and it was difficult concentrating on her aunt's words.

Adam arrived just as Elizabeth groaned and tried to turn on her side. He sat down beside the bed and put on a brave smile. "Hi, darling."

"Hi," she whispered, her spirits brightening.

Adam turned to Lenora. "Can't they give her something for the pain?"

"They already have."

"She needs something more."

Lenora nodded in agreement and called the nurse on duty. The nurse hesitated at first but finally complied, giving Elizabeth a shot of morphine. It soon took effect, and Elizabeth felt herself relaxing again. The hours between dosages seemed eternal.

Dr. Cosgrove entered the room a few minutes later. "How are you doing today, Elizabeth?" he asked, reaching for her chart.

"The needle…helped," she replied, welcoming the relief.

"Good." Dr. Cosgrove studied the chart and looked at Adam and Lenora. "Would you mind slipping out while I examine her bandages?"

Adam held the door open for Lenora, who waved tenderly to her niece.

Once alone Dr. Cosgrove turned to Elizabeth. "I'm just going to have a look. Lie perfectly still."

Elizabeth gritted her teeth in preparation.

Working carefully and quickly, he lifted the edge of a bandage and examined the injury beneath. At length he said, "There, all done."

"What...does it...look like?"

Dr. Cosgrove cleared his throat. "You've received deep lacerations on your face and neck." He lowered his voice. "And your left ear was severed in the accident."

There was a long pause. "Severed?"

"Yes, but they're doing wonders these days with reconstructive surgery," he added quickly.

Elizabeth whimpered and put a hand to her bandaged face. This couldn't be happening. She felt trapped in a nightmare that continued to grow more frightening with each passing minute. She began breathing rapidly, fighting the urge to scream.

Dr. Cosgrove placed a hand on her shoulder. "Breathe deeply, Elizabeth. Slow and steady. In...out. In...out."

When Elizabeth's breathing returned to normal, Dr. Cosgrove patted her on the arm and called the nurse on duty. "We need to cover the wounds with an antibiotic cream," he directed. "Put a new pressure bandage on her ear and light sterile bandages on her face and neck. Monitor for signs of infection. But first, would you call Lenora and Adam back in?"

He made a few notes on Elizabeth's chart.

Adam hurried back into the room, followed by Lenora, and noticed the distress in Elizabeth's countenance. "You told her, didn't you?" he said, taking Elizabeth's hand and looking solemnly at Dr. Cosgrove.

"She needed to know, Adam."

Adam gently squeezed Elizabeth's hand and said, "It's going to be all right, darling."

Dr. Cosgrove jotted a few more notes on Elizabeth's medical chart and then smiled encouragingly at her. "We'll change the dressing and keep you under observation for the next seventy-two hours. Then, with luck, you'll be able to return home."

Elizabeth needed more than luck. She needed God's help, and she offered a silent, earnest prayer for it.

"What about changing her bandages after that?" Lenora asked.

"Soon she won't need bandaging, just antibiotic cream. You can apply it yourself."

"When do the stitches come out?" Adam asked, squeezing Elizabeth's hand again.

"In five or six days. The wounds will be red and very tender for a few weeks after that. And there will be some discomfort when the deeper stitches begin to dissolve."

Shuddering slightly, Elizabeth considered Dr. Cosgrove's estimated time line. A few weeks! Perhaps even longer. Would she be able to endure it? She prayed for strength.

Lenora's voice fell to a whisper. "How long until we know if it was successful?"

"There will be a variable amount of bruising and swelling for the next forty-eight hours. When the swelling goes down, then we'll know."

"Is there a chance of...complications?"

Elizabeth stopped breathing. Complications? She hadn't considered that.

Dr. Cosgrove removed his glasses and looked directly at Elizabeth. "I have every confidence you will make a full recovery, Elizabeth. You're young and healthy, and your skin is in excellent condition. Those are several factors in your favor."

Elizabeth waited for the "But..."

Instead, Dr. Cosgrove said, "And we'll deal with the issue of reconstructive surgery when you're stronger. Now I think we should let you get some rest."

"I'm going to stay," Adam said.

Lenora nodded. "I'll bring you a sandwich when Wil and I come back later." She kissed Elizabeth on the cheek and paused over her for a moment. "We'll get through this together, Elizabeth," she whispered, her lip quivering.

When they were alone, Elizabeth placed both of her hands in Adam's. "Adam," she said softly, "would you pray with me?"

"Of course," Adam said, sliding closer and squeezing her hands reassuringly.

Bowing his head, Adam gave a heartfelt prayer, asking for God's help in Elizabeth's recovery. His words were simple, but his sincerity was eloquent. And while he prayed, Elizabeth prayed too. She prayed that she would awaken and find this was only a bad dream.

CHAPTER 27

WHEN WIL AND Lenora returned, they were able to convince Adam to take a break, so he decided to slip home. On the drive he tried eating the sandwich Lenora had brought him, but his appetite was nonexistent. He finally threw the sandwich out the truck window and watched in the rearview mirror as a crow, sitting on a fencepost, hopped down to investigate.

Maude had already returned from Sid and Alice's by the time Adam arrived home. Her eyes were red-rimmed and puffy, and she looked tired. Adam could tell many tears had been shed.

After inquiring about Elizabeth, she gathered him in her arms and dropped the bombshell. "The family would like you to give the eulogy at the funeral."

Adam pulled back and stared at her in disbelief. "What?"

"They thought that since you were so close—"

"Shouldn't Pastor Wight be the one to do it?"

"He could, yes. But it's a chance for you to honor your cousin's memory."

"But the shivaree—" He dropped his voice to a whisper. "—was Ty's idea."

Maude stroked his arm. "I know you're upset, son. The good Lord knows you have every right to be. I won't try to talk you into doing it, but just think about it, okay?"

Adam nodded grimly. "I'm going to my room."

He slowly made his way upstairs and lay on his bed. Thoughts of his cousin assailed him, and he found himself vacillating between anger and sorrow. It seemed impossible that Ty was dead. Adam had seen death up close and personal in the war, but there had been some consolation because it was for a worthy cause. But to die in a freak car accident—where was the consolation there? And where was the forgiveness for an unfortunate joke that ended up killing Ty, maiming Elizabeth, hurting the other girls, and causing a delay in the wedding?

Adam clenched his fists as a wave of grief and shame washed over him. A lifetime of memories began turning over in his mind, like pages in a book. And written on each one was a unique experience of his and Ty's childhood together: family reunions, sleepovers, boyhood pranks, teen activities…the pages began turning rapidly.

He wasn't sure how long he lay there, remembering. But finally, exhausted and drained, he sat up and rubbed his eyes. Running a hand through his hair, he went downstairs to rummage in the kitchen for something to eat.

He cut a slice of bread and spread butter on it. He'd loved the taste of his mother's homemade bread for as long as he could remember. It was something familiar, something constant in an ever-changing world, and his world *was* changing. Rapidly. Spiraling out of control, it seemed. Being asked to deliver the eulogy was merely the latest example. How could he honor the person who had caused such heartache and grief?

Wolfing down the bread, he headed for the front entrance and grabbed the keys for the truck. Right now Elizabeth needed him. Everything else would have to wait.

Adam spent the afternoon at Elizabeth's side. He read to her from the Bible, shared local news events, and even told her some of his war experiences. Anything to help keep her mind off the accident. Whenever she dozed off, she mumbled fragmented phrases about the car accident, and he knew she was reliving the details, over and over. And so he did what he could to console her and distract her at the same time.

Lee Yang arrived after work to visit. His eyes filled with tears when he came into the room and saw Elizabeth's bandaged head. He forced a smile. "Dry cleaners lonely place," he said. "Both my workers missing."

"Hi, Mr. Yang," Elizabeth said, attempting to smile back. "Thanks for coming."

"This supposed to be happy time. Wedding." He gestured toward the bed. "Not this."

Lee Yang looked so genuinely distraught that Adam found himself feeling sorry for him. Elizabeth was more than an employee to him, and it showed.

"How's the dry cleaners doing?" Elizabeth asked weakly.

"Very busy. Mrs. Murphy bring in another dress and want to see you. She sad you not there. Me too."

"You know what you're going to have to do, don't you?" Elizabeth said.

"No, what?"

"Send for your wife and children. It's time to make it a family business."

Lee Yang's expression suddenly brightened.

A nurse poked her head into the room. "Adam, the patient in room twelve would like to see you." In answer to the question in his eyes, she added, "It's Susan Godfrey."

Adam frowned. "What does she want?"

"She said she needs to talk to you."

Hesitating, Adam looked at Elizabeth. She nodded encouragingly and said, "I think you should talk to her."

Adam didn't need to remind Elizabeth about the last time he'd talked to Susan. The telephone call had changed everything. "Tell her I'll be there in a minute," he said.

The nurse nodded and left the room.

"I go too," Lee Yang said. "See Julie. You get better fast, hear?"

"Hear," Elizabeth replied.

After Lee Yang left, Adam lingered beside the bed, reluctant to leave Elizabeth.

"I'll be right here," she said. "Go ahead."

"All right," he replied, taking one last look at her before closing the door behind him. He walked down the hallway and paused before entering Susan's room, drawing in a deep breath and exhaling slowly. Then, squaring his shoulders, he pushed on the door.

Susan was lying in bed, her arms and legs bandaged, her right ankle elevated and wrapped in a tension bandage. The pain that had been etched in her face the day before was less pronounced, although the dark circles under her eyes indicated a sleepless night. A glass of water sat on the cabinet beside the bed, along with a small paper cup that had contained pain medication. "Hi," she said, her voice raspy and low.

Adam nodded, unwilling to engage in pleasantries.

Susan wet her lips and tried to adjust herself into a more comfortable position. "I've been lying here, doing a lot of thinking."

Adam's stern expression softened slightly. He remembered his own convalescence in the hospital in Italy and how he'd had time to ponder a lot of things. And to strike his bargain with God.

"Elizabeth and Julie and I have known each other since we were kids, Adam. We've been best friends all of our lives and have had our share of laughs."

This is no laughing matter, Adam wanted to say but chose not to make a reply.

"The realization of what we've—I've—done to her...it's so hard. If I could go back and undo things, I would. But I can't. All I can do is to try and makes things right."

"There's no way to make things right."

Susan drew in several breaths, as if preparing herself for what lay ahead. "Dr. Cosgrove was in here to see me earlier. He suggested that I talk to you. It's about something I told him yesterday that he thought you should hear."

Adam nodded stiffly. "Okay."

Susan shifted uncomfortably again. "When we came over the rise, there were cattle on the road. Ty tried to brake but there was no time. He yanked on the steering wheel but the car skidded in the loose gravel. So he swerved into them...on his side of the car, which collapsed on impact. Adam, he deliberately took the full force of the collision."

Adam stared at her intently.

"He did it to try and save us," she added softly.

Adam's vision blurred, and his thoughts began racing. Had Ty actually sacrificed himself in order to save the others? In his mind's eye he could see the events as Susan described them. He pictured his cousin behind the wheel, trying desperately to avoid the collision. And when the collision became inevitable...

Excusing himself, Adam hurried out of the room. Looking up and down the hallway, he noticed a washroom nearby. He stepped inside and closed the door, his breath coming in short gasps. He turned the lock and leaned on the sink, staring vacantly into the drain. His eyes misted over again, and his body began to tremble. Thoughts of Ty overwhelmed him, and he began to weep for the loss of that day. When his emotions were spent, he splashed water on his face and wiped his puffy eyes. Lingering to make himself as presentable as possible, he stepped out of the bathroom and headed toward Elizabeth's room to take his leave of her for a while. He had a eulogy to write.

CHAPTER 28

ONDAY, THE DAY of the funeral, dawned dull and gray. Clouds hung in the air like wads of soiled cotton, strung out in layers. No rain fell, but the air was heavy and somber.

The church was filled to overflowing. Rows of cars and pickup trucks lined the parking lot. Eunice Murphy sat at the organ. The music droned in monotonous tones, matching the mood of the weather, as everyone solemnly filed in and sat on the wooden pews.

The first seven rows were reserved for family members, who had come from far and near. Sid and Alice hunched together on the front bench. They looked tired and stared at the floor as though lifting their eyes required more energy than they held in reserve. Their three surviving children—Tim, Judy, and Rachel—sat beside them and were equally subdued. Hector and Maude sat on the bench directly behind them.

Adam was seated on the stand at the front, looking over his notes and stealing glances at the congregation, which continued to swell in number. There were so many people. Hopefully they would not be disappointed in the words he had prepared.

Julie and her mother sat on the far side of the chapel. Julie's forehead still showed signs of bruising, and it was obvious she was having a difficult time sitting comfortably. Susan and her parents sat directly behind them. Susan was also noticeably bruised and had a bandage on one arm.

Nathan sat on the opposite side, near the back door. His eyes met Adam's at one point, but he looked away quickly.

When the casket was wheeled in, the congregation rose on cue at the indication of Pastor Wight, who stood at the pulpit. Julie and Susan began crying silently, and Ty's mother, Alice, raised her handkerchief and dabbed beneath the netting of her hat. Maude squeezed Hector's hand so firmly he winced.

Pastor Wight gazed solemnly over the congregation, waiting as the organist ended the prelude with a solemn, sustained chord. He motioned for the congregation to be seated. "We are met here this day to celebrate the life of Tyrone Wallace Hansen," he began. "The family would like me to extend their deepest expressions of gratitude for the many kindnesses and considerations shown over the past few difficult days."

As the ceremony continued, Adam took one last look at the notes he'd jotted down after returning home from the hospital when Susan told him the details about the accident. He'd gone directly to his bedroom and had begun to write. Words that earlier refused to come began filling the lines as though dictated like a revelation from Mount Sinai. Before he knew it, he had written five pages.

One of the verses of a hymn now caught his attention and jerked him momentarily back to Italy, to the day the grenade had exploded near him, blowing debris into his eyes:

Through many dangers, toils, and snares
We have already come,
'Twas grace that brought us safe thus far
And grace will lead us home.

Adam knew he could have been killed that day. But grace had brought him safely home, while many of his comrades had fallen on his right and on his left. The *many dangers, toils, and snares* had taken their toll on the battlefield—and now at home with Ty's untimely death. His cousin would never fully experience the gift that grace had granted Adam. The gift of time. Time to improve the family farm. Time to meet someone and fall in love. Time to share a life and grow old together.

Tears formed as Adam contemplated the loss, but he steeled himself and came back to the moment. He had a responsibility to perform, and it would require his ability to control his emotions.

Even now Pastor Wight was glancing at him in a silent signal that the moment to give the eulogy was quickly approaching.

"I have known Ty all of his life," Pastor Wight said, following the hymn. "It was my privilege to baptize him. He was a good boy and followed the rules of the church—" He smiled as an anecdote, not included in his sermon, came to mind. "—if you don't count the time he snuck into the chapel with some friends one evening and played a merry game of hide and seek, in which I was the seeker."

A ripple of laughter went through the congregation. The stage was set for the eulogy, and Pastor Wight nodded to Adam, who drew in a deep breath to steady his nerves as he approached the pulpit. Clutching his notes, he looked out over the congregation.

"Ty was my cousin...and my friend," he began. "We grew up together, and I must confess that we had our share of adventures over the years. My mother always claimed that what one of us couldn't think up, the other could.

"Ty saved my life twice. Once, when I was visiting him at his ranch—I must have been eight or nine at the time—we decided to cut across the pasture to do some exploring. Ol' Brutus, a big and ornery bull, took exception to our trespassing and came after us, snorting like fury. Ty outran me and would have made it safely to the fence, but when he saw Ol' Brutus about to make mincemeat out of me, he pulled out his slingshot and hit the bull in the head with a rock. It didn't hurt the bull, of course, but it distracted him long enough for me to escape. But, you know, it was the funniest thing. Later that morning Ty tried shooting at a telephone pole, and he couldn't hit it for anything. The magic had gone out of his slingshot. But his aim was sure true when it counted, or I wouldn't be here today.

"The other time Ty saved my life occurred when we were eleven or twelve. We were at the dirt hills north of Reunion, making a fort. We tunneled into the side of a hill about six feet. I was farthest in the tunnel, chipping away at the face, and Ty was behind, scooping the dirt out of the mouth of the tunnel. He had just

241

climbed out to spread the dirt around when the tunnel collapsed. I was completely buried. I tried to wiggle an arm free, to clear the dirt away from my face, but I couldn't even move a finger. And the weight was so great that I couldn't breathe. I thought I was going to suffocate. Just as I was about to black out, Ty managed to grab my ankle. When he finally pulled me out, he wiped the dirt from my face and just held me while we both cried."

Adam dropped his gaze and struggled with his emotions, wishing he could have somehow been able to intervene and save his cousin. People around Adam kept dying—in the war, at home—and he was powerless to do anything about it.

Taking a deep breath, he continued his eulogy, talking for fifteen minutes. When he finally took his seat, Maude looked up at him and mouthed, "Ty would be so proud of you." He smiled back and looked at his father. Hector's head moved in approval. And then at the cemetery Hector put a hand on Adam's shoulder and squeezed while Pastor Wight conducted the burial rites. Hector didn't say anything, but the gesture said much.

CHAPTER 29

THE CAR WAS careening out of control.

Julie was falling forward, colliding with the back of the seat and dropping to the floor like a rag doll. Ty was crashing into the steering wheel, his neck snapping violently forward. Susan was recoiling from the impact, doing her best to brace herself with her arms and legs.

Elizabeth felt herself floating over the front seat as the interior of the car revolved around her. Objects swirled in slow motion as though suspended in midair, and she could almost reach out and touch them. Now she was approaching the windshield, which loomed increasingly large until it was all she could see. Suddenly there was searing pain, and everything faded into blackness.

It was the same dream she'd been having since the accident. Every time she closed her eyes, she saw images of tumbling bodies and spinning objects. She heard terrified screams and felt the sides of the vehicle collapse around her claustrophobically. Shards of glass beat against her face and neck, and the sights and sounds mixed together as though they were being processed in a blender.

She jerked awake. She was now home in her own bed, having been discharged from the hospital the day after Ty's funeral. Lenora was tending to her with the fanaticism of a brooding mother hen, constantly disturbing her to see if she was resting comfortably. And as much as Elizabeth appreciated the attention, she was ready to be readmitted to the hospital for some peace and quiet. She felt like she was being smothered.

Lenora had already put antiseptic cream on Elizabeth's wounds and had changed the bandages for the morning. But she hadn't allowed Elizabeth to see herself in the mirror. "You're not ready yet," she insisted.

As Elizabeth now lay in her bed, fighting the dull ache on the left side of her body, she considered the matter. Lenora had just gone downtown to do some grocery shopping, Adam hadn't arrived yet, and Wil was at work. For the first time in days Elizabeth was alone.

She decided to take advantage of this small window of opportunity. She knew her aunt wouldn't approve of what she was contemplating, but she had to see what she looked like...underneath the bandages. *You're not ready yet* provided no clues and gave no satisfaction. She needed to know for herself.

Slowly, painfully, she climbed out of bed and made her way to the vanity table, surprised at the effort it required. Sitting stiffly down in front of the mirror, she pulled her hair back into a ponytail. Then she removed the bandage on her left cheek, wincing at the tenderness of her injury.

The pad came off, revealing an ugly cut across her left cheek, held together by black sutures. She whimpered, not so much in pain as in shock. The bruising and redness added to the grotesqueness, and she blinked in disbelief. Drawing in a determined breath, she removed the gauze pad from the left side of her neck, being careful to not to touch the wound and possibly contaminate it.

She whimpered again.

Staring back at her was the reflection of a stranger. It was horrifying to realize the disfigured image gawking back at her was...herself.

Taking a moment to steady her trembling fingers, she began carefully undoing the pressure bandage around her forehead. The bandage was wrapped in folds and made her feel like an Egyptian mummy. She continued until the bandages lay bunched on the table. Then she cautiously removed the heavy gauze pad that covered her left ear.

She let out a scream and stared in transfixed horror at her reflection. The gaping wound where her ear should have been...the red and swollen tissue surrounding it...the scars on her neck. The damage was worse than she imagined. Burying her face in her hands, she began to sob.

Lenora rushed into the room moments later, grocery bags in

both arms. "For heaven's sake, Elizabeth," she gasped. "What have you done?"

Elizabeth turned toward her in despair. "Aunt Lenora! Just look at me!" She collapsed inwardly, and her shoulders slumped in misery.

"Stay right there," Lenora said. "And for goodness sakes, don't touch anything."

She set the grocery bags down and hurried into the bathroom.

Elizabeth heard the water run in the sink and knew her aunt was scrubbing her hands. Lenora returned with antiseptic cream and applied it to the wounds. Then she put fresh gauze pads in place and rewrapped the bandages. Elizabeth sat still in compliance, like a disobedient child, wincing only slightly as Lenora tweaked and fussed until she was satisfied.

"My stars, Elizabeth! What ever possessed you to do it?"

"I just had to see."

Lenora stroked Elizabeth's hair. "I didn't want you to look yet."

A tear trickled down Elizabeth's cheek. "Oh, Aunt Lenora. My face!"

Lenora embraced her gently.

"What will Adam think of me?" Elizabeth sobbed.

Lenora held Elizabeth out at arm's length and looked at her sternly. "What kind of a question is that?"

"But I'm not—" She searched for the right words. "—whole anymore."

"Stop talking like that, young lady! You are still the same beautiful young woman you've always been. And if people can't see that—" Here her voice rose to a screech. "—then a pox on them!"

Elizabeth caught her breath. This was strong sentiment coming from her aunt, whose language rarely varied from that reserved for polite circles. So if her aunt could voice an opinion *this* strongly, what she said must be true.

Elizabeth found a degree of comfort in that thought.

When the time came for the stitches to be removed, Adam accompanied Elizabeth and Lenora to the medical clinic. So far there had been no sign of infection. Elizabeth's wounds were still discolored and tender, but the pain was lessening daily. This allowed her to sleep more comfortably through the night.

Despite her improvement, however, Elizabeth found it difficult to leave the privacy of the house and walk down the front walkway. The bandages made her feel self-conscious, and she constantly glanced around to see if the neighbors were watching. Julie and Susan, along with Pastor Wight, Lee Yang, and other well-wishers, had dropped by during the past few days. She had felt conspicuous under their curious and sympathetic stares. Still, she was determined not to hide in the house for the rest of her life.

When they arrived at the clinic, Elizabeth steeled herself for the walk into the front entrance. She took hold of Adam's hand and squeezed firmly as he opened the car door for her.

"Hey, you're cutting off my circulation," he said, causing her to smile.

"Sorry."

As they entered the lobby, the receptionist at the front desk looked up and beamed. "Elizabeth, it's so nice to see you up and about. How are you feeling, dear?"

Elizabeth had been asked this question so many times that she'd run out of energy to make anything but a token response. "Fine," she answered.

"Glad to hear it. Just have a seat. Dr. Cosgrove will be with you in a minute. Mrs. Jackson, could I see you about some information on the insurance papers?"

Lenora spoke with the nurse while Elizabeth perused the waiting room, disappointed to see it was occupied. She had hoped to slip in and out unnoticed.

Two women were sitting near the windows, reading magazines and making comments to each other. A young mother with a little boy on her lap was trying to comfort him while keeping an eye on a slightly older girl, who was walking around with her arms outstretched, pretending to be an airplane.

The little girl suddenly looked up and stopped her play-acting mid-flight. She dropped her arms and ran to her mother. "What happened to her, Mommy? Is she wearing a mask? She looks scary!"

Elizabeth flinched. The mother looked up apologetically and quickly silenced her daughter with a firm squeeze on the arm.

"Let's sit over here," Adam said, quickly guiding Elizabeth to some vacant chairs partly hidden behind a tall, mahogany planter filled with artificial flowers.

From the other side of the planter, Elizabeth heard the whispered conversation of the two women.

"She was such a pretty young woman."

"Wasn't she, though?"

"They were to have been married the next day."

"The accident was horrible. Simply horrible."

"She would have made such a beautiful bride."

Elizabeth stared at the floor, pretending she hadn't heard. Adam squeezed her hand, but she continued to stare at the floor and said nothing.

Finally the receptionist said, "Elizabeth, Dr. Cosgrove will see you now."

Adam helped Elizabeth to her feet again and walked her to the front desk. Lenora took her other arm and assisted her down the hallway. Dr. Cosgrove appeared in his office doorway and greeted them warmly before conducting Elizabeth inside. The moment of truth had arrived.

Adam and Lenora sat together on a bench outside the door and waited in silence. Normally Adam would have been uncomfortable having to sit beside Lenora and make conversation. But with his thoughts so preoccupied, he hardly noticed her presence.

After an interminable time the door opened, and Adam and Lenora both rose expectantly. Dr. Cosgrove emerged first, followed by Elizabeth. She had her face turned away, but after another step or two, she turned self-consciously and looked at Adam, maintaining eye contact only briefly. It was as though she stood in judgment, awaiting a final verdict.

Adam breathed in slowly. The wounds on her cheek and neck were now exposed. The train track marks that everyone had feared would result from the sutures were negligible. But the edges of the incision were still red, and there was noticeable bruising. She had her hair brushed forward, deliberately covering her left ear and the side of her neck. She stared at the floor as though interested in the tile pattern. And in the air hung an unspoken: *Well?*

Adam embraced her tenderly. "Dr. Cosgrove did a great job, darling." He held her at arm's length and looked into her eyes. "But considering the amazing quality of the subject he had to work with…"

Everyone shared a laugh.

Lenora looked at Dr. Cosgrove appreciatively. "Thank you, Benjamin. For everything."

"I am pleased with the results," Dr. Cosgrove said.

Holding out his arm, Adam escorted Elizabeth toward the front desk.

As they rounded the corner, Adam spotted Nathan coming down the hallway. Nathan stopped abruptly when he saw them. The motion of Elizabeth's body caused her hair to lift, exposing her neck and ear. Nathan caught his breath and stammered a greeting, then dropped his gaze and examined the front of his shirt.

Elizabeth let out a sob and covered her ear and neck with her hands, hurrying toward the front door.

Adam rushed after her. "Elizabeth, don't mind him." He followed her out to the car. "Don't mind any of them. They don't understand."

Elizabeth climbed in the car and buried her face in her hands. "You're the one who doesn't understand, Adam. Nothing will ever be the same again. People will always look at me like that little girl did, like I'm a...freak." She began crying. "Those two women said as much."

"It was just idle chatter."

"And Nathan couldn't even bring himself to look at me."

Adam sat beside her and embraced her. "He just feels guilty because of the way he behaved."

Elizabeth was inconsolable, however, and went directly to her room when they got home. Adam tried to follow, but she closed the door and leaned against it. "I want to be left alone, Adam."

Adam stood helplessly in the hallway.

Lenora gently motioned him away from the door. "She just needs some time. Why don't you come back tomorrow?"

Adam left reluctantly, confused and upset. He slowly drove the three-mile stretch home, his mind churning. He thought about what had just occurred at the medical clinic. He could excuse the little girl's bluntness. But how could the women in the waiting room have been so judgmental? And how could Nathan have been so cruel? Elizabeth's wounds were now more than skin deep. She had been cut to the core. Pounding the steering wheel in frustration, he wished he could have spared Elizabeth's feelings. But how could he fight thoughtless gossip or defeat rude behavior? For all his military training, he felt helpless against an enemy like this.

CHAPTER 30

HOW COULD IT *have come to this?* Elizabeth asked herself for the hundredth time.

Less than two weeks ago she had been busily planning and working with all the energy that only a young woman passionately in love can exhibit. Her wedding was going to be a magical occasion. But in an instant her world had been turned upside down. Literally. What had started out as a prank to draft a marriage contract had ended in disaster, and no wedding would be occurring now. How could it, when she was no longer the same person? Her future had been permanently changed.

What happened to her, Mommy? Is she wearing a mask? She looks scary! The little girl's words echoed in Elizabeth's brain, as did the conversation of the two women in the waiting room. *She was such a pretty young woman. She would have made such a beautiful bride.* And the image of Nathan's reaction to her appearance played over and over again in her memory. As a result she ate little the following week and only emerged from her bedroom to use the facilities.

She didn't allow Adam to see her either, even though he came calling every day. Why should she? He was only coming out of a sense of obligation. And if given the opportunity, he would bolt out of the engagement and find someone who wasn't...damaged.

The more Elizabeth studied herself in the mirror, the darker her thoughts became. Perhaps time would heal the wounds on her cheek and on her neck, but she'd always have an unnatural-looking ear. She would be scarred for life, and how could she expect Adam to love her now?

Besides, how could she be certain that Adam's feelings for her didn't hinge on duty or pity? Naturally he'd be poorly perceived if he deserted her in her hour of need. But would he feel cheated by having to settle for someone who was blemished?

The best course of action, Elizabeth decided, was to spare everyone the misery. So she remained in her bedroom and refused to see anyone, especially the man she loved with all her heart. And with her seclusion came a pain deeper than anything she had ever experienced.

It was the longest week of Elizabeth's life, but she stuck resolutely to her decision not to allow visitors. It was hardest refusing to see Adam, who continued to come every day. And each time she turned him away, she spent the next hour in tears.

On the afternoon of the eighth day, a light triple knock came on her door. She recognized Adam's greeting. Staring sadly at the door but setting her jaw in determination, she prepared herself for what needed to be done.

"Elizabeth," he called softly. "It's me, darling. Please open the door."

The doorknob turned slightly, and Elizabeth was out of bed in an instant. She threw herself against the door and said, "I can't, Adam. I just can't."

"Please, Elizabeth."

"I'm not ready for this."

"But I want to see you. It's been over a week."

A louder knock sounded on the door. "Land sakes, Elizabeth!" Lenora called, knocking once more. "You can't keep yourself locked up in there forever."

"Please, leave me alone. Both of you."

"But Elizabeth," Adam said. "It's...me."

"Oh, Adam," Elizabeth replied, as the tears began flowing once more. "I can't let you see me yet."

"But I love you, Elizabeth. We're to be husband and wife. Let me help you through this."

Wiping her eyes with the edge of her sleeve, Elizabeth said, "I just need more time."

She was hurting inside, and she could tell by the tremor in his voice that he was too. And it was all she could do to stop herself from flinging open the door and embracing him. But when she thought of Nathan's reaction at the clinic and remembered the comments from the women in the waiting room, the urge to open the door disappeared abruptly.

Pressing harder against the door, she heard her aunt Lenora whisper, "She'll hardly even let me in the room now unless she's wearing a head scarf."

"You mean like a veil?" came Adam's reply.

"Doctor Cosgrove is the only one she'll allow to see her without it."

Adam spoke to Elizabeth again, and she could almost feel the warmth of his touch through the panel. "I brought you something, Elizabeth. I'll leave it here on the floor." There was a brief pause and then he added, "Good-bye, Elizabeth. I'm leaving now. Just look at what I brought, okay?"

"Good-bye," she said, her hand poised above the doorknob, her resolve weakening.

She heard footsteps retreat down the hall. Waiting a few moments longer, she cautiously opened the door and peered out to check the hallway both ways. Then she looked down and saw a package wrapped in tissue and decorated with a bow. Quickly picking it up, she closed the door immediately.

She carefully removed the bow from the package and unwrapped the tissue paper. She caught her breath and put a hand to her throat when she saw the contents. Inside was a copy of their wedding invitation, and taped to the front was her mother's wedding band. An arrow drawn at the bottom of the invitation indicated she was to look on the back.

Turning the invitation over, she found a message that read:

> *Darling,*
> *A wedding band symbolizes the love between a man and a woman, for better or for worse, for richer or for poorer, in sickness and in health. I was prepared on our wedding day to make a vow to love and cherish you 'til*

death do us part. I am still determined to make and keep that vow, Elizabeth. I love you more now than I did the night you and I danced alone in the pavilion; more now than the day we rode down to the river and both ended up in the water. Keep this wedding band as a constant reminder of my love and devotion, and know that I long for the day when I can slip it on your finger... as your husband.

Adam

She pressed the invitation to her heart and cried for a long time. Then she sat down at her desk, reached for a pen and a piece of paper, and began to write a reply.

CHAPTER 31

THE FOLLOWING AFTERNOON Adam returned from another unsuccessful attempt to see Elizabeth. Changing into his work clothes and a jacket, he went directly to the barn. Breaking open a bale for Snowflake and Babe in the far stall, he stabbed the straw repeatedly with the pitchfork to scatter it around, badly startling the horses. Then he attacked the floor in the near stall, tossing the matted straw through the barn window.

Maude appeared in the doorway, wearing a woolen sweater and carrying a basket of eggs. "She still wouldn't see you?"

Adam shook his head and continued working.

"Do you want to talk about it?" Maude asked.

He worked a few moments longer and then paused to wipe his forehead with his sleeve. "I'm just frustrated and tired, I guess."

"There's something more, I can tell."

He looked at her miserably. "Is it that obvious?"

"If you scrape any harder, the floor boards will be going out the window next."

He smiled thinly and set the pitchfork aside. His expression darkened and he blinked several times, rubbing his eyes wearily. Reaching into his back pocket, he pulled out an envelope and handed it to her. "I got this today," he said. "Elizabeth slid it under her door."

Maude undid the flap and took out a single sheet of paper. It was wrinkled, as though it had been folded and refolded a number of times. She walked over to the window and held it up to the light. Adam knew its contents by heart.

My Darling Adam:
    It is with unbelievable sadness and regret that I write this letter, for I realize that I'll never be able to satis-factorily explain my decision. First of all, please know

that I love you with all my heart and soul. You'll doubt this, I know, but I pray you'll understand some day. It's very important to me that you do. It's because I love you that I'm releasing you from our engagement. It's because I care so deeply for you that I'm calling off the wedding. Because of the accident, I'm not the same person you were going to marry. I've changed. But I know you well enough to realize, darling, that you'd still insist on going ahead with the wedding, despite everything. My fear, however, is that you'd do so out of duty or, worse, pity. And I'd never want to hold you to a former promise.

I know I haven't let you see me since I got home from the clinic. And I realize this has hurt you. For that, I apologize with all my heart, and I pray, in time, you can forgive me.

I release you so that you may get on with your life and find someone who can complete you. Someone who is complete herself.

Elizabeth

Maude lowered the letter and looked solemnly at her son. "What are you going to do?"

Adam shrugged miserably and slumped against the stall railing. "What *can* I do? She won't even let me see her."

"Do you still love her?" Maude asked gently.

His head snapped up. "How can you even ask that? Of course I do."

"Then it would seem you're going to have to get creative. Like you did with the penny auction."

"But...how?"

Maude walked over and looked encouragingly into his eyes. "I can't begin to answer that question, son. That's for you to figure out."

Adam looked disappointed. "That's it? That's all the advice you can give me?"

"*Love finds a way,*' the saying goes. And I, for one, happen to believe it."

"But what is the way?"

She patted him on the chest. "Search your heart, son, and see what you can find." She picked up the basket of eggs and started for the door.

Adam kicked at a matted lump of straw. "Some help you are, Maude Carlson."

She smiled apologetically and stepped outside.

Adam sat down on a bale of straw and tried searching his heart, whatever that meant. He hoped to hear a voice, like God speaking to Moses from the burning bush, imparting wisdom and offering instructions. But no voice came. The heavens remained sealed; no revelation arrived to satisfy or to guide. Not even a whinny from the horses in the next stall.

As he turned to leave, his glance fell on a pile of boards that had been thrown haphazardly in the far corner, waiting for someone to rebuild the wood-worn stalls. He decided to give the voice another chance, so he lingered long enough to stack the wood in a neat pile.

But when he finished, he was no nearer an answer than he'd been before. In frustration he slammed the barn door behind him on the way out.

Adam picked at his food during dinner, drawing crisscrossed lines through the mashed potatoes with his fork.

Hector cleared his throat. "When you were a boy and played with your food like that, we'd throw it in the pig bucket and send you to bed hungry."

Adam looked up absentmindedly. "What…?"

Maude smiled thinly. "Of course, one of us would usually end up sneaking him a plate of something or other later on."

"Not me," Hector said in protest. "If he chose not to eat, that was up to him. I wasn't going to coddle him."

"Hec Carlson, I'm going to have to start calling you Fibber

McGee. I know for a fact that several times I went to set a plate outside his bedroom door, only to find a plate already there."

Hector waved a hand in dismissal and returned to his food.

Adam looked from one to the other, pleasantly distracted by their banter. It reminded him of his childhood, when his parents weren't so worn down by life, when the conversation around the dinner table had been more...alive.

He tried to envision a younger Hector talking to his bride as they sat around the dinner table or in front of the fireplace at night, sharing his dreams and looking forward to the future. Had he set out to become a grumpy old man, critical of everyone and everything? Had he decided to stop courting Maude after they were married and act as if the words *I love you* had become a foreign language? Had he determined that he'd have a son but stop developing a relationship with him beyond that of a hired hand? Where had dreams succumbed to reality? Where had intentions given in to compromise?

And what of his—Adam's—own path? What was he setting out to be, and how would it end? Dared he be critical of his father, when Hector at least had a wife and child of his own? Adam started playing with his food again, struck by the irony. Here his father had a wife but took her completely for granted, while he—Adam—desperately wanted to love and to cherish Elizabeth but couldn't have her. Sometimes life just laughed at you right in your face.

Following the meal, Adam helped his mother with the dishes. Hector sat at the table, browsing through an agricultural magazine and commenting on the cost of new machinery.

"Did I ever tell you the story of Sid and Alice's courtship?" Maude said, washing a glass bowl and putting it in the drainer.

Adam shook his head and reached for the bowl.

"No need to go over that old story again," Hector said without taking his eyes off the magazine.

"When Sid first came calling on Alice," Maude said, ignoring

Hector, "he found out she already had a beau. Charles Edgely was his name. He was a year older than she was—"

"And a real dandy," Hector added. "I remember him."

"A dandy?" Adam said, drying the bowl and setting it in the cupboard.

"He always wore nice clothes and a straw Panama," Maude explained. "He went to college in Great Falls—"

"And let everyone know it," Hector added, still pretending to read.

"Charles and Alice weren't officially engaged," Maude continued. "But pretty close to it. She thought of him as the young man she'd eventually marry. But Sid had different plans."

Curiosity piqued, Adam looked at her and said, "Like what?"

She submerged a pot in the sudsy water and began scrubbing. "When Sid arrived at our place that first time, he rang the doorbell as bold as brass. Mother escorted him into the living room, where Alice was already entertaining Charles. My sister suddenly found herself sitting between two gentlemen callers." Maude laughed. "I remember peeking in on her and seeing how awkward things were. And, needless to say, Charles did not appreciate Sid's presence."

"So what happened? A fist fight...a duel...some kind of challenge, winner take all?"

Hector snorted. "Sid could have taken Charlie boy with one hand tied behind his back."

"Actually, Alice tried to discourage Sid from visiting her again," Maude said. "She was happy dating Charles and felt like there wasn't room for anyone else."

Adam took the pot from his mother and dried it. "So she broke it off with Uncle Sid—"

"There was nothing *to* break off. Charles Edgely was her steady. Sid was someone who happened to drop by. And after that night, she never thought she'd see him again. But the very next evening, there he was back on our doorstep. Mother invited him in again, and Alice found herself sitting between two suitors once more."

"Did she still try to discourage Uncle Sid from coming back?"

"Yes, but he didn't seem to get the hint. He came calling the next afternoon, before Charles arrived from college. From that day on she began to see more and more of Sid, and less and less of Charles. Finally Charles stopped coming altogether."

"Well, there you are," Adam said. "Uncle Sid persevered and won her over. *Charlie boy* didn't have true feelings for her, or he wouldn't have let her go so easily."

Maude wiped her hands on a dishtowel and patted Adam gently on the chest. Then giving him a wink, she left the room.

Hector set the magazine down and scratched his stubbled chin. "What was that all about?"

Adam didn't reply. Another voice was beginning to speak to him. He raised his hand to his chest and felt the beating of his own heart.

CHAPTER 32

FOR CRYING OUT loud, Elizabeth!" Lenora said. "You can't stay in there like this." She stood outside Elizabeth's bedroom, talking through the door. "Julie's here to see you."

Elizabeth climbed into bed and pulled the covers around her. "I don't want to see her. I don't want to see anyone."

The doorknob turned and Lenora called out, "Julie will wait right here, Elizabeth. But I'm coming in."

Lenora opened the door and stepped inside. Silhouetted in the hallway light, she blinked in the dimness and reached for the light switch.

"Don't," Elizabeth said softly.

"But it's like a tomb in here."

Elizabeth groaned.

Lenora walked over and sat beside her. "It would cheer you up to have a visitor. Julie could comb your hair and help you change into some fresh clothes. Land sakes, you look like a pile of laundry that's been unceremoniously dumped in a heap."

Elizabeth turned away.

"I know a terrible thing has happened," Lenora said softly. "But you're not like Job, from the Bible, who lost everything. You still have a family who cares for you and a young man who loves you. Don't shut us out."

Elizabeth didn't want to hear about Job and his trials. She had plenty of her own. Nor did she want to hear about how lucky she was to still be alive, to have people around her who loved her. She didn't want to be told the accident could have been worse and they *all* could have been killed. These were expressions Elizabeth had heard repeatedly since the accident, but they gave her no consolation. She was beyond the reach of hackneyed words of comfort. True, she hadn't lost everything, but she had lost much, and things would never be the same again.

She had done what she thought best, with the letter to Adam. And since sliding it under the door, she hadn't heard from him. But what did she expect? She might as well have started the letter with *Dear John*.

Self-pity had become her constant companion, crowding out everyone else and leaving nothing but emptiness and mourning for her unrequited dreams. She was aware of her emotional descent but was unable to stop it. She retreated further into herself each day, and the thoughts of ever being lovable again disappeared, lost in a void of despair. How could she discern now between expressions of love and acts of pity? How could she divine between glances of encouragement and stares of curiosity? She was unlovable, and suspicion and doubt grew like a thickening mist, blotting out any rays of hope or promise.

Lenora sat with her fingers interlaced, staring at her. "Talk to me, Elizabeth. What can I do or say to help you?"

Elizabeth shrugged, tears forming in her eyes.

"It's breaking my heart to see what you're doing to yourself," Lenora continued. She gently stroked Elizabeth's hair. "Scars will heal; injuries can be surgically repaired. You're still the same amazing young woman you always were. But you just can't see it. Or won't."

"Aunt Lenora, I know you mean well. But I just can't do this right now."

Lenora's chin trembled. "In the past we've always been able to talk, Elizabeth. But now it's like there's a wall between us, and I don't know how to break through it." Pausing briefly, she said, "Julie, step in here, please."

Julie appeared in the doorway. "Hi, Elizabeth."

Elizabeth pulled the bed sheet up around her face.

"I just wanted to see you," Julie said.

Elizabeth glared at her aunt in an expression of betrayal and turned away.

"I'm so sorry, Elizabeth," Julie said, tears forming in her eyes. "The shivaree was only meant in fun. It wasn't supposed to turn out like this." When Elizabeth didn't respond, Julie's composure broke and she said, "Say something, Elizabeth. Yell at me, tell me you blame me, tell me you hate me. Just say something, anything."

Elizabeth lay down on her pillow. "I'm tired and want to be left alone."

Julie took a step closer. "Please, Elizabeth, let's just talk, you and me. Like old times."

"The old times are gone, Julie. Please leave now, both of you."

When Julie opened her mouth to respond, Lenora shook her head and said, "We're leaving, Elizabeth." She crossed to the door and rested her hand on the doorknob in invitation for Julie to follow.

With tears rolling freely down her cheeks, Julie appealed to Elizabeth once more, but Elizabeth turned toward the wall and pulled the covers around her shoulders.

"I'll escort you out, Julie," Lenora said. Then to Elizabeth, she added, "I'll be back later, dear. Right now I've got a telephone call to make."

The door closed quietly, enveloping Elizabeth once more in darkness.

The telephone rang as Adam came into the house, wearing a pair of work gloves and a light jacket. The weather was uncharacteristically mild for October, but the chill in the evening air was a promise of colder weather to come.

Maude, who was sitting at the kitchen table darning a sock, answered the telephone on the third ring. "Hello?" There was a pause and then she said, "I'm fine. But tell me, how is Elizabeth doing?"

Adam was beside his mother in an instant.

Maude listened a moment longer and then said, "Oh, the poor dear." She glanced at Adam. "Yes, he's right here, Lenora. I'll put him on."

Anxiously pressing the receiver to his ear, Adam wet his lips. "Hello, Mrs. Jackson."

Without returning the greeting, Lenora spoke rapidly. "Adam, it's growing worse. It's like Elizabeth has lost herself in mourning. She's hardly eating a thing, and she's not sleeping through the night. She'll burst into tears suddenly and then sit sullenly for hours and not make a sound. I don't know what to do."

Before Adam could respond, Lenora continued, "I know she wrote that letter to you. But you have to understand that she's not herself. You can't take stock in what she said. She's confused and hurt and won't listen to reason. No matter what Wil and I do, we can't seem to reach her. But we have to do something, or we're going to lose her, Adam." Her voice broke.

Adam spoke in determination. "I'm not going to let that happen."

He heard Lenora sniff back her tears. "Wil and I are at our wit's end."

"I have a plan, Mrs. Jackson. As a matter of fact, I was just getting things ready. It's a bit drastic, but considering the situation..."

"Let's hear it," she said anxiously. "We're fresh out of ideas."

Maude sat at the kitchen table, darning the sock and listening as Adam spoke into the telephone. The longer he talked, the wider her smile grew. She nodded in approval several times and laughed aloud at one point. Finally setting the sock aside, she walked over to him. Tears glistened in her eyes as she waited for him to end the conversation.

When he finally hung up the phone, she embraced him. "Didn't I tell you that love finds a way?" She wiped her eyes with the corner of her sleeve. "It's a wonderful idea, son."

Too excited to sleep, Adam stepped onto the front porch and surveyed the yard. The light from the full moon cast a silver glow over the landscape. He proceeded to the truck and started the engine, backing up to the barn door and turning off the ignition.

He slipped on a pair of worn work gloves and began carrying out the boards that he'd stacked the day before.

He didn't notice his father's arrival.

"If you're planning on fixing the stalls, the lumber's going the wrong way," Hector said.

Adam looked at his father sheepishly. "Hope I didn't wake you up."

Hector shrugged. "I don't sleep much most nights anyway."

Motioning toward the boards, Adam said, "I was hoping to borrow these for a while."

"I know. Your mother told me about it." He pulled a pair of gloves from his back pocket. "There are a few sheets of plywood in the woodshed. You'll need them too, I reckon. Let's throw them on first."

Adam stared at his father in surprise and followed him to the woodshed. "I'm glad I'm going with you to get plywood instead of *leather*," he said, referring to the strap that still hung on a nail inside the small building.

Hector grinned in response.

Together they carried three sheets to the truck, laying them flat in the bed. Then they began stacking the boards on top.

"What do we need for tools?" Hector asked.

Adam noticed the *we*. "Just the basics. Hammer, saw, tape measure, square. Maybe a chalk line." He finished loading the boards as Hector rounded up the tools.

When they were done, Adam said, "Guess that's it." He hesitated, still uncertain of his father's intentions.

"What time do you want to leave in the morning?" Hector asked.

"Sun up. It's a big day tomorrow, and I've got a lot to do."

Hector sniffed into the back of his glove. "I suppose things would go that much faster if you had help."

"They sure would."

"I'll have toast and coffee ready for us at six."

Adam felt a tingle run up his spine, and he glanced at the old poplar tree, silhouetted in the moonlight, which held the remnants of the tree house he and his father had built years earlier. They worked on it three days, and when they finished, they sat on the platform and surveyed their handiwork. It was the last thing they built together.

Hector took a step toward the house and stopped. Turning slowly to face his son, he said, "About what I told you awhile back. You know, about my staying on the farm instead of going to California that time? I know you have plans to go to agricultural college and then come back here. But your mother and I want more for you than this old place has to offer. Think about it."

"Don't need to. My mind's already made up."

Hector smiled and gazed at the ground for a moment. "See you at six, son," he said, heading into the house. "Night."

"Night, Dad."

Adam lingered to savor the cool night air and contemplate what just occurred. His emotions were very close to the surface of late, and it didn't take much to bring tears. They flowed once again, and he sniffed into his coat sleeve, fighting to regain control. At length he tossed his work gloves into the cab of the truck and leaned against the fender. The release of emotions seemed to clear his head, and an additional idea for tomorrow occurred to him. He hurried into the house to find an empty picture frame.

CHAPTER 33

THE SUN WAS beginning to set the following evening as Adam, dressed in his uniform and service cap, stood beside the horse trailer outside the pavilion. Maude, Wil, and Lenora—looking tired from the day's exertions but pleased nonetheless—watched as Adam and Hector attached the ramp to the back of the trailer and opened the end gate. Snowflake, already saddled, was inside, eating oats from a feedbag.

Maude looked at Adam proudly. "What young woman will be able to resist a handsome young man in uniform?"

Adam smiled in anticipation.

"Our prayers are with you," she added.

Hector helped back Snowflake down the ramp and patted the white stallion on the neck as Adam climbed into the saddle. "Godspeed, son," he said, looking up at Adam in encouragement.

"I don't know if I can stand the suspense," Lenora said, the anxiousness evident in her voice. "I'm sitting here on pins and needles."

Adam shifted in the saddle. "Will Elizabeth be presentable?"

Lenora nodded. "Before I left this morning I made her change into a dress. I don't know about presentable, but at least she won't have on her nightgown. I hid it."

Wil gave a half-chuckle and put an arm around his wife. "Good luck, Adam. We'll be waiting for you next door in the mayor's office."

Adam drew in a deep breath and turned Snowflake around. Digging in his heels, he urged the horse into motion. Moments later the sound of horse hooves clattering on the bare asphalt echoed through the night air, gradually fading as they receded down Main Street.

Elizabeth jumped when a knock came on her bedroom window. She paused in the dimness, listening, wondering if her mind was playing tricks on her.

The knock came a second time.

"Who's there?" she asked anxiously.

"Prince Charming."

She blinked in surprise and lifted a corner of the curtain. She saw Adam, in full uniform, sitting on Snowflake. He smiled at her, and she caught her breath, releasing the curtain. She pressed herself against the wall and placed a hand to her throat.

"Open the window, m'lady."

Elizabeth began breathing in short gasps.

"I've come for you...this time," Adam called, tapping on the windowpane again.

She hurried to her vanity and turned on the lamp. Looking at herself in the mirror, she felt torn between wanting to send him away and wanting to open the window to him.

"I'm not leaving without you, Elizabeth."

Elizabeth ran a hand down the left side of her face and felt the unevenness of the flesh. Her heart fell when she lifted her hair and looked at her damaged ear, gruesome in the stark and unflattering glare of the lamp. She turned helplessly to the window. How could she open it to Adam in her condition? She buried her face in her hands and began to cry. Making her way over to the bed, she climbed in and pulled the covers over her head.

She heard a clink against the windowpane.

"Elizabeth," Adam called, "I have this key and permission to come in and get you if you don't cooperate."

"Go away," she called from under her covers.

"You have ten seconds to open the window."

"I can't, Adam."

"Ten...nine...eight..."

"I don't want you to see me like this!"

"Seven...six...five..."

"Please, just leave me alone."

"Four... three... two..."

"No, Adam!"

"One!"

Elizabeth felt rather than heard the horse's hooves thud away from the window. Silence returned to the yard, and she listened, wide-eyed, to the sound of her heart beating in her ears. Had Adam given up and ridden away in discouragement? The answer came a short time later when footsteps sounded in the hallway.

Tossing back the covers, she rushed to her bedroom door and flung herself against it as the doorknob began to turn. "No, Adam!" She felt pressure on the door. "Please, Adam. If you love me, you'll leave me alone."

"It's because I love you that I can't."

She braced her feet and leaned against the door, but it was no use. Inch by inch, the door opened. Squealing in impending defeat, she ran back to the bed and disappeared beneath the covers.

She heard his footsteps cross the room.

"Elizabeth—"

"Please go away."

He rubbed his hand over the covers, trying to soothe her. "Elizabeth, there's something I need to say to you. Please hear me out."

She didn't respond, and so he continued. "Ty sacrificed his life to save you and the others. He didn't do it just to have you lock yourself away from those who love you. He wanted you to live and be happy. So do I."

She held her breath and didn't reply.

Leaning closer, he asked, "If it had been the other way around and I was the one who'd been injured, would you have given up on me and left me to face it alone?"

"No...," she replied haltingly, her voice muffled in the blankets.

"Then you must have a pretty low opinion of me."

Elizabeth drew back the covers enough to look at him. "I don't, Adam."

"Then how can you expect me to walk away when *you* wouldn't?"

"But the little girl and the women said—"

"Are you going to let a few idle comments determine the rest of your life?"

She lowered the covers further. "Nathan couldn't even bear to look at me."

"I've got news for you, Elizabeth Baxter. None of them will ever be able to see you through the eyes that I do. I love you, and I have no intention of losing you."

At his words she dropped the covers and pulled herself up to lean against the headboard. Steeling herself, she flinched slightly as Adam reached up and gently ran the back of his fingers across her cheek and down her neck. She stifled a whimper and sat statuesquely as he lifted her hair.

"Adam...," she moaned.

"It's okay, Elizabeth."

She closed her eyes and held her breath, expecting him to recoil in horror. Instead he leaned forward and lightly kissed her on the cheek. Then, without warning, he picked her up in his arms.

"What are you doing?" she gasped.

"Taking you away from here."

Her eyes widened at the prospect of leaving the sanctuary of her room. "Adam, I can't!"

"We're just going for a little ride," he said, carrying her down the hallway and into the living room. "It'll be all right, Elizabeth. I promise."

He helped her into a jacket and then led her onto the front veranda and down the steps to where Snowflake waited, tied to a newel post. Lifting her into the saddle, Adam untied the reins and climbed up behind her.

"Where are we going?" she asked.

Adam reined the horse around and headed through the crisp, fallen leaves to the street. "To where it all started," he replied.

She looked back at him quizzically.

"Miss Elizabeth Baxter," he said, "I'm hoping for the honor of a dance."

"We're going to the pavilion?"

Adam nudged the horse into a faster walk. "Hang on."

They covered the three blocks to Main Street quickly. Once there, he slowed Snowflake to a gentle walk. As they approached the pavilion, which was momentarily blocked from view by the town office, Elizabeth said, "What's that sound?"

"Part of the surprise."

Elizabeth listened intently. "Big band music."

"Kenny Jones and His Moonlight Orchestra."

As they rounded the corner of the town office, Elizabeth caught her breath. The pavilion gleamed like a jewel set against a backdrop of black velvet. A soft glow emanated from the interior, and a lighted pathway made of lanterns led to the front door.

Reining up, Adam dismounted and tied Snowflake to a tree on the boulevard. Then he held out his arms to Elizabeth.

"Adam, people are in there. I can't do this."

"Yes, you can, darling. You're the most courageous person I know."

"Courageous? You can't be serious."

"I *am* serious."

"But I haven't left the house in almost two weeks. I've locked myself in my room—"

"And you were doing it for me. You were willing to sacrifice your happiness, thinking it would allow me to find mine. Misguided though it was, that took courage. The only problem is, I could never be happy without you."

She looked at him for a moment. Then she slid off the saddle, into his arms.

He led her up the lighted path to the front door, around which the lights had been arranged to form an archway. Allowing her to linger a moment to listen to the music, he opened the door and escorted her into the warm interior. She gasped in surprise and turned in a full circle, staring as though unable to believe her eyes.

A glass chandelier hung from the center of the room, from which radiated crepe streamers, fanning out like the spokes of a gigantic wheel. Decorations, equally spaced throughout the room, hung on the walls. Kenny Jones and His Moonlight Orchestra sat in the far corner of the room near the gas heater, arranged in a semicircle and cloaked in the soft glow of the lights clipped to their music stands.

Along the center of the back wall was a raised platform, upon which stood three tall rectangular columns, covered in muslin and lighted from within so they appeared to hover in the air. A wicker basket of flowers sat on top of each column, and streamers hung between them, forming two graceful arcs. A decorative floral arrangement was positioned at the far front edge of the platform, and a small table, covered with a lace tablecloth, stood at the other end. In the center of the small table sat an empty picture frame and a vase containing a single white rose.

"It's so beautiful, Adam," Elizabeth whispered. "Who did all this?"

"Some people who love you," Adam replied, helping her off with her coat.

"But...why?"

"Shh, no more questions." He pressed a finger to her lips and held out his hands in invitation. "Would you do me the honor, Miss?"

Hesitatingly, she took his hands, and they began moving slowly in rhythm to the music. At first she kept glancing around as if expecting the entire town to burst upon the scene at any moment. But Adam spoke reassuringly to her, and soon she began to relax, allowing herself to move as one with him.

He pulled her close and gently stroked her hair as they made their way around the room. She melted into him, and they danced in silence, conversing through their feelings.

At length he whispered, "Remember the night of the hayride when we came here? It was our first dance together."

"How could I ever forget?"

"That was the night I fell in love with you, Elizabeth. On this very spot." They danced in silence for a while longer. Finally, he released her and said, "Wait here a moment."

He approached the orchestra and spoke briefly with Kenny Jones, who listened and then turned to confer with the musicians. Adam rejoined Elizabeth as the orchestra began playing "Believe Me, If All Those Endearing Young Charms."

"There's something I want to read to you, Elizabeth. Don't say anything. Just listen."

She nodded.

He pulled a piece of paper from his pocket and read:

> *Believe me, if all those endearing young charms,*
> *Which I gaze on so fondly today,*
> *Were to change by tomorrow, and fleet in my arms,*
> *Like fairy gifts, fading away,*
> *Thou wouldst still be adored as this moment thou art,*
> *Let thy loveliness fade as it will,*
> *And around the dear ruin each wish of my heart*
> *Would entwine itself verdantly still.*

"Thomas Moore," she said.

"Yes, but tonight consider it Adam Carlson."

She looked deeply into his eyes and pressed her lips against his.

How long they kissed, she did not know. Time lost all meaning, consumed in the *now*.

Finally Adam led her over to the table upon which sat the empty picture frame and the single white rose. Getting down on one knee, he looked solemnly up into her eyes. "There is something missing in this picture frame, Elizabeth. A photograph of the bride and groom on their wedding day. You once did me the honor of agreeing to become my wife. I know things didn't work out as we had planned. But I want you to know that I love you more now than I did then. And tonight I reaffirm my love and ask again: Elizabeth Baxter, will you marry me?"

Emotions choked her response as tears filled her eyes. The most she could manage was an enthusiastic nod.

Adam stood and embraced her tenderly. "The first time you said yes, you made me the happiest man on earth. Tonight I'm even happier, if that's possible."

She smiled and wiped her teardrops from the front of his uniform.

He lifted her chin so he could look into her eyes. "I know four anxious people who are waiting next door in the mayor's office to hear the news."

Elizabeth looked around the interior of the room again. "The other people who love me," she said, almost to herself.

"First, let's thank the musicians. Then we need to talk on the way next door."

Elizabeth hesitated briefly before putting her arm through his. It was time to start facing people again.

"They're here!"

Lenora stepped away from the door in Wil's office and tried to put on an air of nonchalance. But her restless pacing and the wringing of her hands betrayed the pretense.

Maude rose from her chair in anticipation, and Wil and Hector, who had been sharing a drink, turned expectantly toward the door.

Elizabeth came into the room first and stopped when she saw the others. Her hand instinctively went to her hair, pulling it down over her neck.

She was immediately swarmed as Lenora rushed toward her, arms extended, followed by Wil and Maude. Hector remained near the desk, toying with his drink.

"Oh, Elizabeth, I can't tell you how overjoyed I am to see you here," Lenora said, tears in her eyes. She turned to Adam and mouthed, "Thank you."

Wil embraced Elizabeth tenderly. "What did you think of Adam's *little surprise?*"

Elizabeth held out a hand to Adam and pulled him into the circle. "It was wonderful. Thanks for all your work. I don't deserve it."

"Of course you do, dear," Maude replied.

Adam walked over to his father and put an arm around him. "And it gave Dad and me a chance to build something together again, even if he did cut a board too short and I had to remind him to measure twice, cut once."

Everyone laughed, and Hector allowed a smile to play across his weathered countenance.

A momentary pause followed. Lenora looked from Elizabeth to Adam and back to Elizabeth again. Extending her hands dramatically, she said, "Well?"

"Well, what?" Elizabeth said, looking innocently at her aunt.

"Oh, Elizabeth, you're such a tease."

Elizabeth embraced her aunt again. "The answer is yes, Aunt Lenora. Adam and I are going ahead with the wedding."

Lenora looked heavenward and whispered, "Praise the Lord."

The three women embraced again, and Wil gave Adam a congratulatory slap on the back.

Adam glanced at his father, who nodded in approval and looked at the women, rolling his eyes at how they were carrying on. Adam laughed and nodded back in agreement.

"When is the wedding?" Lenora asked. "Next month sometime?"

"Tomorrow evening," Elizabeth said, taking Adam's hand in anticipation of what she knew was coming.

"Tomorrow evening!" Lenora gasped. "But that won't give us time to send out new invitations or make the necessary arrangements."

"I don't want to send out new invitations. I want a small, private wedding. And the arrangements have already been made—the pavilion is beautiful." Lenora opened her mouth to protest, but Elizabeth took her aunt's hand in hers. "Please, Aunt Lenora, that's how Adam and I want it."

Lenora looked at her niece earnestly. "Are you certain, dear?"

"Yes. Most everyone I want to attend is right here in this room. There are just a few others to invite, and that's all." She embraced her aunt. "Adam and I will be just as married as if it was a royal wedding, attended by thousands."

Wil lifted his glass into the air. "I propose a toast. To the happy couple."

"To the happy couple," Lenora, Maude, and Hector repeated.

As they stood together, Adam felt his father's arm around him. The warmth worked its way through his uniform and into his very being. And although Hector never expressed himself vocally, Adam understood the unspoken message. It had been years in coming and arrived on this special evening like a wedding present, held in reserve as the most valuable gift his father had to bestow. And Adam received it with all his heart.

The moment was broken when Lenora suddenly announced, "Wil, we've got to get home right now. I've got a thousand things to do before tomorrow evening."

"You go ahead, Aunt Lenora," Elizabeth said. "Adam and I have a few more stops to make."

"Don't be long, dear," Lenora said. "I need your help if we're going to be ready in time."

"We'll hurry," she replied, winking at Adam. "We have the fastest transportation in town."

Julie gasped in surprise when she opened the door and saw Elizabeth and Adam standing there and a white horse tied at the front gate.

"We're going through with it, Julie," Elizabeth said excitedly. "Adam and I are getting married!"

Julie blinked as if she hadn't heard correctly. "When?"

"Tomorrow evening."

"Tomorrow evening? But only yesterday—"

"—I was being an idiot," Elizabeth said.

Julie looked at her warily, as though wondering if this was a prank to get back at her for the shivaree.

"Adam and I *are* getting married," Elizabeth said reassuringly, "and I need a maid of honor."

Julie's eyes misted over, and she put a hand to her mouth. "But after what I did..."

Elizabeth stepped forward and embraced her. "All you did, all you've ever tried to do, was be a friend."

Julie began crying. "Oh, Elizabeth. I feel so bad. Can you ever forgive me?"

Elizabeth was crying now too. "And can you ever forgive *me?*"

Julie pulled away and looked at her in surprise. "Forgive you? There's nothing *to* forgive."

"You were hurt too, Julie. And I wasn't there for you. I shut out a friend—" She glanced at Adam. "—and everyone else who loves me, and for that I'm truly sorry."

Julie embraced her again and looked at Adam over Elizabeth's shoulder. He smiled in a gesture of reconciliation, and she returned the smile, an expression of genuine relief playing across her face.

Later, as Adam and Elizabeth rode Snowflake toward Susan's house to ask her to take the wedding photographs, Elizabeth said, "That takes care of the maid of honor, but what about—" She dropped her voice to a reverent whisper. "—the best man?"

"I've been thinking about that," Adam replied, nudging Snowflake into a trot as they made their way down the street. "I'm not going to have a best man exactly."

Elizabeth twisted in the saddle to look back at him. "What do you mean?"

"Well, it may be unorthodox...but I'd like my dad to stand beside me."

CHAPTER 34

THE CEREMONY WAS scheduled for five o'clock. Two rows of folding chairs had been set up in the pavilion near the front, with an aisle down the center. Eunice Murphy sat at a portable organ positioned close to the platform. The prelude music wafted through the pavilion, and the streamers seemed to sway in rhythm.

Susan was situated at the front door, greeting the few invited guests and taking impromptu photographs.

Maude sat with Sid and Alice. She wore her regular Sunday dress, along with the brooch that had belonged to her grandmother.

Dr. Cosgrove and his wife sat in the second row beside Lee Yang. Adam and Elizabeth had made two final stops on their way home from Susan's to extend the personal invitations.

The wedding party was positioned on the platform, standing in front of the three illuminated columns and facing the audience.

Adam was dressed in his uniform and stood at attention. His eyes were fixed on the front door, through which Elizabeth would be coming at any moment from the town office, where Lenora was helping her put on the veil.

Hector stood beside Adam and shifted uncomfortably as he tugged on his necktie. Maude smiled encouragingly at him, and he managed to relax somewhat.

Julie, wearing a full-length blue dress, was on the other side of Adam. She too was staring expectantly at the front door, where Wil now stood peering anxiously out while waiting to walk Elizabeth up to the wedding platform.

Pastor Wight sat on a chair near the organ, awaiting his cue.

All eyes went to the front door moments later as Lenora entered, beaming proudly. She wore a formal dress and diamond jewelry. Motioning enthusiastically to Pastor Wight, she hurried to get seated so she could watch the grand entry.

Eunice Murphy began playing Mendelssohn's "Wedding March" as Wil held out his arm to Elizabeth. A collective sigh went through the room. Elizabeth's dress and veil seemed to capture the dreamlike tones created by the lighting, and to Adam, she had never looked more beautiful. She wore the two-strand pearl necklace Lenora had promised to give her on her wedding day, and she held a small bouquet of flowers.

Wil walked her to the front without incident. There, he proudly released her to Adam and took his place beside Lenora, who patted his hand in approval.

Adam assisted Elizabeth onto the platform, and they stood between his father and Julie.

Hector anxiously felt his pocket for the tenth time to make certain he had the wedding band, which Adam had gotten back from Elizabeth when he had taken her home last night.

Pastor Wight faced the wedding party, his back to the audience. He held a single sheet of paper that outlined the ceremony, which had been significantly trimmed. He nodded to Eunice, who ended the march with a sustained note, and then smiled at Adam and Elizabeth. With a clear, practiced voice he began the brief ceremony.

Adam and Elizabeth each said *I do* at the appropriate moment. Lenora dabbed her eyes when Hector handed over the wedding band and Adam placed it on Elizabeth's finger. The tears ran more freely when Elizabeth held her hand up to show off her wedding rings.

Maude reached for her handkerchief when she saw Hector turn and embrace Adam. As Hector was about to let go, Adam pulled him closer. Tears ran down Maude's cheeks as she watched the two men she loved most in the world slap each other on the back affectionately. It was this moment, she knew, that would linger foremost in her heart for the rest of her days.

Following the ceremony, Susan stepped forward to take the formal photographs. Adam and Elizabeth posed together, and with family members, in a variety of combinations. Elizabeth ensured that her left side was always turned away from the camera. There were some things she was not ready to have immortalized in photographic form.

When the pictures were over, the happy couple walked toward the door. Elizabeth paused, holding the wedding bouquet in the air. Julie and Susan gingerly moved forward as she turned her back and threw the bouquet over her shoulder. Both young women managed to get hold of it. They laughed at one another and held it aloft triumphantly, amid applause from the onlookers.

Adam led Elizabeth to the black Buick Roadmaster parked out front. Wil had insisted they take his car on their honeymoon and had spent the afternoon polishing it, inside and out. Everyone followed them out to the boulevard, watching as Adam held the door for Elizabeth, making certain her dress was gathered inside before closing the door. He smiled at his parents and hurried around to the driver's side. Starting the car, he looked over at Elizabeth. "Ready, Mrs. Carlson?" he asked.

Elizabeth smiled. "Ready."

As they drove away from the pavilion, she turned and gave a final wave to those huddled on the boulevard, who were waving in return and straining to see the happy couple until the last possible second. Adam rounded the corner and stepped hard on the accelerator, and the pavilion and well-wishers disappeared from view. Elizabeth turned back around in her seat and reached for Adam's hand. He smiled at her and squeezed her hand firmly. She slid over to him and leaned on his shoulder. Together they settled in for the drive, their eyes fixed on the road ahead.

Epilogue

October 28, 2006

ONCE THE DISHES were done and the house tidied, everyone left for home. Adam and Elizabeth sat together on the couch in the soft glow of the brass floor lamp. Lost in their own thoughts, they looked at the decorations in the living room: the banner that read *HAPPY ANNIVERSARY*, the crepe streamers that hung from the center of the ceiling, the balloons that were taped to the walls, the hand-drawn picture labeled *GREAT-GRANDMA LOVES GREAT-GRANDPA* that showed two stick figures holding hands, the floral arrangement on the mantel with the pennant that read *HAPPY 60TH,* the photograph in the old picture frame of Adam and Elizabeth on their wedding day, and the photo album of past anniversaries that sat beside it on the coffee table.

"It was a wonderful evening," Elizabeth said.

"Yes, it was."

Elizabeth leaned her head against his shoulder and closed her eyes. "Do you remember what you told me during our first anniversary dance after we were married?"

Adam chuckled. "I hope it was, 'Happy Anniversary.'"

She nudged him playfully on the arm. "I'd just had the first of several medical procedures on my ear, and I asked your honest opinion about it. You looked at my ear and said that as long as I could hear you express your love for me, I should look on it as a gift, because many people live their whole lives without hearing *I love you.*"

"That's fairly profound...for me."

"You'll never know what your words meant to me."

He held her hand and leaned his head against hers.

"I honestly don't know what would have happened if you had given up on me," she said softly.

283

"I would *never* have given up on you, Elizabeth. You were coming with me to the pavilion if I had to hitch Snowflake to your bed and pull you there."

She nestled against his arm. "I still wonder if people actually believe that you showed up on a white horse."

"What else was Prince Charming supposed to ride?"

Laughing lightly, she said, "Everything was so special—the decorations, the music, the dance."

Adam picked up the old picture frame containing their wedding photograph. "Remember when I proposed to you that night?"

Elizabeth's eyes glistened. "The proposal and the wedding the next day were right out of a fairy tale."

"Except we ran out of money on our honeymoon in Kalispell and had to come home early."

Elizabeth stared at the decorations, remembering. "Those were lean years, to be sure. But once you finished college and got the farm back on its feet, we did all right."

He kissed her on the top of her head. "Three children, six grandchildren, eleven great-grandchildren...and counting. We *have* done all right, Elizabeth."

Patting him on the arm, she said, "I suppose we'd better turn in. It's getting late."

Adam set the picture frame down and helped her to her feet. "Before calling it a night, there's one more thing I'd like to do."

She looked at him questioningly.

Bowing his head slightly, he said, "Would you do me the honor of one more dance, Miss?"

Elizabeth laughed in surprise. Smoothing down her dress and adjusting the two-strand pearl necklace around her neck, she placed her hand in his.

Holding each other close, they began moving in a small circle in the center of the area rug. The light from the floor lamp cast a warm glow throughout the room as he softly hummed "Believe Me, If All Those Endearing Young Charms" once again.

AUTHOR'S NOTE

THIS NOVEL IS a work of fiction, but it is based on events that actually happened in my family history. My father did serve in World War II and was injured as described in the book. My mother worked in a dry-cleaning shop as a young woman and gave me information on how the business operated. My wife's parents lived for many years on a farm and faced some of the adversities mentioned in the novel.

A shivaree was planned for both my parents' and my wife's parents' weddings. For one reason or another the intended shivarees failed to occur. But my sister-in-law was "kidnapped" on the evening of her wedding and involved in a car accident. Fortunately, no one was hurt, but it got me wondering... *what if?*

But for all the family details, the love story is my wife's and mine. And I dedicate this novel to her.

ACKNOWLEDGMENTS

I WROTE, REVISED, AND rewrote this novel over a period of years. Whenever I was writing, I WASN'T mowing the lawn, helping out around the house, or completing items on the "honey-do" list. My biggest thanks goes to my wife, Marsha, for giving me the time to write and for being patient while the grass grew long and the "honey-do" list grew even longer. Thanks, love, for being my biggest supporter...and toughest critic.

A big thanks goes to our children and grandchildren for their love and support. And tech skills! The webpage looks great. You helped me understand Facebook and other forms of social media, none of which existed when I began writing *The Anniversary Waltz*. Thanks, kids. I couldn't have done it without you. Literally.

I want to give special thanks to my parents and my wife's parents. You served as the inspiration for the novel, and your legacy will live on in its pages. Speaking of which—a big thanks to my friends who proofread the pages and offered comments and suggestions. You saw what I could not see: my mistakes. Thanks for helping point out all my flaws!

The Anniversary Waltz would never have seen the light of published day if not for my wonderful agent, Joyce Hart. Thank you, Joyce, for believing in the novel from the beginning and maintaining that belief, even when I despaired of ever finding a publisher. But find one you did. Thanks for your faith and perseverance—and for always answering your e-mails so promptly.

A huge thanks goes to everyone at Charisma House. What an amazing team. Your professionalism and courtesy, efficiency and kindness have been a blessing. I had no idea it takes so many hands to pass a book along through all the stages of publication. To the entire staff: I am grateful beyond words to have your fingerprints all over this project.

I want to mention a huge thanks to my editor, Lori Vanden

Bosch. I am in awe (and somewhat jealous) of your skills and insights. It takes me years to write a novel, but in the space of a week or two you come to know the manuscript better than I do. I'm a schoolteacher by profession, and I can truly say that working with you has been an educational experience of the highest order. Thanks for helping me become a better writer and for your unwillingness to let me get away with anything other than an "A for effort" on my report card.

COMING IN SPRING 2013
FROM DARREL NELSON

THE RETURN OF CASSANDRA TODD

Turner Caldwell could never have imagined that the outdoor training and survival skills he learned at Camp Kopawanee, a Christian summer youth camp where he worked several years as a leader, would one day become so crucial. When Cassandra Todd, the girl associated with making his life miserable in high school, suddenly reenters his life and asks for help in eluding her abusive husband, Turner finds himself entangled in a life-and-death struggle that will require every skill he has in order to survive.

PROLOGUE

S HE LAY BESIDE her husband, listening to his steady breathing. A sliver of moonlight peeked through a gap in the curtain and illuminated his features. He lay on his back with his mouth partway open, his hair disheveled, a two-day growth of stubble on his chin. He snored softly but otherwise remained asleep.

She rolled onto her side and glanced at the clock: 1:27 a.m. After waiting to make certain her movement hadn't disturbed him, she eased back the covers, her bare feet soundlessly touching the floor. She grimaced as the bedsprings protested her departure. Remaining still for a moment, she studied her husband. He continued to snore, and his silhouetted shape did not stir.

Tiptoeing to the bathroom, she quickly changed in the darkness, slipping into the clothes she'd purposefully laid out before going to bed. She rehearsed what she'd say if her husband unexpectedly came in and discovered her...dressed.

Then, with her heart in her throat, she stepped into the hallway as cautiously as though walking through a minefield and went directly to the bedroom next door. Opening the door slowly so the hinges didn't squeak, she listened to see if her husband had noticed her absence.

All remained silent, except for the blood pounding in her ears. Exhaling slowly, she crossed the room and gently touched the little figure huddled beneath the covers. "Sweetie," she whispered. "It's Mommy."

The little boy, only three, rolled over in protest to the interruption.

"Time to wake up."

He opened his eyes and stared questioningly at her.

"Come with Mommy."

"Wheah?" he asked. This was followed by an extended yawn and catlike stretch.

"We're going on an adventure."

"An advencha?"

"Shhh! We don't want to disturb Daddy. Hurry and get up, but be very quiet."

Another yawn. "Isn't Daddy coming too?"

"No, he has to work. So it's just you and me, little man. Now hurry."

After helping her son get dressed, she guided him to the door and peered into the hallway. "Remember," she whispered, "Daddy needs his sleep, so be very quiet."

"Okay."

They went into the kitchen, and she opened the refrigerator door. Grimacing as the refrigerator light blazed on, she grabbed the bag of food she had prepared earlier and closed the door quickly and quietly. Then she went to the home security controls near the interior garage door and entered the code to disarm the system.

"Mommy, I have to go potty."

Sighing, she whispered, "All right, but we won't flush the toilet. We have to be very quiet."

When that chore was finished, she led him into the garage and pressed the remote button on the key fob. The trunk lid of her car opened with a soft *click*, revealing a single suitcase inside. Lifting the suitcase out, she closed the trunk lid softly, not daring to latch it shut. In the stillness every sound seemed magnified.

"Awn't we going to dwive?"

"No, we're going on this adventure by bus."

The little boy's eyes lit up, and he sucked in his breath.

"But we still have to be very quiet, sweetie."

Exiting through the side garage door, she paused to make sure their departure hadn't been detected. The house remained dark and silent.

She pulled her son close and embraced him. "Dear God," she

prayed. "Please guide us and watch over us. We need your care and protection. Amen."

"Amen," her son repeated.

She kissed him on the cheek. "Ready for our adventure?"

"Weady."

Avoiding the streetlight, they crossed to the other side of the street and headed down the sidewalk, remaining in the shadows.

Ahead lay the bus depot. Behind, only heartache.

ABOUT THE AUTHOR

DARREL NELSON IS a schoolteacher by profession and lives with his wife, Marsha, in Raymond, Alberta, Canada. They are the parents of four children and are proud grandparents. *The Anniversary Waltz* is Darrel's debut novel. A second novel, entitled *The Return of Cassandra Todd*, comes out in the spring of 2013.

Correspondence for the author should be addressed to:
Darrel Nelson
P. O. Box 1094
Raymond, Alberta, Canada
T0K 2S0

Or you can visit his website (www.darrelnelson.com) and post comments there.